LAST
OF THE
CRESCENT BORN

CRYSTAL MICHEL

DEDICATION

First, I want to thank you, the reader, for picking up my book and giving it a chance; it means the world to me. Second, I want to thank my friends, Ashley, Mia, and Froggy, for being so patient all these years while I wrote. Third, I want to give great thanks to Becca Fitzpatrick. Buying Hush, Hush was the first book I ever bought. You opened my world, without you, this book may not exist. Lastly, I want to thank my mother, for without you I would not exist

PROLOGUE

Humans have been told stories from the time they are born. They end with happily-ever-afters to give a sense of peace. As humans grow older, surrounded by war and chaos, they say that happy endings never happen. But deep down, it's what humans crave. To have hope to cling onto. The stories that end with happy endings give humans that peace they felt so long ago. The ones with tragic endings make them ask themselves if they will ever have a happy ending. If they can't happen in a simple story, what hope do humans have?

Humans rely on those happy endings. They count on them, they live through them, and most of all, they thrive on them. But what happens when fate decides that you don't get a happy ever after? What happens when fate decides you don't get to be human? Going against fate is like trying to change your very being... Unless, of course, you find a way to cheat it...

ONE

"No! Absolutely not!" I slammed my fork back into my to-go bowl and glared at my coworker, friend, and roommate, Sara. She moved out of her dad's house and stayed with my mom and me a few years ago. She shrugged and continued munching on a bite of her breakfast potato. She kept glancing at me as she did so.

"It's not a big deal, Seine," she muttered.

"Not a big deal? You volunteered to help with some random-ass end-of-the-year celebration planning for school, and now you're backing out so you can go on a date. And you expect me to cover for you just because we're work friends," I argued.

Sara sighed and leaned back in her seat.

"Come on, Seine, it's just a couple of hours out of your day," Sara said.

"A couple of hours while having to deal with preppy overeager people, you mean," I said, taking a harsh bite of a strip of bacon. I couldn't believe she would expect me to cover for her, and she would go out on her date. She was an outgoing person who loved being the center of attention. I was the type of person who would rather be stabbed than meet new people. My idea of fun was curling up with a good book.

"Why can't you do this? Just this once?" When Sara saw that I wouldn't budge, she fluttered her eyelashes at me. She looked slightly more guilty than she should have.

"What are you not telling me?" I asked through my teeth and Sara's eyes widened.

"N-nothing!" She looked down at her phone quickly before looking back at me. I lurched away from my seat and reached over the console. Sara yelped and grabbed for her phone at the same time. She dropped her little box of breakfast potatoes onto the floor where they left little grease stains on the mat.

Sara looked around for another route to get away, but unless she got out of the car, she was trapped. And I knew she wasn't going to brave the twenty-seven-degree weather. Being from South Carolina, it was highly unlikely she would. Unlike myself, who grew up with the freezing winds from Lake Erie in a small town no one had ever heard of- Dalelry, New York. I'd have better chances outside than her.

Sara instead threw herself into the backseat, wiggling hard to squeeze between the front seats. I slapped her ass when it got close to my face, and she yelped and kicked her legs. Sara had made it to the backseat but not without dropping her phone to the floor. I grabbed her arm before she could get the phone, and I stretched out to grab it before her. Sara growled, not wanting to lose, and tucked herself into a ball before wrenching her arm out of my grip.

"You're so annoying! Just tell me what you're hiding!" I said with clenched teeth as I pushed her away from the phone. If I wasn't able to get it, I sure as hell wasn't going to let Sara.

"You're one to talk!" Sara said while pressing my face into the passenger side seat, surely leaving imprints. "It's not like you're ever busy after work anyways!"

"How would you know? You never asked! For all you know, I had other plans!"

"Sitting in your room reading nasty ass smut does not count!" Sara hissed as I lightly pinched her leg.

"You're just jealous that you can't keep a straight face reading it!"

"I'm not a delinquent like you who reads that shit in public!"

My reply was muffled as I took a hit beneath my jaw. My head flung back, and I let out a pained groan. Sara froze in her attempt to get the phone and looked down at me in shock.

"Seine?" Sara asked, worriedly. She quickly got off me and watched as I straightened up in my seat. I rubbed my jaw and a dull pain spread along my jawline.

I looked up at Sara from under my eyelashes. I could use her distraction to my advantage. I threw myself towards her phone and grabbed a hold of it. Victory was mine as I turned to see Sara's shocked face. I scrolled through her phone and found what she was hiding from me. Disbelief flowed through my veins as I dropped the phone as if it were on fire. She lied to me! She volunteered me for two days a week for three months! She was never going to be working for the school celebration. She only volunteered me! I was still stuck doing this celebration thing! AND IT WAS UNPAID VOLUNTEER WORK!

An eerie calm settled over me. Slowly, I looked up at my dear sweet friend, who looked nervous. Sara looked like she was going to book it again.

"Just a couple of hours, huh?" I said sweetly. "You forgot to mention that I will be spending two hours after work every Wednesday and Thursday for three months!" I yelled as I smacked Sara's shoulders repeatedly.

"What in God's name are you two fighting about now?!"

Sara and I froze at our boss's voice coming through the frosted windows. Looking up, I saw our boss leaning against the door that led back to the store. She held a strip of bacon in her hand as she pursed her lips. Her hair was swept up into a tight bun, and her hazel eyes twinkled with mirth. She had a suit jacket draped over her arm, and her blouse was untucked from her pencil skirt. The security light created a halo around her head, making the snowflakes sparkle like a crown.

"Uh, hey Debra," Sara said after I rolled down my window, letting the cold in. She shivered, and I inhaled deeply, enjoying the burn of the cold on my lungs. Yes, it hurt, but it also felt refreshing.

Debra raised her eyebrows at us as she took a bite of bacon.

"You two are turning twenty-four in two weeks. Do you think you can stop trying to kill each other already?" She asked, raising her eyebrows at us. "Now tell me, what were you two arguing about this time?" She asked.

"Sara volunteered me to help with some random celebration planning!" I told her, outraged.

Debra's eyes flicked over to Sara, then back to me. Instead of yelling at Sara for doing something behind my back, she said nothing. She finished off the bacon strip and turned around to unlock the door.

"You knew!" I gasped. I got out of my car quickly, leaving Sara swearing behind me as she crawled back over the console to roll the window back up. "Debra!" How could she know and not tell me?!

"Calm down, Seine," Debra told me as she tucked in the bottom of her blouse and pulled on her suit jacket.

"Calm down? Debra, she didn't even ask me if I wanted to do this or not!"

"Uh, Sean's here, I'll see you at school," Sara said, throwing me my car keys, which I didn't try to catch. Sean Swig, also known as Sara's boyfriend. Sara practically ran from my car and into his. Sean's blue convertible was on the side of the road, and Sara jumped in.

"Wait, Sara…!" Sean peeled down the road and out of sight. Damn you, Sara, and your meddling ways.

"I never understood why she comes with you to work on her days off just to have him pick her up," Debra mused and walked inside the store. I followed, after I picked up my keys off the ground. I rubbed the scar on my palm as a slight pain formed. It randomly hurt when I was too cold or too hot. I had no memory of where I got it from, but it was there for as long as I could remember. I was quiet as she went to turn off the alarm.

"Don't be too hard on her," Debra said, breaking through my murderous thoughts, "she just wants you to meet new people."

"Debra, I'm perfectly fine with my friends," I told her. "Besides, Sara knows that I hate meeting new people."

Debra shrugged her shoulders and set her purse on the counter. After punching in the security code, she turned to me and sighed.

"You never know. You might have something in common with some of the people there," she told me.

"The only thing we'll have in common is the fact that we're stuck working together for the next three months," I whined.

"You might have more in common than you think," Debra muttered under her breath. I highly doubted that. Seeing the doubt on my face, she frowned. "At least make an effort to talk to someone," she said sincerely. Not wanting to hurt her feelings, I nodded. She smiled and wrapped her arms around me in a tight hug. "Good, it worries me that you haven't made any new friends… since it happened," she ended with a whisper.

I frowned over her shoulder. Had it really been so long since it happened? It seemed like yesterday that I was asking him if he was sad to leave. A pang shot through my chest at the thought of him.

Pushing my feelings down, I focused on the other part she said, the part about friends. There was nothing wrong with staying in the same social group. I mean, I guess I could make a few new friends... You know, widen my horizons a bit... Who was I kidding, I loved my friends, I was perfectly fine with them. I pulled away from Debra and gave her a small smile.

"I better get going, I need to count the registers before we open," I told her.

I gave her a peck on the cheek. She smiled and headed into the back office. I grabbed my tattered bag off the floor and made sure I had the necessities: my phone, charger, snack, and supervisor key. Seeing that I did, I started my work for the day, already wanting it to be over.

• • • • •

"What the hell happened to your face?" My kind, blunt friend Naji asked me as she buckled up next to me. Her full name is Najia Johnson, but I call her Naji for short. I had known her since my freshman year of high school ten years ago. It felt like I had known her forever.

"Well, hello to you too, Naji," I said with a roll of my eyes. She flicked her newly dyed purple locks out of her eyes as she peered at me. "Just pick your music for the day so we can go get Yamka." I pulled away from her house and followed the familiar road to Yamka's. Yamka was our friend from high school who worked with her family instead of going to college. Once a month, we got together and hung out at a local club, Secrets of the Night, Secrets for short. It was the only place where we could let go of everything in our daily lives. Sara didn't like loud crowded places, even though we were given plenty of space in the VIP section. But Sara always declined the invitation.

Naji leaned back with a smile and rummaged through the CDs attached to the visor above her. Someday, I would upgrade my car so that it could connect to my phone, but that was money I didn't have. She kicked up her feet as she looked, and I took note of what Naji was wearing today while stopping at a traffic signal. She had on a graphic tee shirt from a band I had never heard of, and around her neck was a choker necklace with Saturn on it, and hanging off the rings was a crescent moon.

"Yo, Seine, I know I'm hot and all, but the light's green," Naji said while sliding a CD in. I snapped out of it and drove.

"The hottest," I smirked.

Naji and I talked about the previous night's homework. After taking a few gap years, we were finally in our senior year of college. We somehow ended up with the same teachers but different mods. It was unfair and unjust. Neither one of us had the same classes except for art, which was our last class of the day. Our art class was over at four, I had the rest of the day off while she had Music Composition. After that, we spent the rest of the night together. It was actually pretty sweet.

I pulled in front of Yamka's house and waited. Naji and I relaxed and listened to some guy singing about lighting something on fire. As we chatted about our art projects, the car door behind Naji was yanked open, and Yamka threw herself into the back seat. She slammed the door shut and quickly buckled.

"Go, go, go, go!" she demanded hurriedly. I looked towards her house as I shifted into drive. Yamka's mother was racing toward us with a bunch of papers in her clenched hand. She was obviously mad about something again. I sped away from the curb, leaving Yamka's mother standing under a streetlight. Looking in the rearview mirror, I saw her get swallowed by the night.

After a few minutes with none of us saying anything, I slowed down to the speed limit. I glanced at Yamka in the rearview mirror. She was frantically smoothing out her long brown hair, only to give up and put it up into a loose ponytail. Her dark skin was flushed red, and she looked on the verge of tears.

Naji replaced the arsonist song with K-Pop. Yamka's lips lifted into a small smile. The girl loves her K-Pop. I looked at the dashboard clock and saw that we still had fifteen minutes before the club opened.

"Yammie, you still up for drinks?" I asked while turning into the small parking lot beside Secrets.

"It'll be my treat," Naji piped up.

"Yammie? Do you want to talk about it?" I asked.

Yamka sighed and unbuckled to lean between the front seats.

"She found some college applications in my dresser, and now she thinks I'm abandoning the family business. That's all. She overreacted. Now let's go get us some fruity drinks and get tipsy." Naji and I laughed as we followed Yamka into the club.

TWO

A few nights later, I turned the corner onto the street our school was on and pulled behind the line of vehicles waiting to get into the parking lot. We inched forward towards the security check, and Naji turned the music down.

"How y'all doing tonight?" The night guard asked us from his booth. He was an older gentleman, maybe in his mid-forties. He had greying hair and a beard that was neatly trimmed which seemed to make his blue eyes brighter. In the last four years that I've passed through the gate, Mr. Scott always greeted me with a smile. He was a good man.

"We're good, how about you, Mr. Scott?" I asked as Yamka and Naji both handed me their student IDs.

"Same old same old," he smirked. "The Mrs. found a new recipe book of Korean cuisine that's ruining my figure."

I slid in my ID with a laugh as I handed them to him. I looked him over and smiled at him. He was full of shit, but he still looked good, and I told him as much. He blushed a little and murmured his thanks as he took the IDs. He ran them through his little computer thing, waiting for our names to pop up.

"Alright, Yamka Sihu, Najia Johnson, and Seine Rudi. You're all good to go." He handed back the IDs, and Naji turned the music back up once again. I smiled and waved goodbye while the security gate lifted to let us through. I found a parking spot next to an old pickup truck and parked. We still had twenty minutes until we had to be in class. Usually, it would take longer to get to school, but on Wednesdays and Thursdays, our other friend Katja got a ride from her mom because she had before-class meetings.

Loud rap music filled the parking lot as Sean pulled in with his crew. He pulled into the slot on my left. Naji, Yamka, and I all groaned. Sean and his twin brother, Jared, were the hottest and cockiest guys back in high school. Girls swarmed them like flies to honey. Personally, they gave me the creeps. With them were Sara and a few cheerleaders that were copied and pasted.

"Oh my God, that's horrible music," Naji groaned. Yamka leaned forward between the two front seats and turned as she looked out Naji's window.

"That's not music. That's a whale that ate too much krill," she quipped.

Naji and I looked at her, then at the Swig brothers. They were currently sitting on the hood talking to the head cheerleader, Layla. Unlike the stereotypical cheerleaders you see in movies, Layla wasn't a "mean girl." She was nice and didn't really hate on anyone. Sara and the other girls got out of the car. The back door opened and there was a loud thud. Yamka and Naji looked at me. My heart felt like it had frozen in my chest as I unbuckled. My car, someone had hit my car.

"Oh shit. Scary Seine is back," I heard Yamka whisper as she leaned back.

"I haven't seen her since she got dress-coded on the last day of high school," Naji whispered back.

"It was ninety-five degrees out, the school air conditioner was broken, and there was nothing wrong with my tank top," I said as I got out of the car.

I raced around the front to the passenger side. A girl stood between my car and Sean's. I ignored her as I inspected the door of the car he had bought me for my sixteenth birthday. Towards the bottom of the door was a five-inch scratch and a dent.

Stay calm, stay calm, stay-

"That's what you get for parking your piece of shit next to a real car," a snotty voice said behind me.

My spine stiffened. I knew that voice. It was the same one that called me names in elementary school. It was the same one that started the rumor that I was an easy lay in high school. I turned to face Peyton, my tormentor from the last sixteen. Fucking. Years. Her bleached blonde hair was a stark contrast against her ebony skin. She glanced at the damage she had caused and her mouth curled into a cruel smile.

I smiled sweetly at her.

"That's funny coming from the spoiled little rich girl whose car is currently sitting in the police department lot after you crashed it when you were drunk," I said.

Peyton's face flushed red as Naji and Yamka chuckled in the car. Peyton glared at them through the tinted glass. When she looked back at me, she was smiling.

"I'll get you back for that," she snarled.

"I'm sure you said the same thing to Aurora after she beat you in the art competition and her painting was 'somehow' destroyed," I snapped.

Peyton flinched away from me and glanced at the Swig brothers who were watching the whole exchange. She stepped closer to me so that her expensive high heels were toe to toe with my sneakers. She grabbed my arm, digging her nails into my skin.

"You can't prove anything," she hissed. I looked down at her hands and back at her.

"I suggest you move your hand before a nail chips or a finger breaks," I threatened.

Peyton tightened her grip before flinging my arm away from her. She grabbed her large bag from the back seat narrowly missing me and strutted away.

"Damn it, Peyton, you need to stop starting stuff. Otherwise, I'll have to kick you off the squad," Layla warned Peyton. They walked away with the rest of the girls while the Swig brothers stayed behind. Sean walked to me and pulled a business card out of his wallet.

"Call this number and tell them that I sent you. They'll fix it up," he told me.

I took the card without looking at it. What I did look at was the parking lot, noticing several people giving us curious looks. Great. Now there would be rumors about how the nobody was seen flirting with her friend's boyfriend. Not that I was, but it was bound to be said somewhere on the grapevine.

"Thanks," I mumbled. *Now go away.*

"Anytime. In return you'll just have to help me break in the backseat," Sean said.

My head snapped up in disbelief. What the hell did he just say? Sean was smirking at my red cheeks. He leaned forward, placing his arms by my head, trapping me.

"Why ya blushing baby? Your friend already broke in the front seats," he whispered in my ear.

"Ugh," I said in disgust. I pushed his arms away from me and walked away to get my book bag out of the car. Unfortunately, Sean followed. He placed his hands over his chest theatrically and pretended to be hurt.

"Aw, come on Princess, don't be like that."

I flinched away from him as I grabbed my bag. Naji saw and scowled at Sean.

"Don't call me that," I hissed at him.

"Hey assbutt, shouldn't you be getting to class?" Naji asked as she got out of the car and stood by me. Yamka followed suit but narrowly missed hitting Sean with the car door.

"Nah, doll face, I was about to treat you like my homework; slam you on a table and do you all night."

My mouth dropped open as Sean walked to his brother, laughing at our faces. Jared looked back at us and rolled his eyes.

"Sean let's go before you get into more trouble this week," Jared said as he scooped up his bag off the ground. "It's bad enough that you got caught cheating yesterday and have to help with that volunteer celebration thing. The next thing you know…" Jared's voice trailed off as both brothers left.

Did he just say what I think he just said? Shit, shit, shit, shit.

"God he's so annoying," Yamka said. "Thank God we don't have class with him."

"I feel bad for the people helping with the celebration planning," Naji added.

I looked up at the bright sky that seemed to be mocking me.

"Fuuuuuuuck," I moaned. The next three months were going to be the death of me.

THREE

At dinner later that night, I sat at our usual table in the corner of the cafeteria by all the windows. Everyone, except our friend Aurora, was in the lunch line and at the salad bar. And Yamka and Naji were throwing bits of food at each other. Each time they hit the other person; they got a point. If a piece of food fell on the floor a point was taken away.

While they were doing that, I watched the lunch line. The sassy-looking girl with tan skin, dark brown hair, and brown eyes was Jazmine. Behind her was a girl of Asian descent who had several facial piercings and a no-shit attitude. That was the stylish Alice. During our sophomore year, Alice had been in a car crash that left scars on her arms and left her orphaned. Katja's parents adopted her. Speaking of Katja, she was in line with them as well. She had been my friend since eighth grade. Her hair was blood red, that, surprisingly, was natural. Her eyes were the brightest green I had ever seen. She was my sister from a different mister.

When everyone was at the table, Yamka and Naji stopped throwing food long enough for me to tell them all what Sara had done. As I finished, the only sound around us was the chatter from other tables. I cleared my throat before asking the big question.

"So… who wants to hang out with me after school to make sure I don't kill myself?"

Then, my great, wonderful friends, whom I love dearly, started laughing their asses off. I glared at them as they laughed at the predicament Sara had gotten me in. They could laugh it up all they wanted because one of them was going with me whether they liked it or not.

"You know what, never mind. I think I heard that the senior class officers wanted to do a flash mob at graduation. I have some great ideas for that. If only there were some fellow friends of mine that could put a stop to it all," I sighed dramatically. "But oh well, it's not like we only get one college graduation… oh wait, ya we do."

Gasps and cries of horror went around the table as they visualized a cringy graduation. All at once they started talking loudly. We were drawing attention to our table, and I tried quieting them down, but they were too busy voicing their outrage.

"Y'all are louder than the football players when there's pizza," I told them and covered my face with my hands. They were my friends, and I loved them for reasons beyond me, but damn they were weird.

"I can stay after with you today, but I usually have work Wednesday and Thursdays," Jazmine told me over everyone.

"I can stay after…" Katja trailed off as she checked her phone calendar, "for half an hour every other Thursday," she finished. "I have to work at the pool," she apologized.

"Um, I can't stay after," Alice spoke up next. "I have Mock Trial and volunteer work on Wednesday. Thursdays I have my fencing practices."

"It's okay Alice because I can't stay after either," Yamka assured her. "You know how my parents are," she rolled her eyes, but we all saw the hurt underneath. Yamka's parents were super strict about everything she did. I placed my hand on her shoulder and squeezed it.

"Welp, I'm free both days," Naji said, shrugging her shoulders. She leaned into my side, tucking her head under my chin. "Looks like you're stuck with me."

"Oh, thank gods, what could I ever do without you?" I said sarcastically. Everyone laughed as I nudged her away from me. "What about your other meetings?" I asked her.

"The Alphabet Mafia meetings are on Tuesdays and Reign of Choir meetings are on Mondays," Naji explained.

"Ah, okay. Well Aurora has Anime Club on Thursdays so that's out…" I wonder if I could just show up for today and tell them that the whole thing was a misunderstanding. I mean, I didn't sign up for it, so why should I be made to stay?

"Wait Seine, what days do you have Yearbook and Creativity Journal meetings?" Jazmine asked me.

"Oh, Yearbook meetings are on Fridays and C.J. only has meetings once every month to check on submissions," I rolled my eyes. "And it's not like I actually get to do my job anyways." I was a bit bitter.

"Peyton still isn't letting anyone do anything?" Katja asked. Yamka snorted out a laugh while I gave her a dirty look. She thought anything that got me riled up was funny.

"No," I answered Katja. I just had to get through today and then I could quit… right?

• • • • •

Two Weeks Later

"Oh, my gods, no," I moaned as I hit my head on one of the fold-up tables.

It had been two weeks since the first time I had to stay after to help with the wretched planning. My birthday had come and passed with little celebration. Naji and I had gone to dinner but that was it. I had been too preoccupied trying to get out of helping with the party. I had spoken with the person in charge of the whole thing. Begged if I was honest with myself.

Which was unfortunate for me because they didn't care if I wanted to help out or not; I was on the list, so I was helping. And now I was stuck with eight other people who constantly made me want to cut my ears off. Not only that, the only thing we had done was argue about what theme the damned celebration would be.

"Oh come on! You say no to every idea!" Peyton said, who was, unfortunately, the second in charge of the whole shebang.

Leaving my face on the table I spoke to Naji, who was shaking with laughter.

"How can she not see how cliché it would be with having a Winter Wonderland theme? In January? Remind me why I still come here."

"B-because the Dean promised you extra special food and to make sure the theme wouldn't suck. B-but the way things are g-going, we're going to be s-stuck with a Carrie prom-styled celebration," Naji said in between laughs.

I smacked my head on the table again. Out of the eight of us here, only Layla, Payton, and I were actually working. Sean would stay until the boss left then come back a few minutes before we all left. Naji was only here to make sure I didn't kill anyone, myself included. There was a guy, I think Layla said his name was Damon. He would come in, grab a bottle of soda, and

Lie down on the bleachers to play on his phone. I had only heard him speak once and that was to tell Peyton to shut up and leave him alone. The rest of the people never showed up. Lucky me.

"What was that?!" Peyton snapped.

I groaned and looked up at her. I was so not in the mood today.

"I said, with you in charge it'll be a miracle if we get anything done." Peyton looked at me dumbfounded, as if she couldn't believe that I had actually spoken back to her. Her eyes hardened and threw a bunch of papers at me. They fluttered in all directions before falling to the floor. She stomped off towards the gym doors with her parting words:

"I'M DONE! YOU'RE IN CHARGE! LET IT ALL GO TO SHIT"

To say that it was quiet after that is an understatement. Sean walked into the gym staring out after her. He raised his eyebrows and whistled the Jaws theme. Layla went after Peyton only to come back looking resigned. Damon looked away from his phone to stare at me. And Naji, Naji looked full-on pumped. What the hell. Fine, I'm in charge? Let's do this.

I took a deep breath and stood up. I'm sure I looked awesome in all my glory with my messy bun and ripped jeans. And let's not forget the red mark that was most likely on my forehead.

"Well, okay, then, you heard her. I'm in charge," I said as I looked at my very pitiful team.

"No offense Princess, but Peyton couldn't get me to stay here, I doubt you will," Sean said. Not one to back away from a challenge, I smiled at him. He looked unnerved as I walked toward him.

"You will stay here for the full two hours. You will do as I say without complaining. And you will buy supplies that we need." I told him with each step I took. "And if you don't, not only will Sara hear about the incident two weeks ago, she will also learn that you're not trying your damnedest to make sure the celebration she was excited about is amazing." I pressed forward more and jabbed my finger into his chest as I said through clenched teeth: "And stop calling me Princess."

Sean backed away from me a few steps and looked around the gym rubbing his chest like my jabs actually hurt him. He shuffled his feet and rolled his shoulders.

"Ya whatever," he mumbled.

Content that he would oblige, I turned to the other lazy male. Damon was sprawled on the bleachers with his head hanging off a step. His light grey eyes watched me as I climbed up. I sat on the step above him so that he had to look up at me. Damon sighed and sat up, bending his long legs under him. He placed his phone on the lower step between us.

Hmmm.

"What?" He asked.

"You seem like a 'no bull shit' kind of guy," I stated placing my arms on my legs and leaning forward.

"I guess," Damon said slowly.

"So, I'm going to give it to you straight." My hand shot forward and snatched up his phone. Damon made a sound of protest and made a move for it, but I held it out of his reach. "You help out for an hour and the second hour you can do whatever the hell you want," I held up his phone. "But you have to give me your phone for the hour your working."

Damon glared at me as I talked. As I finished, he had gone from glaring to straight out scowling. But he had listened and that was all I needed for now.

"You're really fucking annoying. You know that right?" Damon asked and I shrugged. "Whatever, just give me my phone."

I held it out to him but didn't hand it over. I raised an eyebrow at him.

"Do we have a deal?" I asked.

"You're going to regret this when you find out," Damon mumbled. "Yes, we have a… deal."

What the hell did that mean? Find what out? Before I could make sense of it, Damon grabbed his phone out of my hand and slouched his way down the bleachers. I stood up and met Naji back at the table. Layla was there and she had gathered all the papers Peyton had thrown like a child.

"Okay, Layla since you know almost everyone, get word out that the celebration theme is Black Light. That meant neons, fluorescents, stuff like that," I told her. Naji slapped me on the arm and I turned to give her a "what the hell" look.

"Where did you pull that idea from?" She asked.

"I came up with it in Chemistry," I told her and looked at Sean. "I need you to buy all fluorescent and neon paint and markers you can find. Oh, and find some Tonic water. I'll come up with the designs tonight and go over them with you next Wednesday."

"That sounds simple enough." Sean said and walked out.

"Why can't you go over them with us tomorrow?" Layla asked.

"I have to go visit someone, so I won't be in school," I answered and left it at that. Naji threw an arm over my shoulders and hugged me close. She knew what tomorrow was. It was when I went to visit him. It seemed fitting to see him the day he left; his birthday. My mom never visited him because she blamed him for leaving. So, I went alone.

"Okay, enough with the silence," Damon said. "What do you want me to do?"

I looked around the gym… Hmmm, what could he do?

"You could find neon white tablecloths and neon white cloth napkins. And at each table there will be neon markers so that people can decorate their napkins," I told him, coming up with ideas left and right. Holy crap it was going to be cool. Damon nodded and left, leaving just Layla, Naji, and me.

Layla bit her lip as she looked at me.

"Um, what if some people don't want their clothes to, you know, glow?" She asked.

"They can wear normal colored dresses and suits if they want," I told her.

"This is actually really cool, Seine," Naji said.

"Thanks, I just hope everyone else thinks so too."

Now I would have to find a neon or fluorescent dress... Damn me and my ideas

FOUR

Istood outside the barn, not daring to breathe. It was amazing that even after years, the pain in my chest was still raw. That was the price of being human though. Feelings could be sprung on you just by looking at something. Memories flooded in as I opened the barn doors. It was dark inside with little light coming in from the open door. As my eyes adjusted, I could make out the huge object in the middle. A tarp was covering it, but I knew that there would still be dust inside. Slowly I pulled the tarp off and folded it without looking at what I had just uncovered. I wasn't ready to think about it yet. I stood with my back to it, staring at the tarp in my hands. My hands were clutching it tight making my knuckles white.

Why couldn't I do what my mom did? She would get drunk, sit in the house, and look at pictures while eating his favorite foods. Why couldn't I let you go?

I sighed and threw the tarp on his workbench. Slowly I turned to look at it and felt memories invade my mind. Some were old, from when I was just a little kid. Others were my last moments with him.

Like the first time we had gone to the fair when I was eleven, just him and me. There was a stuffed elephant that I had fallen in love with at one of those impossible game booths. He had spent an hour and fifty dollars for that dumb elephant. I was so happy when he handed it to me. I had given it to him before he left… They found it in his pack even though it took up room.

I looked over at the old fair tickets tacked to the corkboard above the workbench. Faded from age and the writing on them was barely legible.

There was also the time when I was eight and had planned a water balloon fight. I had tried a surprise attack approach, but somehow he had known. I had snuck up on him while he was in the garden and he had soaked me with the water hose before I could throw a balloon. I had shrieked and ran away laughing. We spent all day outside pelting each other with balloons.

I felt my lips twitch as I remembered our laughter being loud.

My last happy memory of him was from my twenty-first birthday. I had opened my presents, went out for pizza, and went bowling. He hadn't gone easy on me just because it was my birthday. We were happy. But all day I had felt that something was off. His smile wasn't as full, his eyes weren't as bright, and his laugh wasn't as loud. My mom had stayed in the background and watched us have fun. She smiled and shook her head when Sara had asked her to join.

When we got home after dropping Sara off at her house, my mom had gone to the kitchen. He sat me down in the living room. It was there that he told me that he would be leaving, that he wouldn't be there anymore. A month later, on his birthday, he stood by the front door with his things packed into one bag. We said our goodbyes and he told us that we would see him again. A few months later we found out that we would never see him ever again.

I opened the truck door, sparing a glance at the ratty elephant in the passenger seat. I hopped in, pushing his old soda and water bottles out of the way. His old soccer jersey was in a heap on the backseat. There was an old cooler on the floorboard. It was locked and I hadn't found a key yet. I just hoped there wasn't food in it. There was some loose change in the cup holder; ninety-five cents to be exact. A faded picture of us was pinned to the visor. The steering wheel cover was worn away and needed to be replaced. I placed my phone by the elephant and grabbed the chain hanging from the rearview mirror. I slipped it over my head and clutched the dog tags in my hand, imprinting his name on my skin.

"Happy birthday," I whispered as tears rolled down my cheeks.

A harsh wind blew the barn door shut sealing me in the cold darkness. It was fitting. Where else could I go to let it out? Gradually the tears stopped and the cold became too much for me. I placed the dog tags back and whispered my goodbyes. Climbing out of the truck was difficult since my body was frozen stiff. Grabbing my phone from the seat I felt a warm breeze and I shivered. There wasn't a heater in the barn to create the breeze, but it could have been a cross breeze? I wasn't majoring in science, so I didn't care especially when I was freezing. I covered the truck back up and I trudged out of the barn with my arms huddled close to my chest for warmth. Without looking back, I closed the barn door. Had I looked back, I would have seen the shadows move and seen the man made of smoke and ash watching me.

FIVE

"Seine, Seine, SEINE!"

I bolted up in my bed and pain radiated through my skull. I rubbed my forehead wincing. Sara was standing above me rubbing her own head.

"Damnit Sara," I growled.

"Sorry, sorry. Your mom wanted me to tell you that she has to go into work and that you can get out of bed today." She told me.

After I came home from visiting his truck, shivering and blue-lipped, my mom had scolded me. She told me that I was going to get sick, and me being me I told her I knew what I was doing and a little cold wasn't going to make me sick. Not this northern-born and raised girl. That would be preposterous. Of course that was completely what happened and I had been in bed for the last three days. Doing absolutely nothing. Not even reading, just sleeping, drinking water, and eating crackers.

"Oh, thank the gods," I threw off my floral-designed blanket. That-that right there was why I liked school. It kept me busy and laying in bed was driving me crazy. I swung my legs over the side of the bed and stood up. My vision went black around the edges and I felt as if I had just gotten off a Tilt-A-Whorl. I plopped back on the bed with a huff and blinked to clear my vision.

"Are you okay?" Sara asked.

I looked up at her. She wasn't wearing her glasses and she wasn't squinting as much as usual. Her face was pale and she kept touching her mouth and then wincing.

"Are you okay?" I counter asked.

Sara's eyes widened and dropped her hand away from her face.

"Ya, I'm fine. I think my wisdom teeth are finally coming in. My mouth hurts," she told me.

"Ouch," I could understand the discomfort. Mine had come in at the end of high school. Months of pain and not being able to eat some days because of it. And the constant taste of blood. Yuck.

"Tell me about it," Sara pulled my phone out of her pocket and threw it to me. "Call your dweeb friends. They've been calling and texting you. Do they always text you at the same time?"

Going through my phone I saw twenty-five unread messages from Naji, fourteen from Katja, and ten from Jazmine along with five missed calls. Yamka had blown up Facebook with sticker messages and Alice had direct messaged me several times on Twitter.

"Sometimes. And they have no idea that they do it. It gets confusing when they send the same things as each other at the same time," I told her as I answered my friends.

"I'm sure it does… Do you want to go out for lunch?" Sara asked.

"Yes, I need to get out of the house," I said. "Where do you want to go?"

"Moody's?" Sara suggested. Moody's was a restaurant in town run by an old guy. He was really laid back… Well, unless you don't tip the servers. Then he would get pissed and a pissed old guy was never good.

"Sure," I got up without issues and found a change of clothes.

"Great, but could you shower first? You reek."

I threw my clothes at her as she ran out the door.

Damn her.

• • • • •

"And how would you like that cooked?" The server asked me.

"Medium well," I told him and he nodded before he turned to Sara.

"And you?" He asked.

"Um…" Sara looked at me and looked confused. "Ummm… Rare?"

I felt my mouth drop open as I looked at her. Not once had she ever ordered her meat as rare. She told me once that the sight of the blood made her feel sick. And here she was ordering her steak as rare? What the hell?

"Is everything okay?" The server asked. "I can change the order if you'd like."

Sara shook her head and said everything was fine. The server looked doubtful but left our table. I stared at Sara as she played with her straw. Minutes of uncomfortable silence went by. I could go the rest of the day without saying anything, but Sara couldn't stand awkward silence. I would give her another five minutes before she snapped. As the five minutes were closing, Sara sighed and looked up from her drink. I raised an eyebrow at her and waited. She bit her lip and shrugged her shoulders.

"I don't know," Sara started. "I've been slammed at work and school and I came here the other day and I ordered my usual non-bloody, absolutely no pink steak. And when I got it, it tasted like ash in my mouth. But when Sean cut his steak and the blood dribbled onto the plate making it pink, my mouth watered. And it wasn't like I thought it looked good. My salivary glands actually hurt, I wanted the steak so bad," Sara's eyes glazed over as she talked about the gross bloody steak that apparently called her name.

"So… Did you… You know? Eat some?" I asked. I really wanted her to tell me yes, that she took a bite and gagged. That she went back to her completely dead meat. Sara nodded and cast her eyes to the table. "And…?"

"It was so… Good," Sara told me, her face scrunching up in disgust despite what she said. "It was so much juicier than well-done."

"Oh," was all I said.

"But… It was like the sight of blood made me hungry…" Sara trailed off as my eyes widened as she talked.

"Uh, careful there Sara, you're starting to sound like a vampire," I said jokingly.

Sara's skin paled even more than it was and she shot out of her chair like a bullet. Startled, I stood as well.

"Sara?"

Sara grabbed her purse and ran out of the restaurant. Everyone watched her flee. After a few seconds, they turned to look at me. I was trying to figure out what the hell had just happened. Maybe she remembered that she had something to do?… Or had someplace to be? It couldn't have anything to do with what I said, right?

"Seine, is everything okay?" I turned to see Jared standing by the now-empty table.

His dark green eyes trailed across my face seeking an answer. Unlike his brother, Jared was actually sort of nice. In an intimidating way.

"I… I have no idea," I told him. I reached into my pocket and pulled out a couple of twenties. I handed them to Jared. "Can you give these to Moody? I need to go." Jared took the money and nodded.

"I hope she's okay," he said as he left to hunt down Moody.

I did too.

I left the restaurant and looked for my truck which was gone. My eyes burned with anger and whipped my phone out of my pocket. There was a voicemail from Sara.

"Hey, I know you're going to be angry, but I took your truck. I called Naji and she's going to pick you up. I'm sorry but I remembered that I had something I needed to do," Sara's voice said.

I called her back and left a voicemail in return.

"If you scratch it, I will kill you," I threatened. I hung up and soon after Naji pulled up in her black and purple Jeep. She rolled down her window and the cold wind tossed her hair in every direction. Her clothes were wrinkled from the wind.

"Hey, so Sara's lost it," Naji said, rolling her… Purple eyes?!

I stared at her. What was up with people today? Sara was craving blood and running off. And now Naji's eyes were purple.

"What's wrong?" Naji asked.

"Did you get contacts?" I asked. She must have.

Her face scrunched up with confusion.

"No, why?" Okay, now that really confused me.

"Really?" I asked.

"Yaaa, why?"

"Your eyes, they're purple," I said slowly and Naji lifted a hand to her face. Understanding glowed from her and she lowered her hand.

"Oh, yeah. I did get contacts. We need to go to Alice's house," she said as I swung into the Jeep still boggled out of my mind.

"Why? What's wrong?" I asked.

Naji looked for traffic before pulling away from the curb.

"Nothing. We need to get Alice's car since Sara has your truck and pick everyone up."

"Again, why?"

"So, we can go shopping of course," Naji chuckled as we sped off.

Whoooooo.

• • • • •

At the dress shop, Layla tried on a dark wine-red strapless dress that would glow. It was fitted to her chest and flared out at the waist. The skirt of the dress was poofy, but not over the top. The top layer was lace that parted in the front of the skirt. The material of the bodice was twisted delicately. The dress caused Layla's hair to look coppery.

Jazmine bought a short neon purple dress. It had a silk bottom layer with a lace top layer that had rose designs. At the top of the skirt in the back was a small lace bow. The back of the dress was open showing off Jazmine's caramel skin. Some straps covered her shoulders. The front was lace-covered silk with the same designs as the skirt. Jazmine also bought a black beaded necklace with purple stones in the center with matching earrings.

Aurora got a black strapless dress that clung to her hips and bust and it ended just above her knees. Neon blue and white lightning decorated it. When she wore it at the celebration, she would look like she was wearing a dress made of lightning.

Naji got a black dress that ended below her knees. The skirt had small ruffles that were pulled up to reveal purple ruffles beneath. On the bodice were three stylishly placed black bows.

The sleeves were just long enough to cover her shoulders. Every shadow that the ruffles cast had been sprayed with a neon purple translucent spray that would glow under the black lights.

Yamka fell in love with a floor-length dress. It had a white bodice with small silver beads sewn on with some strings that dangled. The back was see-through and had one thin strap on the left shoulder. The skirt flowed down in all its purple glory. The bottom of the skirt lay on the floor, looking like purple water. There was a slit in the skirt on the left side that stopped above the knee. Yamka's leg would show when she walked. The skirt would glow vibrantly.

Katja chose a red ball gown-type dress. The bodice was tight showing her hips. The top of the bodice was dark red with red fabric crisscrossing over it. On the left on the top were some large beads with lace work sprouting out like leaves. Towards the waist, a dark red created the illusion of a belt. The skirt of the dress had sideward ruffles in red, plum, and dark magenta lace. The edge of each ruffle was silk. The colors made Katja's green eyes brighter. The salesperson had assured Katja that only the ends of the ruffles would glow.

After my friends found the dresses of their dreams, it was my turn. Despite having ideas about the celebration and helping everyone with their dresses, I hated clothes shopping. And dress shopping, I usually just find something simple. But no one would have it. Jazmine threw a purple dress at me to try on. Naji topped it with a black one, which Katja buried under a red one. Layla found a yellow dress, one I'm sure she put there as a joke. Yamka threw a silver and rose dress on the ever-growing pile. Aurora even threw in a few dresses like hers.

I tried on every single one of them. They looked good, but none of them spoke to me. We were about to leave the store for a new one when a man came in with a rolling rack filled with dresses. He went to the salesperson with them. Everyone stopped at the door as I went after the rack. The man was telling the salesperson that the dresses were from an old ballet show.

"Uh, can I look at these?" I asked tentatively.

The man and the salesperson both looked at me, smiled their "yes", and went on talking about a show where two brothers died a lot while hunting.

I went through the dresses hanging and some of them were trashy. Others were too girly. But then my hand brushed against a soft fabric that was crushed between two fluffy dresses. I pulled it off the rack to reveal a dark blue and black dress. It had thin straps with lace that led to more lace that covered the chest. Under the gems, the fabric went from black and through shades of blue until it was white and began to darken again. Before the fabric reached teal again, the waist had a two-inch area covered in gems. From the waist, the skirt flared out, but not drastically. The skirt faded from teal to white back to teal much like the bodice, but sideways. Crescent moons and stars lightly decorated the skirt and bodice. I felt the fabric between my fingers lovingly.

"You should get it," I jumped to see Naji standing beside me.

"You think?" I asked.

"Look around. Is there any other dress that makes you smile? Or feel that it is the one?" She asked.

I looked around the store. There were a few I liked. The peach one with the skirt that flared back. The black one with the gems on the top. But I kept looking back at the dress I had in my hands.

"That's what I thought," Naji grabbed the dress from me and handed it to the salesperson. "She'll be buying this."

Soon we were heading to Layla's to pick out shoes. Why Layla's? Because Layla loves buying shoes, even when they are not always in her size.

SIX

“Hey Mom, what's wrong with Sara?” I asked as I pulled on my jacket. She looked up from her bowl and frowned.

“It's her wisdom teeth. They're really bothering her this morning,” she told me.

“Oh… Um mom, did Sara tell you why she flipped out yesterday?”

“No, as a matter of fact, she didn't,” my mom said, spearing a piece of honeydew. “I hope it's not drugs.”

“Really Mom? Drugs? Sara has a hard time taking ibuprofen for headaches. I doubt it's drugs,” I told her with a roll of my eyes.

“Well what else could it be?”

“I don't know. You're the mom, do mom things. Investigate,” I said, giving her a kiss on the cheek. “Love you. I'll see you when I get home.”

“Love you too,” she said looking towards Sara's room.

I ran to my truck which Sara had thankfully returned without any new scratches. I picked up Naji and her purple eyes. Yamka was next and apparently, she too had gotten contacts. But unlike Naji, Yamka's contacts were golden yellow. It had creeped me out the way they reflected light at first, but after a few minutes, they were… Coolish. She had shared a glance with Naji and assured me that everyone was wearing contacts lately.

I wasn't stupid. Their glances with each other had given them away. Something was obviously going on and I would find out. One thing I couldn't stand was secrets and the fact that my friends were keeping some bothered me.

When I pulled up in front of Jazmine's house, her lawn was covered with tall plants with small purple flowers. Jazmine opened the back door bringing in a scent that burnt my nose and throat. I felt it twitch as a sneeze threatened. I could feel three pairs of eyes on me as I held it back.

"What?" I asked pulling away from Jazmine's house and the dreadful flowers.

"You okay there?" Jazmine asked.

I looked at her in the rearview mirror and groaned. Her eyes were the same color as Yamka's. I may not be up to date with most trends, but I would have heard of this one. And my friends have never really cared about trends. So why start now?

"Not you too," I said.

"Not me too, what?" Jazmine asked.

"Uh, Seine is just realizing colored contacts are in," Yamka said emphasizing colored contacts. I kept stealing glances in the rearview mirror. Jazmine looked at Yamka and Naji in shock.

"No shit," Jazmine exclaimed.

"Is there anything else that is 'in' that I should know about?" I asked sarcastically.

My new trendy friends were silent on the way to Layla's. Every now and then I would hear their phones buzz. They would look at their phones and look between each other and me. I had a sneaking suspicion that they were texting each other about me. I pulled onto Layla's street and there were three collective gasps.

"We forgot about Layla," Yamka hissed as I pulled to a stop across from Layla's house. I unbuckled and turned in my seat to glare at them. They looked nervous about something.

"What the hell are you guys up to?" They ignored me as their fingers flew across their phone screens. "Hellooooo? Confused driver here," I snipped.

"Shit, here she comes," Naji said.

Soon Layla, Jazmine, and Yamka were in the backseat while Naji was breathing heavily next to me.

"Hey guys…?" Layla's voice trailed off as she noticed the tension. "What's wrong?"

I rolled my eyes and turned more in my seat to look at her. There were three cries from my friends.

"No!"

"Don't look at her!"

"Layla, she can see!"

Naji even tried forcing me to turn me away.

"What the hell is wrong with you guys!?" I snapped, pulling away from Naji. I looked at Layla and saw her covering her face with her hands. What I could see of her was that her hair was down for once and it was long. Longer than I would have thought possible with tiny curls.

"Layla, unless you've grown a third eye that leaks pus, uncover your face," I said angrily. It was deathly quiet as Layla lowered her hands. Layla's cheekbones were incredibly sharp as if they were chiseled out of stone. Her lips were a shiny blood red. Her skin was pearly white. Layla's face was hauntingly beautiful. To be honest, it was kind of hot, but I wasn't sure what to make of it.

"Um… What no contacts?" I asked, unsure of what else to say and Layla blinked in surprise. Uneasy chuckles filled the truck as I turned around and started the drive to school. "Is that a new trend as well?" I asked. "First colored contacts, then new uh, makeup fashions. It's as if you guys suddenly care what is trending."

"Not… Exactly. We're just…" Naji trailed off.

"You're just what?"

"Trying things out for the celebration," Layla said.

"Okay, I understand trying contacts, but Layla… Why the makeup? Don't get me wrong, it's hot, but why wear it today?" Yamka laughed and Jazmine chuckled. I looked over at Naji to see her smiling. "What?" I asked.

"Her… Makeup is going to be an everyday thing from now on," Jazmine said.

Ummm, okay. I loved my friends and everything, but damn. I wasn't sure Layla's new look would go well. But she could take care of herself. And if she couldn't, we would back her up. By making sure she didn't hurt anyone…

• • • • •

I threw my Algebra 2 and Trigonometry textbook into my locker. Stupid letters and numbers. Solve your own damn problems. I slammed the locker door shut. I was decent in most classes, excelling in English and art, but math hated me. I had almost failed a test yet again. You'd think with my mom being a bank teller I would be great at math. Nope. I sucked.

The warning bell rang causing first-year students to scramble to their classes. The sophomores fast walked. The juniors walked at a slow pace and we seniors stood in the halls, not caring if we were late.

All day I had been seeing people with contacts, not a lot, but enough to notice. And no one cared about Layla's new look. In fact, no one blinked an eye at her. Everyone who wore contacts though, did give me looks when I stared. I couldn't help it, some of the contacts were odd. One person had all-white contacts, and another had reptilian ones. Most had the same contacts as Jazmine and Yamka.

"Hey Seine," Aurora said, walking up to me. By now I wasn't surprised to see her eyes a teal color. Oddly enough the contacts brought out the blue tips in her hair.

"The teal looks good," I told her and Aurora's eyebrows shot up at my remark as we walked to the cafeteria together.

"Uh thanks," she said. "So how did the test go?"

"Ugh, don't get me started," I complained. "I don't know how you know everything."

Aurora smiled as we got out of the way of a bunch of guys. One bumped into my shoulder causing me to stumble back. Piercing brown eyes stared at me. His hair was shorter than it was before. He was taller than I remembered.

"Watch where you're going," he snapped. I blinked. Brown eyes were replaced with black and Damon stormed away.

"What was that about?" Aurora asked, placing a hand on my shoulder. I watched Damon turn the corner and was gone from my sight.

"I thought I saw..." I shook my head. There was no way that was him. "Never mind. Let's go eat barely edible food,"

When we got to the table everyone was staring at Alice. Aurora and I took our seats. Alice speared a leaf of lettuce and chewed it as we stared at her.

"Sooo, why are we staring at Alice?" I asked.

"She just told us that she'll be leaving tomorrow to go to some prestigious fencing school," Layla said.

"That's cool. Where at?" I never understood fencing, but to each their own and all that jazz.

"Europe," Alice mumbled.

"What?! That's awesome!" Aurora said.

Apparently, Aurora was the only one who thought so. Katja looked disappointed. Jazmine, Yamka, and Naji all looked sad, yet excited.

"She's going to the fencing school and I'll be attending the boarding school connected with it. It has a great archery program," Katja said.

We all stared at her now, including Alice. It was obvious that Alice didn't know that particular detail. My eyes landed on the table cringing at the awkwardness that was about to happen.

"You're what?" Alice asked. "But the celebration is this Friday!"

"It's fine." Katja shrugged. "I'm pretty sure that even in Europe they have celebrations. Besides, the only reason I was going this year was because someone bought an extra ticket," she said.

"But your dress-" Katja cut Alice off.

"My dress will be fine for any celebration."

They stared at each other until the bell rang and they went to their next class. Jazmine, Yamka, Naji, Layla, Aurora, and I sat in silence as the cafeteria emptied. I couldn't believe that Katja and Alice were moving to Europe. Their junior year was almost over. Katja had bought her dress and picked out her shoes.

I guessed if it was what she wanted…And it would look good for future jobs. A deep part of me though, a selfish part, wished Alice was going alone. But the selfish part was drowned out by my understanding that Katja needed to go. It would be beneficial for her… I wondered how long they knew that they would be leaving…

"So, farewell pa-"

"SEINE RUDI!" A deep voice boomed from the cafeteria entrance. I, along with everyone else in the almost empty room, turned in that direction. Standing in the doorway was Jared. He stalked towards me and my friends. Those left in the room watched him, trying to figure out why he wanted to talk to some girl who wasn't worth talking to.

He straddled the empty seat next to me with his back facing my friends. He crossed his legs and folded his hands as he looked at me. His green eyes were now a burgundy color. He smiled at our discomfort.

"Ladies," he greeted. I looked at my friends quickly while pursing my lips. Ooookaaay?

"Uh, hey Jared? What's up?" I asked.

"So, this celebration idea of yours is really neat," he said.

"Thanks, I guesss." *What's your point?*

"You're welcome. But see, I already bought my suit, so nothing is going to glow," Jared said, spreading his hands out. "So now I have a problem."

"And? What do you want me to do about it?" I asked and Jared raised his eyebrows.

"Change the theme."

… What? Was he- was he serious? Hell no.

"No, no way," I told him.

"Why not?" He asked.

"Seriously? You have had a month to buy a new suit. It's not my fault you didn't. So, either you deal with your non-glowing suit or," I reached into my book bag and pulled out a white package. "OR you can take these and stop whining to me," I set the box on the table between us. Jared looked at it uncertainly. He reached for it and pulled it to him.

"What is it?" He asked.

"Open it and find out," I said, wiggling my eyebrows. Naji chuckled next to me. She knew what it was because she helped me order them.

"It's not going to blow up is it?"

"Only one way to find out."

Jared slowly opened the top lid of the box. When he pulled on the tissue paper, my awesome friends all yelled:

"BOOM!"

Jared jumped in his seat dropping his leg and sat up straight. We all burst out laughing at the look on his face. I leaned into Naji as my sides ached and tears ran down my face. Through blurry vision I watched Jared glare at us. He stood up and I grabbed his arm as he went to leave.

"Oh come o-on! That was f-funny!" I told him. He looked at where my hand touched him. Next to my fingers was a tattoo. It was a navy blue watercolor splatter. I let go of him and smiled. "Are you going to look in the box or do I have to give It to someone else?" I asked.

Jared scowled and picked up the tipped-over box. He pulled out the tissue paper glaring around the table, daring us to laugh. Jazmine snorted out a laugh and Jared looked at her; she waved teasingly at him. Jared pulled out a dark blue tie that unrolled as he lifted it out of the box. He felt the fabric between his fingers. Jared laid it over his shoulder. Next, he pulled out a matching handkerchief that was folded neatly. He raised his eyebrows at me and tipped the box so that matching cufflinks landed in his hand.

"Okay how are these going to help?" He asked.

I grabbed the black light pen from my bag and held my hand out for Jared to hand over the tie and handkerchief. I clicked the top of the pen and shone the light on them. The navy blue fabric turned to a glowing blue color.

"Holy shit that's cool," Jared said as I turned off the pen and smiled at him.

"Ya, they are pretty cool," I told him. I handed back the tie and handkerchief. He took them and put them back in the box. "The cufflinks glow as well."

"Cool. How much do you want for them?" Jared asked.

"Free, but you have to send some of your friends, them I'll charge."

"Why don't I have to pay?"

"Because I'm a businesswoman and this way I'll make more money. Plus once you lose the contacts, the glowing blue will look good with your green eyes and your blue tattoo," I told him.

"Ooookaaay," he was silent for a few seconds sharing a look with my friends. "So I guess I'll see you at the celebration then. Save me a dance," he winked and walked away.

My mouth dropped open and… And…

What the hell was that?

I looked around the table and saw matching looks. Except for Naji who was smirking and wagging her eyebrows at me. I looked at Jared's retreating back in confusion.

Did… Did he just flirt with me?

SEVEN

There was an hour and a half before the celebration started. I had on my dress and my hair was up in a bun of loose ringlets. I was putting in earrings when I saw a large dark blue mark on the inside of my wrist. It almost looked like a bruise was forming. Frowning, I rubbed at it. I didn't remember hitting it on anything. As I racked my brain as to why it was there, the Jaws theme went off through my phone speakers.

"Uugh," I complained. But I still answered it. "Yes Peyton, what do you want?" I had given her my number when she wouldn't stop bugging me. After word spread about my glowing merchandise, she wanted some for her date. Unlike everyone else, I had charged her fifty dollars for each item in the box. She was pissed when she found out, but oh well. With the two hundred dollars I got from her, and with the seven hundred-and-twenty I got from everyone else, I didn't care what she thought. I had made a five-hundred-and-forty-five-dollar profit.

"Since I'm the official person in charge, I'm the person peo-ple call. And I don't really fe-"

"Peyton, what do you want?"

"Ugh, you're so rude. Anyways, I just got a call asking me what the tonic water was going in. I told them to leave it in the bottles on the tables."

• • • • •

"You told them to leave it in the bottles… Even though we or-dered specific glasses… What the fuck Peyton?"

She laughed through the phone.

"It's your problem now," she said and hung up.

I stared at my phone.

"Stupid petty bitch," I moaned. I grabbed my heels, keys, and my purse. Walking out of my room I came face to face with Sara. She had a towel wrapped around her with her hair pinned up.

"Where are you going?" She asked.

I rolled my eyes and Sara raised her eyebrows.

"Peyton is trying to make sure the tonic water is being served in their bottles. Normally I wouldn't care, but other people would. And I don't want Peyton to be smearing my name the whole night."

"Ew, what are they supposed to be in?"

"Plastic champagne glasses," I told her as I went down the stairs.

"Like that's any better!" Sara yelled as I shut the door.

• • • • •

I pulled up to the school and saw an empty lot. Which was odd since teachers were supposed to be here.

Carefully I walked into the school trying to avoid ice patches. It was sort of creepy being the only one at the school. The lights were on, but it was silent unlike during the school day. Once inside I slipped off my heels, no need to get a head start on sore feet. My feet slapped against the floor tiles as I walked.

When was the last time the floors were cleaned?

As I walked down the hall towards the gym, the lights flickered. Thinking of all the corny horror movies I've seen, I laughed quietly at my racing heart. I opened the doors to a dark gym and found the switch for the black lights and flipped it. Chairs glowed at tables, and balloons on poles cast lights across the room. Green, yellow, red, and purple lights shone up from the floor and onto the walls. Each table glowed neon white allowing me to see the vases of neon markers.

There was a fridge splattered with glowing paint sat in the back behind tables set out for food. I opened it… To see it completely empty. Dammit Sean. Under one of the tables was a box with the plastic wine glasses I had ordered.

"Thank you gods," I said, my voice echoing.

I went around the room straightening placemats, correcting silverware, and cleaning up the DJ booth. I turned on some music and continued to fix things.

"When we're apart
There's something missing in my heart
I see everything anew
-my feelings are true
-I become someone new
You make me forget my troubles and worries
I'm myself with you
You don't have a clue
About the things you give me the courage to do
When we're apart
I only see the storm

but when I'm there with you
I see the rainbow
-Oh, oh, oh,
But you don't have a clue
The ways you make me feel..."

"Heehehehehee."

I looked up from the table I was at, the hair on my neck raising. I placed the plate down and looked towards the doors. The lights in the hall were flickering again.

I will not ask who's there, I will not ask who's there, I will not-

Footsteps sounded behind me. I turned around and didn't see anyone there. The music shut off with a screech.

"Shit," I whispered.

The skin on my neck warmed and I turned around. Again there was no one there. Crash! I spun to see an overturned table. Plates lay on the floor broken along with the broken vase. Crash! The table further down was tipped over. Markers flew across the room. The tablecloth bellowed as it floated to the floor. A light buzz came from the hallway as the lights flickered faster and faster. Static came from the speakers. The lights by the walls went out one by one with a hiss.

My heart pounded in my ears. Sweat beaded at my hairline. What the hell was going on? The black lights started to flicker. At first, they were flickering, but as the seconds passed they began to pulse faster. If I wasn't terrified out of my mind, I would have thought the strobe light effect was neat. POP! With every balloon that popped my heart jumped in my chest. Soon the balloons dangled on the poles in shreds.

"Heehehehehee," the laugh sounded from behind me.

Oh, fuck no!

I grabbed the skirt of my dress in my fists and hiked it up to my thighs as I booked it the hell out of the gym. The black lights cast disfigured shadows as I ran. My feet pounded against the polished wood, barely heard over the static and buzzing. The hallway was only lit by the flashing lights from the gym. I could see the side door that would lead me to freedom. I was so close. Just a little faster. Come on, co-

Pain radiated through my skull as my hair was yanked back. My feet flew out from under me and my chance at escaping was gone momentarily. I was thrown back and I slid across the floor. I came to a stop halfway down the hall on my side.

I groaned and grasped my head. The skin on my legs was raw from where they hit the floor while sliding. I looked down the hall to see a figure standing still. With every flash of the light, the figure appeared closer. I tried to scramble to my feet, but my dress was caught on a locker.

Frantically, I ripped free only for the figure to grab me by my throat. They lifted me like I weighed nothing as I clawed at the hand that obstructed my air. They tilted my head back so that I was looking at the ceiling. When the light flashed again I was unable to see my attacker. When it was dark again I was brought close to the person. I caught a whiff of clover before I was airborne.

I flew through the gym doors landing on a table and sliding onto the floor. The broken glass cut my arms and legs. Hissing in pain I pulled bits of glass out of my skin. Blood smeared on my skin and the neon white tablecloth. The black lights made the blood glow a sickening color.

Markers were kicked across the floor as the person walked toward me. I took a running start toward the men's locker room. The only reason I didn't go this way before was because the attacker was closer to it earlier. But now that they were closer to the gym entrance, I could make a run for the door that led to the football field.

The automatic light flashed on, making me squint. I weaved my way around benches and open lockers. My arms pumped

at my sides. Again freedom was feet away when I was slammed into the lockers. My head bounced off the ridges, ripping out hair in the process. I cried out and my legs collapsed under me. Warm blood dripped into my blurring vision. I saw leather-clad legs walk up. I was grabbed by the throat and picked up like a rag doll. I got the faint impression that they were toying with me like a cat and mouse. The wind blew around us and I was standing next to the stalls. Bewildered, I looked around me. The stalls were right next to the door that lead to the gym. There was no possible way I could have gotten here in just a few short seconds. What the hell? I was picked up and thrown into the mirrors above the sinks. The glass cracked and my body laid across the sinks painfully.

"Uuuuuh," I lifted myself up on one arm only to have an elbow rammed into my spine. "Ahhhhh!" A new pain sprouted as the force pushed me against the sinks. They creaked and water sprayed everywhere. My foot was grabbed and my hands scrambled to hold onto the sink. The water made the porcelain slick and I was pulled off the sinks. I fell onto the wet floor, and they flipped me onto my back. Dark red eyes peered at me. Every other detail was blurred out and smoke clung to them so that I couldn't tell who they were.

"W-who-??" I whispered in shock.

They smiled evilly and revealed bright white fangs. I stared at them in horror and fear. What the actual hell? Those were fake, they had to be... But they looked so real compared to cheap Halloween fangs.

"If I didn't know any better, I would have said that you looked surprised," they said in a gravel voice.

"Who are you? Why are-"

They threw me out of the locker room and into the gym. I laid on one of the broken tables in stunned silence while a ringing filled my head. In a flash, they were towering over me. They reached down and grabbed me by the front of my dress, only to toss me again. I hit one of the poles and landed awkwardly. Fire shot through my side and each breath that I took burned. Again they were standing over me. They grabbed my arm while stepping on my leg. They pulled up quickly, letting go when I screamed as my shoulder dislocated. I held my arm and sobs racked my body.

"The Temnaya Koroleva says hello," they chuckled. They lifted their leg and I could see the bottom of their shoe. They stomped down on my chest and there was a crack. With my next breath liquid came out of my mouth.

"Looks like you punctured a lung. My job is done," They turned and walked away with a laugh. "Sweet dreams, Princess,"

Blood splattered with every breath I took. I was drowning in my own blood and by the time the first person would appear, I would be... Dead. I was dying in the middle of my school gym. Naji was right, we did end up with a Carrie theme.

My eyes grew tired and I knew that I couldn't sleep. I had to stay awake. Must keep eyes open. Must keep eyes open. Must eyes keep. Eyes keep must... What was I supposed to be doing? I was so tired... Sleep, I needed to sleep. I let my eyes drift shut.

"Don't you dare."

My eyes opened at his voice. At first, all I saw was a light, but it soon faded. Left in its place was a man in camouflage pants and a white muscle shirt. His hair was shaved and his muscles were more defined. He looked down at me with concern. "Don't you dare give up on me Princess," he said, placing his hands on me, spreading warmth through my chest.

"D-D-" When I tried to speak my chest tightened and coughs racked my body. Blood stained his white shirt as it flew from my mouth.

"Shh, don't try to speak," Not one to always listen, I tried anyway. His look of concern turned to the oh-so-familiar look of disapproval. "What did I just say? Stop moving, I'm trying to heal you."

Where his hands rested on my chest the warmth turned cold. My eyes grew heavy once more and they slid shut against my will. He swore and pressed harder on my chest. The feeling of fire chasing after the coldness in my body felt strange. When the fire reached a cold spot in my body, it would move. My body was in chaos and there was nothing I could do about it. Finally, the fire chased away the coldness. My eyes shot open and he fell onto his ass. Suddenly the fire was gone. He got on his knees and looked at me with a smile on his face.

"Welcome back. Go ahead and sleep, it's safe now," he said.

"But D-Dillion-" he kissed my forehead.

"Sleep little sis. When you wake up, you'll understand."

EIGHT

Jared got out of his car and slammed the door shut. He was wearing his suit without its jacket because he had forgotten it at home. He had been getting ready when he heard Sean swear from downstairs. Apparently, Sean had forgotten to bring the tonic water earlier in the day. Sean had said that he would have brought them himself, but Sara wanted him at her house for pictures.

Which led to Jared being in the school parking lot with three large boxes of tonic water. On his way into the main entrance, Jared saw Seine's truck in the parking lot. He smiled remembering the way she had looked when he flirted with her. Jared liked her, she was feisty. And didn't take any shit. Jared's smile faded. There was the little mystery of how and why she had been able to see his "tattoo."

As soon as Jared opened the front door he smelled it: blood. He sat the boxes down and followed the smell down the hallways that led to the gym. Cautiously, he walked down the last hallway until he saw a particularly dark area by the lockers. Upon inspecting it, he saw ripped blue fabric stuck on a hinge.

Jared followed the smell of blood through the gym doors where the smell was stronger. He took a step forward and was blinded. When he could see again he looked around the gym in surprise. For someone who didn't want anything to do with setting up, Seine had done an awesome job.

One of the tables closest to the door was on its side. Broken plates, along with markers, littered the floor. The tablecloth glowed a light blueish color with dark glowing smudges. The sound of water spraying came from the men's locker room. Weaving his way around the tables slowly Jared saw a table split in half. The tablecloth reeked of blood. Jared followed a blood trail to a pole that resembled a stripper pole. On the floor beside the pole covered in blood was Seine.

Oh my God.

Jared ran to her side and dropped to his knees. He checked her pulse, finding it weak, but there. Jared ran his hands over her. There were deep abrasions on her legs. Three of her true ribs were broken. Her sternum was fractured and her shoulder was dislocated. When he was sure she wasn't in danger of dying, Jared pulled out his phone.

"Change of plans, the extraction is happening now," he said.

"Now?" The person on the other end asked.

"Yes, right now. She's been attacked. Call the rest of the guard and her mother. Let them know that I'll meet them there."

"Will do. The jet will be at the landing strip in twenty minutes with your medical supplies."

"Make it fifteen," Jared said looking down at Seine. He couldn't believe that they had found her. After all, he had done to prevent this.

"Right away, your Majesty."

Jared hung up and scooped up Seine in his arms bridal style minding her injuries. Her blood transferred onto his shirt staining his tie.

"Let's get you home Princess," he whispered.

• • • • •

Days Later

"Najia, you need to calm down," Jared said from his comfortable spot on the floor.

"Calm down? CALM DOWN? MY BEST FRIEND IS LAYING ON THERE IN A BLOODY MESS! AND WE CAN EVEN HEAL HER RIGHT!" Najia glared, her purple eyes flashing and the coal-like parts on her skin burned bright.

"He already told you. We can't heal her our way because she's not fully transitioned," Jazmine spoke up from the doorway.

"And when will she transition?!" Najia asked.

Jared rolled his eyes and laid on the floor. He looked up at the bed with the sleeping Seine. He had gotten her to the jet without any problems. They took off and he had treated her the best he could. When they had landed, the family doctor had taken over. Seine was hooked up to an IV while she was… Sleeping. And Najia has been freaking out nonstop. Which was getting really annoying.

"Najia, why don't you go play FO in the game room and stop hovering. She's not going anywhere," Jared told her.

• • • • •

One Month Later

"Will you all get the hell out?!" Jared yelled at the girls crowding his room.

Aurora, Jazmine, Layla, Yamka, and Najia stopped their endless chatter. They looked at Jared as he rubbed his temples. There was only so much a guy could take hearing about "hot" book characters. And he was a little annoyed with them comparing fake guys to him. He wasn't a book character, he was going to have flaws.

They looked put off, but he didn't care. More than a month of them bickering and gossiping was driving him mad. He just needed peace and quiet. They must have seen something on his face because they left without saying anything. The door closed behind them and Jared sat heavily in the chair.

After weeks of barely sleeping and finally having quiet, he felt exhausted. He looked over at Seine, who was slowly healing, and let his eyes close. Jared felt bad for her. When she woke up she would be confused. And when that passed, she would be angry. But what did he know, humans never did what he expected. He opened an eye and looked at the inside of her wrist. An aquamarine blue splatter that marked her skin. Then again, she wasn't human.

NINE

Everything was stiff and I couldn't move without wincing. Opening my eyes was difficult, but when I did, I wanted to close them once again. It was too bright. Slowly, I cracked my eyes open. It took forever, but finally, I could see where I was… Which was not my room. The walls were coal black, as was the carpet.

Did I get drunk at the celebration? How stereotypical… Oh gods, whose room am I in!?

I sat up and looked around. A large floor-to-ceiling window lit up the room. The walls were black, but not a horrible shade, it almost made the walls look soft. There was a fancy bookcase to my right with various pieces of pottery and large books. Small lights on cables hung over the bed. On either side of the bed that I was in there were some lamps. A leather chair next to the bed looked worn out. The whole room screamed "guy."

I heard the sound of a shower turning off behind a door. The door opened and a guy walked out with a towel wrapped around his waist. Water dripped down his chest drawing my attention to things I shouldn't have been looking at. His head was covered by a towel as he dried his hair. I watched him walk to a dresser that I had failed to see. He pulled out some clothes and it dawned on me that I could feel the sheets on most of my skin. Lifting the sheet covering me, I saw dark purple and red scars covering my legs. My ribs were a light purple. My shoulder was the ugly yellow color of an old bruise. I was in nothing but my underwear. My eyes widened and clutched the sheet to my chest.

Oh, gods. What the fuck did I do?

The guy pulled the towel off his head, leaving his hair a mess. He let the towel lay off his shoulders as he turned around. And when he did, everything became worse.

"Shit," I whispered. Or at least I tried to whisper. My throat was the desert and my tongue was lead in my mouth. I must have made some sort of noise though because Jared's head jerked up.

"You're awake." He sounded shocked. He left and came back a second later with a glass of cold water. He handed it to me and I reached for it with shaking hands. My plans of taking a small sip went down the drain once the cold water hit my tongue. I drained the glass and Jared took the glass from me to refill it once more. My eyes followed him, taking in the way his muscles shifted in his back.

"Did I get drunk? I never get drunk. Hell, I never drink. Why did I drink?" My eyes widened. "Oh, oh no. Did we use protection? I can't be a mother yet. I can't-Oh gods."

Jared stared at me freaking out and busted out laughing. He grabbed his clothes and went back to the bathroom.

"We didn't do anything," he called out.

"Where are my clothes then?"

"About that, they had to be thrown away. They were… Ruined," he said, coming out of the bathroom and pulling on a shirt.

"Ruined? What the hell happened last night?" Even to myself, I sounded hysterical.

"Maybe I should start from the beginning." Jared sat in the chair and scratched the back of his neck. "Right. So on the night of the celebration you were attacked." He paused and looked at me. "You sustained some injuries and when I showed up you were unconscious. I carried you to my car and drove to the air strip, where we boarded a plane. In the air I stopped your bleeding and when we finally got here, the family doctor took over."

As Jared retold the details I saw flashes of it all happening again. The flickering lights, the footsteps following me. The tables were knocked over, and water spraying. And…

"…What was wrong with their teeth?" I whispered. Jared's eyebrows shot up, then scowled.

"Of course, it makes sense now."

"I'm glad it does to someone," a slightly annoyed voice said. Jazmine stood in the doorway with bags under her eyes and a pile of clothes in her hands. I smiled at her and she sat down beside me.

"How are you feeling?" Jazmine asked.

"A bit sore, and confused," I told her, sneaking a glance at Jared.

Jared stuck his tongue out at me, obviously trying to make me smile but he didn't look into it. I looked at him closer and like Jazmine, he too had bags under his eyes. His hair was disheveled, unlike the usual style it had at school. It was almost like he didn't care about his looks anymore. Jared's normally tan skin looked pale and malnourished.

"Well, that's to be expected after all that you went through," Jazmine told me with a sad smile. "I guess we should tell you why what happened, well… Happened." She scooted back against the headboard and let out a sigh that sounded exhausted. "I guess we should start with the fact that you're currently on an island in the middle of the Pacific Ocean that no one knows about. Before you say anything, we're relatively safe, but there can't be any communication outside of the island to keep it secret. If you try it won't work. You know the Bermuda Triangle?"

I closed my mouth and cut off the questions that were brimming my lips. I could wait to ask them, I had plenty of practice from being a curious child. I nodded.

"Okay, so, you've heard about ships disappearing, UFOs, and the like, right? This island is like that. It can all be explained by non-believers; those who don't believe in magic. The ships were sunk because they came too close to our island. The UFOs were actually our private planes scouting out for danger. Everything can be explained by what we are. You, your family, all of your friends, some people at school, we are not... We're not..." Jazmine seemed to be having a hard time saying what she wanted. She looked like she wanted to puke. She looked over at Jared for help. He sighed and leaned forward in his chair with his hands folded in front of him.

"What she's trying to say is that we're not human. And before you start denying that you're one hundred percent human, have you noticed people's eyes? You have, I can see it on your face, not to mention you commented on my eyes while we were at school," Jared looked at me hard, daring me to challenge him.

"Those are just contacts, a new fad, it'll be over in a month or two," I said quickly. There was no way that I was going to accept this. I was human, as human as they were. But they were saying that they weren't... And if they weren't human, what were they? What was I? I had to be human. Jared shook his head while Jazmine placed a hand on my covered leg. My heart was pumping hard enough that I could hear it in my ears. I felt my hands shaking as my body raged between being cold and hot every twenty seconds.

"What do you think we are?" I whispered.

"Well, you're a lycanthrope, also known as-"

"A werewolf," Jazmine finished for Jared.

"You…you think I'm a werewolf?" I asked. There was no way they believed what they were saying. Maybe I was dreaming, that was highly possible. Maybe I actually went into a coma from being too cold and this was the result. That would be the only way that one of my friends and some guy from school, would try to convince me that I was a werewolf. Werewolves were made up, a thing of myths, and every girl's dream in 2006. Reading about monsters was completely different than being told that you were one of them.

"It's okay if you don't believe us, you have plenty of time to understand," Jazmine said.

"Uh-huh, riiiight." My doubt hung in the air between the three of us for a few seconds before Jared cleared his throat.

"Like you said Jazmine, she has plenty of time, so why don't you give her those clothes so she can shower and get dressed," he suggested, looking away from us, a blush covering his cheeks.

Oh. I was practically naked…in what was most likely his bed… Oh, gods. I felt my own face redden and pulled the sheet tighter around me. Jazmine smiled a little at my discomfort because she found my being embarrassed funny. She held onto my clothes and slid off the bed to allow me to awkwardly maneuver my way off without flashing anyone. I took the clothes from Jazmine and walked into the bathroom holding onto my makeshift toga with help from her. As soon as I closed the door I pinched the skin on the inside of my elbow. Pain radiated from the spot, the skin instantly turning red. I was still standing in the bathroom and not waking up. I leaned against the door, letting out a breath that came from my toes. This was real, this was really happening. My friend had drunk the crazy juice and wanted me to join the crazy train. Pushing myself away from the door I took stock of the bathroom.

The walls were covered in large black and white wooden tiles, there being more black than white. The floor was a white marble before leading into the floor-to-ceiling glass shower where the floor became tile. Straight across from where I stood was a pure white porcelain tub that looked heavenly. On the coinciding wall was a cabinet with a sink and a still fogged-up mirror from Jared. Below the mirror was a large crystal bowl with a faucet that had a waterfall-type spout that didn't seem all that necessary in my opinion. All in all, it was very stylish and it made me a little nervous to touch anything should something break. Very carefully I placed the clothes on the cabinet.

I walked over to the shower and looked at the several different knobs for a few seconds before I made a guess at how to turn it on. Why couldn't showers have the same workings? There was a fifty-fifty chance I could have messed something up. The water put-putted before a heavy stream rushed out. Feeling the water to make sure it was comfortable, I discarded the little clothing I had on and stepped into the shower. There was a railing attached to the wall that I held in case my legs gave out. My aches and stiffness melted away, but I discovered more bruises along my skin. When I started worrying about the cost of the water bill, I got out of the shower. I found a couple of towels hanging on some hooks on one of the glass walls. I wrapped one around my body while tying my hair up in a towel turban.

I went to pick up the clothes Jazmine had given me when my hand knocked over a blue hair gel container to the floor. I cringed at the loud smack it made against the floor and counted my blessings that it didn't break. Bending at the waist, I picked up the gel and straightened.

Glancing into the fogged-up mirror I saw a figure standing behind me. I dropped the gel once again and screamed. The container broke, gel splattering my feet and floor. The guy flinched away from me before stepping closer. I spun around, slipping on the slick marble and falling onto my backside. Twisting around I saw the bathroom door fly open, hitting the wall. Standing in the doorway was a white dog with black paws twice the size of a husky. Beside it was a very pale and scary-looking Jared. The dog tackled the person to the floor while Jared rushed to my side and helped me up. He stood in front of me as growls filled the room.

I peeked around Jared's shoulder and squinted at the sight in confusion. The dog was on the person's chest, but the person looked blurry; as if I suddenly needed glasses. I blinked a couple of times in a quick recession trying to clear my vision, but the person remained blurry while everything else stayed in focus. The dog's muzzle was pulled back from its teeth and looked ready to lunge forward. The person reached up and held the dog by the throat and flung it away from them. A cry escaped my mouth as the dog crashed through the shower walls. Glass rained down around the dog and across the floor. The person did a fancy ninja flip so that he was standing on his feet and turned to face Jared and me.

"That wasn't very nice," a familiar voice mocked. The blurriness surrounding the person slowly receded to reveal an annoyed Damon. He looked around Jared to glare at me and I shrank back in fear. "You've caused a lot of trouble for me little girl,"

I stared at him, my fear fading. Damon was just some punk kid from school with a bad attitude. I had nothing to fear from him. The whole blurry thing was some sort of trick of the light. I glared right back at him with as much dignity as I could while wearing a towel. He raised an eyebrow at me as if daring me to say something back to him.

"I'm so very sorry to have made a hassle for you in your such important life that would somehow qualify you the right to come into the bathroom where I'm currently naked. How sad for your poor, important, perverted life," I sneered, still from behind the safety of Jared's back. I wasn't afraid, nope not me. It was just better to be safe than sorry.

The dog appeared from the shattered shower stall and shook out its fur. Glass tinkled to the floor. Damon glanced behind him at the dog with a look of disgust. As if the mere sight of it deserved the wrath of the oh-so-important Damon. The dog stood on its back legs and took a step forward. As it did, the air around it seemed to shimmer. By the time the other foot moved, Jazmine stood in the dog's place.

My brain couldn't understand what my eyes were seeing. Jazmine was the dog… The dog was Jazmine… The dog was a wolf? Which meant Jazmine was a wolf. And if she was a wolf, that meant that she was a werewolf. Werewolves, which were apparently real. Which meant Jared and Jazmine didn't drink the crazy juice. I put my head in my hands and let out a moan of despair. It was official, I had lost my ever-loving mind. I looked in time to see Jazmine snap her teeth at Damon, who in return wiggled his fingers at her in a mocking wave. She walked around Jared and took hold of my arm, pulling me from the bathroom. Jared let out a groan as he looked over his now-wrecked bathroom before following us out.

When we exited the bathroom, Damon was lounging on the bed looking as if we were late. He looked me over, rolled his eyes, and snapped his fingers. The air around me warmed and my skin tingled. The towel that was wrapped around me was replaced with the clothes Jazmine had given me. My hair tumbled down my back in soft waves, no longer wet. My mouth filled with the taste of copper as if I had sucked on a penny. Jazmine shook her head at him and threw herself onto a beanbag chair I had previously overlooked.

"Show off," Jared whispered.

I stared at Damon in shocked disbelief. He smiled smugly from his spot.

"You're a wizard Harry," I whispered.

Jared choked on a laugh and Damon's smug look vanished. He glared at us and Jazmine stuck her tongue out at him. I looked at the three of them. They looked completely at ease while my world was fragmenting around me. One of my friends from the past several years was some sort of mythological creature. And if what they told me was true, then every single one of my friends was one as well.

All the people I thought I was close to, were perhaps, the farthest from me. They kept who they were secret from me for so long. It must have been so hard to be around me without truly being themselves. How exhausting for them to pretend to be someone they weren't. I thumped on the floor next to Jazmine with this new realization. Now that I knew, they could be themselves, they could be true to their hearts. I glanced at Jazmine with tears in my eyes. She looked concerned at the tears in my eyes.

"I'm sorry," I whispered.

"For what-?" Jazmine started to ask when there was a commotion at the doorway. Yamka, Naji, and Aurora burst into the room. They were talking with one another, but when they saw me they stopped. They stopped walking, and they stopped talking, I think Naji might have even stopped breathing. A few seconds passed in complete silence before I raised my hand in a little wave. Naji let out a little yell before charging at me. She threw herself at me and we fell backward. Laughing I hugged her to me and let the tears fall. One of the most precious people in my life was in my arms, so everything would be okay. Yamka and Aurora walked in more normally while smiling.

"Seine! Seine! SEINE! You're awake! Goddess it's about freaking TIME!" Naji smacked my arm lightly.

"Sorry, sorry! Must have needed some extra sleep after dealing with you every day," I teased while sitting up with her still hanging onto me.

Aurora sat on the bed next to Damon, who in turn scowled and moved away from her. There was a story there that I would get after things settled down. Yamka squished herself in the chair with Jared. They both looked cozy which raised some questions, but later, I would ask later. I looked over at my friends and Damon. They were all some sort of beings that stories were written about.

"So," I started, "Jazmine is obviously a werewolf. What are you?" I asked.

Jazmine made a low sound in her throat causing me and everyone else to look at her. She looked a little uncomfortable despite being in what looked like the softest bean bag ever. Damon laughed from the bed and Aurora, bless her soul, smacked him with a pillow.

"I'm technically not a werewolf, I'm what South America calls a lobisomem; a wolf shifter made the old fashion way instead of being born one," Jazmine explained. "You could be turned into one by being bitten, getting blood on you, being the seventh son, or having sexual relations with a priest. Basically what movies are really based on."

"… Did you say lobby some men?" I asked, trying to lighten the mood. Jazmine smiled and shook her head at me.

"No you dork, a lobisomem" she repeated. "When I was seven, I visited my grandmother in Brazil and got lost. I somehow ended up in a cultist gathering where they were screwing with things they didn't understand. They decided a lost kid would be the best test subject. They poured blood on me and it changed me. Unfortunately, or fortunately, depending on the way you look at it, my screams called attention to their gathering and they fled. I was left half transitioned into a lobisomem when some old natives found me. Grandma was among them, she was the great-great-granddaughter of a lobisomem chief. You could say it was fate that I got lost. Grandma knew of this place and sent me here to get me used to being around those sorta like me. When I was twelve I was able to control my shifting, so I was able to go back home, where I met you."

I didn't know what to do with this information. Part of me was sad for young Jazmine, the other part, a selfish part, was glad she went through it so that she was here. The others in the room -well except Damon, I think he was sleeping- nodded like they knew the story. Yamka nudged Jared in the side and whispered something. He laughed and nodded, his hair falling into his face. A small tinge in my chest caused me to furrow my brow. I wasn't jealous, was I? That wasn't fair to them, I had no right.

"My turn!" Naji sang in her singsong voice. She pulled away from me and spun on the floor so that she was laying on the floor with her feet on the bed. "So you noticed my eyes right? When I picked you up after Sara ditched you? Well I guess you know now that I wasn't wearing contacts. I'm actually the daughter of dragons! Exciting, I know. My mom is a Fire dragon, while my pops is a Water dragon. They aren't completely dragon, which is why I'm not a giant lizard. That would be hard to explain while in town! LOL. But they were enough for me to hoard things, and I have some magic. Hence the purple eyes. Oh! And now that you know about it all, we don't have to glamour ourselves anymore so you can see our true selves." Naji tossed her arms in my lap where they were covered with black marks. The black glowed faintly, moving fire under it. Like cooling embers of coals. I lightly touched her expecting it to be hot to the touch, but it was surprisingly cool. Naji spoke all the while, swinging her feet in the air. "It gets hotter if I'm emotional."

I stared at her in shocked silence. My best friend was a freaking dragon. A small, purple-eyed dragon that hoards. That definitely explained why she had a bunch of jars in her room of random things… Well, I guess they weren't really random after all. Wait… I squinted at my dear sweet hoarding dragon friend.

"In eighth grade you totally snagged my crystal ball with the bird knuckle in it, didn't you?" I accused playfully.

Naji looked at me from her odd position and smiled sheepishly. She somehow managed to shrug while laying on the floor.

"It's highly possible that I might have taken it before I had a better handle on my hoarding issue," Naji said apologetically. "But hey, we became friends because of the great search for it,"

"You're so lucky I love you, you crazy girl," I said fondly, shaking my head. "Okay, so we've got a werewolf, a dragon, and a professional ass. What are the rest of you?" I asked. From the bed Damon lifted his arm slowly and flipped me off, only proving my point. Aurora shook her head at him before turning her attention to Yamka and Jared. She shrugged and Yamka chuckled. I watched her in surprise.

"I'm pretty much human except for my eyes. I'm from angelic lineage, but it's from so far up the family tree all I have are the eyes," Aurora told me and I fought to keep the shock off my face. That meant angels were real. Did that mean demons were too?

"What about Layla?" I asked. From what her "makeup" looked like, she had to be something exotic.

"She's a banshee," Damon said. "If she screams people die. It's great in battle,"

I… Noted. If I ever went to battle I would make sure to have Layla join us.

"Why isn't Layla here?" I asked suddenly.

"Layla's family belongs to a different court," was all Jared said.

"Oh… What about you and Yamka?"

"He's a vampire," Yamka answered for Jared. "I'm the same as Jazmine except I was born, like, everyone in my family is born a werewolf. Mom is a purebred which is why she's always hard on me and stuff. Mom sends me here every break to 'properly' become a werewolf." Yamka rolled her eyes and Jared laughed. "No big background story, sorry." She jabbed Jared in the shoulder hard. "Let's blow this popsicle joint, they can fill her out. Besides, it's not like you need to be here anymore." She told him.

I glanced at Naji at the same time she shot me a look. This was not the Yamka that I knew. This was a snippy and borderline rude Yamka. Unlike when we were at school, she seemed more carefree and happy. Which was the real Yamka? The one who always made us laugh or the one who hasn't looked at me once in the last ten minutes? Naji smiled at me but it didn't reach her eyes. So it wasn't just me who noticed.

The old chair creaked as the two of them stood and drifted towards the door. Jared paused at the threshold. He looked like he wanted to say something, or maybe that was my imagination. Yamka pulled on Jared's arm and he resisted for a few seconds before rolling his eyes slightly. He let her pull him out of the room, leaving me slightly more confused than before. The silence in the room was thicker than my book collection. I glanced down at my hands, which I had subconsciously folded in my lap. My nails were chipped and there was something brown under one of them. There were crisscross scars on my arms that were a faint pink. Exactly how much time had passed?

"You guys are such a bore, I wanted at least one fist thrown." I looked up to see Damon getting up from the bed.

"Who's throwing down fisticuffs?" Naji asked then promptly backward somersaulted into a sitting position next to me once more.

Never mind the fact that she told me that she was a dragon, she seemed the same. I didn't know what I would do if she started acting differently. Damon towered over her with a look of complete disdain. He dug around his dark jean pocket for something. He pulled out something that looked like an old chocolate roll, the size of a pencil and an inch thick. Damon lifted it to his nose and smelled it? He literally smelled something that looked like it belonged in a sewer.

"What the hell is that?" Aurora asked.

"It's a cigar…"

"But why though?" Aurora asked.

Damon ignored her and twirled the thing in between his fingers as he turned his gaze on me. Damon sighed before sliding it back into his pocket. Just like back in school, his eyes were black. I guess with a color so close to brown, he would fit in more than, say, purple.

"I suggest talking to her sooner than later," he turned towards the door, crooking his finger at Aurora, telling her to follow. "Because since you're finally back where you belong, the Crowned Head isn't going to let you leave. I also recommend someone making you a map of the manor, or else you may end up somewhere you'd wish you hadn't." He and Aurora left the room, leaving me staring after them.

Jazmine laughed from the beanbag, causing Naji and me to look at her. Earlier she had looked stiff, but now she was spread out and looked a lot more comfortable. Her golden eyes shone with tired amusement. She waved a hand lazily gesturing around the room with a small smile.

"That was more awkward than showing up to the wrong class senior year," Jazmine tittered.

My look of confusion transformed into one of annoyance. I had gotten lost the first week of my senior year despite being there for three previous years. It had been humiliating having to get directions from a first year. Getting lost in general aggravated me and caused anxiety, which coincidentally led to my being lost.

"Totes agree," Naji said. "I nominate myself for the map making, because let's face it Jaz, you're artistically challenged."

Jazmine nodded and shrugged, saying:

"That's fair," she looked back at me with a small smile. "Damon wasn't joking when he said they wouldn't let you leave. While you were out in lala land, the Crowned Head told everyone that you aren't allowed to leave the premises before he lost service while doing Crowned Head things." She smiled sadly. "So you might want to get used to seeing us every day."

My eyes narrowed at her. Damon had said "Crowned Head" as well, only he sounded a little sarcastic about it.

"Crowned Head?" I asked. "Who is that and why are they telling people not to let me out of here? They have no right to do that. Hell, they had no right to bring me here without my permission." I said with barely controlled anger.

Naji and Jazmine shared a look with each other that sent a shiver down my spine. Naji rubbed the back of her head while Jazmine looked everywhere but at me. They both looked like they had been asked to hand in homework they hadn't done. Whatever they were going to say, it wouldn't be good.

"Well," Naji drew the word out, causing my worry to intensify. "It so happens that the Crowned Head might sorta um…" She trailed off and looked at Jazmine for help.

"He's you're um… Dad?" Jazmine finished and leaned back as if she was afraid I was going to explode.

I blinked once, twice, three times. My… Dad? The one that I was told was dead? My dad, a man I've never known, was supposedly a "Crowned Head." A king. Alive. And he was telling people to keep me locked in? Oh heck to the no. I squinted at my friends.

"What?" That was my brilliant response.

Jazmine looked away from me and glanced around the room.

"Your dad is the king of the Rudianda Kingdom, the home of Criaturas mágicas de luz," Jazmine said. "Which makes you, Seine, the Princess. The first one we've had in over a century. Which is why you must be protected."

"Cri- what?" I asked. "And me, a princess? Are you kidding? I am the least qualified to be a princess."

Naji rolled her eyes and flopped back onto the floor. She looked like she was seconds away from making a snow angel.

"Jazmine's just showing off her Portuguese. It means 'Light Magical Creatures,' it just sounds better in Portuguese. We usually just say 'L.M.C'. or 'C.L.D.' And you're more fit to be a princess than Payton." Naji said.

What???????

TEN

I stared around one of the many marble pillars in the lobby. Standing at the door were Samuel and Hunter, two soldiers that have gotten to know me very well in the last few months.

After I had calmed down from Jazmine's little bomb, she informed me that I had been put into a medically induced coma for almost three months. Which meant my senior year of college had finished without me, and the world went on. Naji told me that my mom knew that I where I was, and that she couldn't join me because she wasn't "part of the court." Sara was currently missing along with Sean. Jared's theory was that they ran off together, but it didn't sit well with me. Not that I could ask Jared about it, he and Yamka were never to be found. At least, not where I looked. I was reassured that there was a team out looking for them, though. Aurora was always with Damon for some unknown reason and I didn't want to be near Damon.

After a week I tried to leave the manor, but true to what I was told, I wasn't allowed to. I had even tried to escape out a window, but they were apparently spelled against me. I could open the windows and feel the fresh air. That was it though. If I wanted to, I could open the window in my room on the second floor. From there I could see a couple of miles away. Unfortunately, it wasn't very interesting though. The manor was surrounded by trees and more trees. So the only ones I had talked to in the last six months were Jazmine, Naji, and the soldiers. Though I'm sure that the soldiers would rather never see me again.

Samuel had a short and scrawny build that looked sleek in his Victorian-style suit and coattails. His untamed red hair seemed to shine brightly against the whites and greys of the suit. In one of our… meetings, he told me that he was eighteen. Next to him, standing stiff and proper, was Hunter in his matching suit, but in black.

Unlike Samuel, Hunter was tall and filled out his clothes. His brown hair looked darker next to Samuel's head. He looked weary as he listened to Samuel talk. Hunter didn't talk much, so I didn't know as much about him as I did Samuel. My guess was that he was in his mid-twenties, an only child, a momma's boy, and secretly played some sort of instrument. But it was only a guess.

I snuck from behind the pillar to the next, careful not to make any sound. I wasn't going to make that mistake again. I looked behind me to make sure the coast was clear before speeding to the next pillar. By then I was about twenty feet away from Samuel and Hunter. It was probably the closest I had gotten in the past week. I took a step and Hunter's back straightened. Samuel stopped talking and looked at him strangely. I froze behind the pillar, not daring to move. Hunter was the one to worry about while Samuel was still in training so he wasn't as experienced. Hunter turned away from the door and lifted a hand to the sword on his hip. He looked over the lobby, pausing at where I was hiding before moving away. Samuel looked around the room as well, clearly confused about what he was looking for.

After what felt like ages of standing still and hardly breathing, they turned their attention back to the front doors. Daylight shone through the glass windows and cast shadows across the floor. I peeked around the edge, noticing that Hunter didn't take his hand off of his sword and Samuel was more alert. I slowly inched my way to the last pillar, finally making it there after stopping several times. The last time I had gotten this close to the doors, I had given myself away by tripping over my own feet. It was not a proud moment. Today though, I would touch the door, I owed that much to myself.

With a deep breath, I braced myself before sprinting toward Samuel and Hunter. My bare feet brushed across the floor silently; shoes made too much noise in the quiet room. A few feet away from them, I threw myself at Samuel. He stumbled, unprepared for the onslaught. I pushed past him and my fingers brushed the shiny knob.

This was it, I was finally going to be able to step foot outside. I was going to be able to take a breath of fresh air without a screen in the way. I would be able to see the sky. The knob turned and-

My hand was pulled off the knob and my freedom was gone. I was twisted around in a flurry of movement. My hair fell into my face and I was trapped in the arms of a very stern Hunter. I blew the hair out of my face with a huff and was able to see an embarrassed-looking Samuel in front of me. I gave him a small smile and tilted my head back to see Hunter looking down at me. His bright orange eyes stared at me and I shrugged. Hunter rolled his eyes, removed his arms from me, and went back to his post. I smiled at his back and turned my focus on Samuel.

"You did better than the other day," I told him.

Samuel shook his head sadly and looked at Hunter briefly before running a hand through his hair, making it stick up every

which way. His golden eyes closed for a few seconds before looking at me with a small smile.

"You know Princess, you've been more trouble than I thought you would be," he mumbled to me.

I leaned up against the wall next to his post and shook my head at him.

"How many times are you going to make me tell you to call me by my name and to stop with the princess crap?" I asked exasperated.

Samuel shrugged and turned to his post while trying to fix his hair.

"Sorry Princess, but my life was subtly threatened if I ever called you by anything else but your formal title."

"Now who would do su-" a deep professionally detached voice cut me off.

"Princess," Hunter stated, "perhaps you could go bother someone else, maybe explore the manor, read a book about the proper etiquette of an actual princess."

I smiled at him, not bothered, and raised my shoulder in a half-shrug.

"Why do that when I can do two of those things right here, three if you're feeling spontaneous," I said. "I can bother you while you inform me of my 'princess' duties since you seem to have so much to say on the matter."

Samuel stifled a laugh and Hunter turned to glare at us. Samuel paled and shot me an apologetic smile before turning into a statue, staring out the window. Hunter fixed his look on me and a shiver traveled down my spine. I pushed myself away from the wall and blew out a breath. I waved my hand at Hunter as I turned away.

"I'm going, I'm going," I said and walked away, with nowhere in mind.

I pulled the map Naji had made out of my pocket. It was wrinkled from all the times I had folded and unfolded it. There were three floors and a basement. Naji had drawn a very detailed map, showing where the main rooms were, such as bathrooms, kitchens, and friend's rooms. There were also some weird things. Such as an indoor soccer field, a basketball court, an arcade, and a laser tag obstacle course. Some of which I visited just once to see what they looked like. But after I was noticed, people in the room would stop what they were doing and stare at me. It was awkward for everyone involved. So I didn't go anywhere that had large groups of people.

Looking over the map, I tried to find a place to go. The basement was off-limits to me for some reason. I knew Jared's room was down there because after it was decided that I was healthy, I was brought upstairs. The only places I hadn't been that I liked were the pools, the greenhouse, and the library. I didn't have a bathing suit and there was no way I was going swimming with a bunch of strangers. The greenhouse was on the second and third floors. And it did cross my mind once before, but when I visited I couldn't cross the threshold. The floor was made out of glass that looked down at the entrance of the lobby. There was no way in Hell I was going in that room for any reason whatsoever. Which left the library, a room that I would have visited first, but according to Naji there was a huge shipment of books that had to be sorted through. I had offered my help, but I was informed that the person in charge was gravely picky and that I would just get in the way. But I was bored again, so whether the books were sorted or not, I was going to the library.

I walked up the grand staircase to the second floor and instead of exiting off the right side towards my room, I went to the left. I passed the kitchen I made frequent trips to, passed the pool that Jazmine used for laps, and passed a weight room where the quiet sound of weights clanging drifted out of the closed door. The soccer field was next to the weight room and on the opposite side of the pool; the kitchen was down a different hallway. Low thuds came from the wall as I walked passed and I tried not to flinch at each one. I took another left at the end of the hall, and I ended up at the library.

Large double doors that were currently closed greeted me. I was almost, almost, afraid to touch them. I lightly pushed open one of the doors and quietly shut it behind me. Turning towards the library I felt my mouth drop open in awe. The large room was lit by several crystal chandeliers equally placed along the ceiling, along with large bay windows. Bookshelves were everywhere, filled with books. In front of me was a huge wooden desk littered with boxes and books. I drifted to the right, pulled by some unknown force. The smell of the books caused something to tickle at the back of my mind. Somehow it smelled familiar... Maybe all libraries smelled the same. My hand trailed the spines of books as I passed, taking random twists and turns. Some books looked brand new, while others looked ancient and seconds from falling apart. There was an occasional ladder braced against a shelf with books stacked by the bottom. It had an air of tranquility.

I ended up in the far right corner in the back where it was a little darker and seemed colder. Against the wall was an old mid-thigh wooden bookcase with glass doors. The glass was spotless, the wood polished, and dust free. The doors didn't have any handles, but there was a small keyhole on one side. Inside one of the shelves was an old copy of a child's book with a family of bears on it. The cover had yellowed and it looked water stained. Next to it was what looked like a retro doll in a rainbow dress, the hair up in a child's attempt at a ponytail. One of the shelves held a broken plastic jump rope. Along with it was a faded green leather-bound diary that was closed by a matching leather strap.

A silver glint caught my eye. Laid carefully on the shelf was a silver chain with a small locket. There was an engraving on it, but in the dim light, I couldn't make it out. Below it was a dull yo-yo that was probably shiny at one point. The string was knotted several times. On the bottom shelf lay a broken Etch A Sketch, a candy dispenser, discolored chalk, a few cars, playing cards, and an old sketchbook that was closed.

On the very bottom shelf lay a metal plaque that read: "Belongings of the Lost Princess."

An uneasy feeling settled in my bones the longer I looked at the case. Goosebumps decorated my arms and I shivered, suddenly cold. Everything felt familiar in a creepy sort of way. I bent a little to get a better look at the lock. It looked like a three-prong kind of key was supposed to be used. The hair rose on the back of my neck and I straightened. I looked around the dark corner, and the feeling of being watched filled my veins. Not seeing anyone, my body began to tremble.

I turned away and rubbed my arms, trying to warm them up. I started for the way I came, walking quickly, trying to put space between the bookcase and myself. As I rounded one bookshelf I bumped into what felt like a solid wall. There was a faint "oof" as I lost my balance. Books and papers fell around me as I fell backward. I was grabbed around the waist and I landed on something softer than the floor. As the papers settled to the floor I pushed my hair out of my eyes and I came face to face with a pair of bright neon blue eyes with white rings around the irises, similar to Aurora's. And they looked very annoyed.

I pushed myself away from them and awkwardly sat next to them. They sat up and I looked them over. They were a he. He had a light complexion and his hair was shaved on the sides while long on top with blue highlights. There was a feather earring that hung in his ear and his septum nose ring shone in the light. His jaw was sharp enough to cut glass. He had two barbells through one eyebrow, which was scrunched up as he glared at me. Like the library, he too, seemed familiar. Images of a little boy in a white sweater flashed through my mind. I was chasing him through the library. The boy had the same eyes and highlights. I called out the boy's name as he laughed and ran faster.

"Luke," his name slipped from my lips in a whisper and his eyebrows shot up. He tilted his head to the side as if to evaluate me.

"Princess," he said flatly.

I blinked in quick bursts.

"How? How do I know you? Why do I have a memory of us here?" I asked in confusion and just like that, a guarded expression slammed down on his face.

"Right, I guess you wouldn't remember everything, Princess." Luke spat the word like it disgusted him. "You seem to remember my name though… I was your best friend when you lived here as a child. I was supposed to be your undercover guard, to be with you at all times to keep you safe." Luke pushed himself to his feet and dusted his black jeans off. He shook his head at me. "You promised that we would be together forever, and then you left. Now if you excuse me Princess," he bowed mockingly, "I have more work to do now thanks to you."

With that he walked away, leaving me sitting on the floor. Naji found me a few minutes later still picking up the fallen books. She danced up to me waving her hands and the remaining books went back to their original places.

"Whatcha doin'?" she asked, lifting a book from my hands, and skimming the cover before tossing it over her shoulder. I gaped at her while it sailed to a table and gently settled on it. I shook my head at her with a small roll of my eyes.

"Apparently making the bestest friends with the librarian," I sniffed crossly.

Naji smiled at me and looked towards the desk with a knowing glint in her eyes.

"Luke has his… Issues," she said cryptically. She shook her head and glanced at me with a wide smile. "We've got plans today girly, so no lurking around anymore." Naji hooked her arm around mine and tugged me towards the front door.

"Lurk? I don't lurk," I told her, rolling my eyes.

"Ya you do, but no more," Naji held up a finger and in a mocking voice she continued. "We must get you a proper education that you were deprived from so that you may be a fitting young Princess." Naji lowered her hand and snorted as we walked past the library door and to the left of the room. "Not my words, obviously."

I looked around nervously for Luke.

"Uh, Naji, where are we going?" I asked as she led me to a spiraling staircase that looked seconds from collapsing.

"Didn't you get the memo? We're getting you a good edumacation to get you all sorts of smarticles," Naji said as we went up the stairs.

Which, it turned out, led to a small room that was brightly lit. There was a desk in the center of the room with writing supplies, another bookshelf, and a couple of desks. The desks looked identical to the ones that haunted every high school student. Next to the desk was a rolling chair that looked comfortable. On the wall in front of the desks was a dark green chalkboard. And before my eyes, a piece of chalk floated and wrote on the board.

"Welcome Seine Rudi, please sit to begin your lesson for the evening"

I stared at the words and slowly they disappeared, leaving the board clean. Standing beside Naji, I could feel her body shaking with laughter and I turned to glare at her. She held her arms up, still laughing, and stepped away.

"You read the board, go sit down," Naji said as she plopped herself in the rolling chair and patted the books on the nearest desk, dust going up in a small cloud.

Waving the dust away I cautiously sat in the cold seat. Instantly the dust disappeared and the top book on the pile opened. The title page said that the book was of proper etiquette. I groaned internally and tried to turn the next page, but it wouldn't move.

"You have to read the whole page otherwise the page won't turn," Naji informed me while looking up from a book with a faded moon on it that popped into existence in front of her. She shrugged and flipped through the mystery book.

Muttering about having schoolwork while being out of school, I started reading. After what felt like ten minutes, I wanted to hit my head on the cold desktop. The book said that a woman wasn't allowed to kiss another woman. That it was "frowned upon" and to do so would mean to be outcasted by everyone. I rolled my eyes at how out of date-it was. If I wanted to kiss another woman I would damn well do as I pleased. Neither the book nor anyone would tell me not to kiss another person. The next paragraph was common sense about how women weren't to be late with an "appointment" with a guy.

But the part that made me snort was that it also said that women couldn't go to the bathroom while with the guy. Naji raised an eyebrow at me, but other than that she stayed glued to her book. I sighed. This was going to be a long hour. There was what I would call the "no duh" passage where it said that playing in traffic was a bad idea and gossiping wasn't ladylike. There was also a part that talked about how if a friend or family member was having issues but hadn't mentioned it to you, you weren't supposed to bring it up. You were to pretend to be oblivious to it until it was brought up by that person.

There was also a page that had me rolling my eyes at it. A woman's exercise was dancing, swimming, archery, lawn tennis, or crocheting. How was crocheting an exercise? The others I understood because that was at least a physical exercise that got you sweating. The most crocheting could do was give you stiff fingers and a new blanket.

Beneath the ridiculous exercises was how a woman wasn't supposed to show curiosity. Doing so would mean that you were surely possessed by an evil force. Getting rid of the evil would involve an exorcism with water of the holy and a transfusion with the blood of the first angels. There was even a picture drawn to show a woman tied to a post to show said exorcism. Although it looked like a witch burning.

Just as I started to read about how puns weren't punny, the book slammed shut causing me to jump. Naji jumped as well and her book fell from her hands, a thudding sound filling the room. I stood to stretch as she picked up her book with a grimace. I caught sight of it as she slid it onto the table; the cover had ripped.

"The library is gonna be mad," she muttered. Naji sighed and looked at me with a smile. "Guess what."

I looked at her warily, at what she could possibly be about to say. With Naji, she could be thinking of absolutely anything that could range from art to alien creatures from West Playground. I cracked my back and rolled my neck before answering her.

"Chicken butt…" when she didn't laugh I sighed. "What?"

Naji grinned and bounced on her feet, full of sudden energy, and threw her hands to the sides. Her eyes seemed to be a brighter purple as she bounced and her short hair floated around her head.

"We get to go on a trip now that you've technically started your lessons." She squealed.

I blinked at her stupidly, not quite grasping what she had said. When I did, my eyes widened and my mouth dropped open a little. Naji grinned at me and danced around in a weird dance of hers. My lips twitched and a smile filled my face. She grabbed my arms and twirled me around in a circle.

"You weirdo," I told her laughing. I pulled her to a stop and we headed back downstairs. "Why am I allowed to leave now that I read some of that old-as-dirt book?" I questioned. Naji shrugged and we began the long walk downstairs taking our time, but I noticed that Naji had a little more pep in her step.

"I dunno, that's how it was for all of us. We read a little every day and we got to be able to do more things. The book decides how much you read each day based on how you're feeling. Before you ask; magic. It knows because of magic," Naji informed me. "We're going with Jazmine to her granddad's house. There was an accident a few months ago involving a warlock… He was killed, but not before he took out the warlock as well…" Naji trailed off as we came up behind Jazmine, who was leaning against one of the pillars.

Jazmine smiled at us with a proud smile, pushed herself away from the hard marble, and made her way toward us. Hunter and Samuel stood at the windows still behind her. Jazmine was dressed in her usual attire of blue shorts and a flowy shirt. Her yellow eyes glinted as she passed by a stream of sunlight coming in through one of the windows.

"Granddad was a badass and was so strong when he kicked that warlock's ass. He wasn't prepared for it, heck, none of us were. But he fought for months, before his power failed him and they both died." Jazmine shrugged. "We have lunch every couple of weeks though, so he can help train me."

I gave her a worried look. Her granddad had died, but she had lunch with him??? Jazmine laughed at me and Naji smirked while patting my shoulder. I glanced between the two of them, my eyebrows scrunching up in confusion.

"Her grandad has visiting rights from ἄγγελος." At my blank stare, Naji sighed. "It's Greek for 'angel'. It's not exactly what you think an angel is, but close enough. They're sort of jerks with wings that make the rules for the supernatural."

"Angels are dicks, got it." I nodded slowly and I could have sworn I heard Hunter snort. "Shall we hit the road?" I asked, rubbing my hands together in excitement.

Jazmine smirked at me and nodded her head, gesturing for me to go first. I walked ahead of them and practically skipped to the doors. Hunter and Samuel turned to face me. Hunter frowned at me and looked over my shoulder to glance at my friends. Samuel sneaked a peek at Hunter before smiling at me. He still looked a little bothered by my attempted escape earlier.

"Twice in one day, how lucky we are to be in your presence once again Princess," Hunter drawled.

Naji snickered and I threw a glare at her over my shoulder, before turning my attention back to Hunter. I bowed mockingly to Hunter and grinned at his disapproving look.

"Au contraire, it is I who is blessed by being in the same room as the most witty gentleman within all the lands," I said dryly. I straightened in time to see his lips curl in what might have been the beginning of a smile before his face smoothed out again. I quirked an eyebrow at him. Maybe he wasn't made of stone.

"Are they taking you for a walk? Need a leash or do you already have one?" Hunter directed the second question to Naji.

I was wrong; he was made of diamonds.

"Excuuuuuse you? I am not a dog that needs to be put on a leash!" I said outraged.

Uncomfortable silence met my words. I looked at everyone in the lobby. Everyone except for Hunter looked like they wished they were somewhere else. Samuel was staring at the floor as if it held all the secrets. Jazmine had taken a keen interest in the chandelier above her. And Naji looked like she was about to be sick.

"I already have one," Naji whispered in a small voice.

My head whipped to look at her, but she avoided my gaze. She held up her hands and they started to glow. A long purple tether appeared between her hands. She looked apologetic as one end flew around my wrist and tied tightly. I instantly tried to pull it off, but it held strong. I shot a betrayed look at Naji and she looked remorseful. The other end of the tether was wrapped around Naji's wrist as well. The whole scenario reminded me of a movie I had once seen.

"Seriously?" I shook the tether. "An actual leash, are you kidding me?"

"It is a precaution," Hunter said with the same seriousness as if this was normal. "You are going out on a new continent you have never even heard of, let alone where to go if you were to get lost. With the leash, you will be able to follow it back to Naji. If you get into trouble, she will be able to tell."

"And a glowing purple leash won't be weird to see? No human will question it?" I questioned while eyeing the tether.

"Once you step outside of these walls the tether will become invisible to everyone but the two of you," he said and I snorted. Hunter rolled his eyes at me. "You have not been outside since coming here. Are you going to stand here and bicker about something that will keep you safe, or are you going to leave so I can get back to doing my job?"

I didn't respond to him. Instead, I looked at the door with longing. Hunter wasn't going to stop me this time. I wouldn't have to try to sneak around them. Fresh air, no walls, unfiltered sunlight, bright skies. So why, why was I hesitating? After an internal war, I reached for the doorknob and when no one tackled me, I opened the door. As soon as I smelled the fresh air, I ran out down the steps. Forgetting everyone behind me and my earlier fears, I took a deep breath.

After a few seconds of me being an abnormal person, I became aware that everyone was looking at me. My face burning,

I looked away from them. I heard Jazmine say something to Samuel before Naji and Jazmine joined me outside. Naji still looked upset and I hated seeing her like that. I brought her in for a hug showing her that I understood and forgave her. She instantly looked relieved and smiled at me. Jazmine had started walking down a long driveway to a cobblestone path through some woods. I gave a quick look around, noting for the first time that there wasn't a single vehicle to be seen.

"Uh, we're walking there?" I asked while we caught up to Jazmine. Naji's laugh tinkled through the air, and Jazmine smirked at me.

"You wanted out so badly, enjoy it. It's a seven mile walk to Granddad's house," Jazmine said.

I stared at her and then at the path ahead. It was full of hills and rocks and who knows what. I was more of an "on the path" type of person. What lay ahead held untold promises that would trip me up. I sighed. When I wanted out, I was thinking more along the lines of laying in the grass. Finding a pond to dip my toes in. Hell maybe even swim in it too if it looked clean enough. Oh well, I was out and that was all that mattered… Even if I would without a doubt, fall at least once.

ELEVEN

Two hours later I had fallen a grand total of six -six- times. Naji and Jazmine were a lot more agile than I was. I knew this, yet I was still annoyed when they hadn't even tripped or stumbled once. When we finally came out of the horrible terrain, I was a mess and they looked like they were ready for a photoshoot. We had come up to a quaint little house that looked like a grandparent's house. It was a nice pale yellow, flowers were in full bloom by the stairs, and a swing moved lightly in the breeze on the porch. There was even a birdbath next to an old oak tree.

Jazmine opened the door and instantly the smell of old people came from the house. It brought me back to when I visited my Papa, the smell of soda, laundry, and cigarettes. It was wonderful and I missed it. I followed into the house and we were greeted by an older gentleman that was… Transparent. He was playing a game of chess by himself as we approached. We were a few feet away when he checkmated the white King.

"Hello girls," he said looking up. He had kind eyes and a warm smile.

"Hey Granddad," Jazmine said, moving in to hug him. I watched carefully, thinking that she would pass right through him. To my surprise, she hugged him without an issue. My eyes bugged as Jazmine became blurry around the edges as they hugged. They parted and Jazmine's granddad looked at Naji and me. He nodded at Naji and smiled wider.

"Ah Najia, how are you dear?" he asked.

"I'm good Mr. Bradwell, how was your fishing trip last week?" Naji sat in the chair opposite of him and started resetting the game board. Mr. Bradwell grinned and leaned back in his chair. He waved a hand in the air and the chessboard was replaced with Checkers. Naji blushed slightly and smiled at him gratefully.

"It was fantastic, all the fish were pretty cool with me swimming with them," he chortled and looked over at me.

His face drained of the little color that he had. His eyes looked haunted as he looked me over. I shifted nervously and he followed my every move like a hawk. A chill started at the base of my spine and slowly made its way up. He went from an everyday old person to someone who looked like they'd seen a ghost...

"Uh, hello?" I said and looked over at Jazmine who looked just as confused as I felt.

Mr. Bradwell jerked in his seat and whatever magic that held him in his seat vanished. He fell through the wooden chair onto the floor where he stayed for a few seconds before rearing up.

"Gran-" Jazmine's concerned voice was cut off as Mr. Bradwell lunged up and flung himself at me. Too shocked to move, he flew through me. Coldness spread throughout me and my head felt as if I had a brain freeze, but only worse. My lungs refused to bring in air, leaving me gasping. My legs turned to jelly and I fell to my knees, my hands bracing myself up.

"Seine!"

"Granddad!"

My eyes found my friends just in time for the same coldness to go through me for a second time. Mr. Bradwell appeared in front of me and spun with his hands outstretched, his fingers curled. Jazmine wrapped her arms around him, but he flung his head back and Jazmine flew. Checkers flew everywhere as Jazmine slammed into it. She groaned and held her shoulder, where a table leg protruded from it. Red blossomed around the leg. Naji threw herself at Jazmine and placed her hands on her. The same purple glow from the leash appeared from Naji's hands. I struggled to my feet with difficulty. Once standing I tried to make my way to them. Mr. Bradwell turned on Naji and she looked at him in fear.

"Please, Mr. Bradwell, stop this," Naji begged.

For a second, I thought she had gotten through to him because he paused. But then he growled, growled. He raised his hands and Naji flew away from Jazmine. A cry escaped me as she flew through a wall. He turned on me and I took a trembling step back. His eyes were wild as he came towards me.

"M-Mr. Bra-" I stuttered out as I continued to back up. He matched me with every step I took.

"You will not kill again," he hissed as he stalked my way.

"Ki-kill? I haven't killed anyone!" I cried.

"Don't lie." His hand shot out and grabbed my arm. He used his grip on me to pull me close to him. "You've killed them all," he hissed. He was so close that I could see myself in his eyes. "You'll kill them all again."

The purple tether materialized and unwound itself from my wrist to wrap around Mr. Bradwell's shoulders. I looked over to where Naji had fallen to see her make her way out of the hole gradually, plaster raining down silently around her as she moved. Her purple hair was covered in white powder and her usual laid-back nature was momentarily replaced by anger. Her eyes glowed brighter, casting a shadow across her cheekbones- which seemed to sharpen before my eyes. In fact, the bones in Naji's' face seemed to be shifting, more elegantly than Mr. Bradwell's' had. Purple scales decorated her cheeks and her eyes narrowed at the corners, giving her an elfish look. She appeared from the hole taller with a purple hue around her as she held her tethers tight.

She stood behind Mr. Bradwell breathing heavily, blood on the side of her face. As she pulled on the tether Mr. Bradwell lost his grip on me and stumbled back. The tether pulsed at an angry pace and he struggled to get free. My arm throbbed where I had been grabbed. Glancing down at it I saw nail marks that were frosted around the edges and were bleeding. There was a howl and I looked up to see Naji tying the tether around Mr. Bradwell to a chair. He yelled and hollered as his movements were restrained. Once he couldn't move, Naji went over to check on Jazmine. Their conversation was muffled, but Jazmine stood up with the help of Naji. They made their way over to me and Naji placed a hand on my shoulder.

"Are you okay?" She asked but it sounded as if it came from underwater.

"Yes," I responded slowly. I rubbed my arms trying to get rid of the goosebumps still there from when Mr. Bradwell grabbed me. Warmth spread from Naji's fingers to my shoulders and soon the chill faded from me and my vision became clear. Naji removed her hand and stretched her fingers out as if they were cramping up. Swallowing hard I glanced back at Jazmine who was currently pulling the wood out of her shoulder. She grimaced while bile rose in the back of my throat as she dropped it to the floor. Jazmine placed her hand on the wound and the blood that stained her skin slowly retreated back into her body. She looked me over to make sure that I was okay. Jazmine gave me a small smile that faded when Mr. Bradwell made a noise that reminded us what had just happened. Almost silently we looked towards Mr. Bradwell. He was no longer yelling but he was staring widely at me with his teeth bared in disgust. Jazmine crouched in front of her granddad and I moved closer to Naji.

"Granddad, look at me please," Jazmine said, trying to shift Mr. Bradwell's attention away from me. He growled in response and continued to stare at me. His edges flickered in time with the purple tether holding him in place as if they were feeding off each other's energy. Jazmine reached out and Mr. Bradwell's head whipped over to look at her and she faltered. Jazmine withdrew her hand, sadness flickering over her face before it faded.

"Granddad, who is it that you think she is?" Jazmine gestured to me and Mr. Bradwell's eyes swung back to look at me. He glared at me, growled again, and it was like he was staring into my very being. I suddenly had no secrets while our gazes were locked. Every thought, every feeling, and every emotion that I ever had felt like they were rushing through my head. Swirling together to the point that I couldn't tell which feeling was what, except for being disoriented.

"Granddad! Look at me! Stop digging around and answer me! Who did you think she was?" Jazmine laid her hands on his knees and the swirling emotions and thoughts stopped as soon as she touched him. The bile that I fought off earlier came back up and I pitched away from Naji just in time to hurl the contents of my stomach into the nearby trash.

"She is the end. She killed us then and she'll kill us again. It's only a matter of time. But her. This one. She might be different from last time. She might save us with help. But she'll have to make a sacrifice. She'll have to decide. Him or her. She needs to decide when the earth bleeds red and the moon turns black or else- or else…" Mr. Bradwell trailed off as I stood back up wiping my mouth discreetly. He blinked a few times looking around the room and then down at the tether tying him down. "Jazzy girl? What's going on? What happened?"

Naji moved closer to me as Jazmine smiled sadly at Mr. Bradwell. She patted his legs lightly before nodding to Naji and the purple tether slid off of Mr. Bradwell but kept them nearby.

"Granddad, do you know Seine?" She asked while nodding back at me. I tensed as Mr. Bradwell followed Jazmine's line of sight. He frowned as he looked at me partially cowering behind Naji.

"I do not believe we had the pleasure of meeting before now. Why don't you step out dear so I may look at you better." Mr. Bradwell gestured for me to step out from behind Naji. "Come on out dear I won't bite."

I swallowed hard and looked at Jazmine and Naji checking their faces to see what they were feeling. Jazmine gave me a small nod of encouragement but her eyes were tight with worry. Naji barely took her eyes off Mr. Bradwell as she inched away from me but kept the tether closer, preparing to use them if needed. I stepped a few feet away from Naji and with each step, the tether followed me. Mr. Bradwell looked me over, his gaze lingering on my face. At the blue mark on my wrist that refused to disappear. A week after waking up the blue splatter turned into wrapping lines crawling up my forearm. It wasn't often that someone blatantly gawked at it, but when they did I was reminded of it. Of its stark color against my pale skin… The bright blue pattern disturbingly looked like an exposed vein. One of the constant reminders of what had happened permanently to my body. I lightly brushed my fingers over it, crossing my arms to try and cover it the best I could.

"You don't seem familiar to me, but perhaps we have met in the past…" Mr. Bradwell trailed off as he watched me hide the mark. "Nothing to be ashamed of my dear, they say our marks are reminders of what killed us in the past. Have pride in having been reborn." He smiled at me, a completely different person than only moments before. "I am pleased to meet you Seine." He held out his hand and looked at me expectantly.

I started and rushed forward to shake his hand, but Naji's tethers wrapped around my wrist before I could take his hand. Mr. Bradwell raised an eyebrow at her reaction. I looked back at her and she had a grimace on her face as she pulled me back a few steps until I was back at her side.

"Sorry Mr. Bradwell, but you went a little poltergeisty earlier and I can't take any chances," Naji said and grabbed my hand as if she was making sure I was alright. Looking down at our hands I saw tiny purple sparks dance across our skin. I swallowed hard as my heart skipped a beat and looked back at Mr. Bradwell, who was watching us with careful eyes.

"I see… Was I quite bad? You all seem to be standing in one piece at least. I apologize for my behavior. It may be best if you lot take your leave early, it seems the fishing trip took more out of me than I thought." Mr. Bradwell turned to Jazmine. "My Jazzy girl, I apologize again for my actions. Make sure to visit me soon… It may be time for me to leave."

Jazmine let out a whimper and brought a hand to her grand-dad's cheek. Tears fell down her face as she looked at him.

"No. It hasn't even been a year yet! You have at least half a year left before you have to leave!" Jazmine sobbed.

I gave a confused look at Naji but she shook her head at me.

"It was good to see you, Mr. Bradwell, we'll be back before the season is over." She stopped for a moment and gave a small smile. "Don't go anywhere until I get my rematch," Naji said tilting her head at the scattered checkerboard. "Jazmine, we'll wait up the hill for you." And with that Naji practically dragged me out of the house.

• • • • •

Much to my dismay "up the hill" actually meant up several hills until I was once again soaked in sweat. When I was doubled over trying to catch my breath, Naji sat on a nearby rock covered in fuzzy moss, the tether glowing between us. She sighed deeply and leaned back on the rock looking over at me with tired eyes. Wiping sweat from my eyes I sat beside her on a tree that grew sideways into an "L" shape- a chair made from nature itself. The bark scratched lightly against my palms as the silence stretched between us.

"Soooooo," I began, "He seems extremely nice when he's not trying to kill me." I leaned against the side of the tree that reached for the sky and swung my feet in lazy kicks while trying to catch my breath.

Naji let out a harsh laugh that ended in a sigh. "I promise Mr. Bradwell isn't always like that. But since he's been here be-tween realms he's wasting energy. And when he does that he ends up channeling the spirits around him. Which makes him basically lose his mind for a few minutes. If it helps, whatever Mr. Bradwell says when he's off his topper, it doesn't normally mean anything." Naji paused and looked up at the sky.

I followed her gaze and looked up as well. The leaves of the trees around us blended together in a canopy of greens, reds, and purples. There was sunlight streaming through the leaves decorating the ground and the both of us in their colors. It was… Peaceful. I closed my eyes and inhaled deeply so that I could smell the earth and the slightly sweet smell the breeze car-ried to me.

"He was right, you know. About the marks. There is a tale that says the marks are from what killed us in our past life. Yours is… Not the worse I've seen Seine, trust me in that." I opened my eyes and looked at her to see her gazing at the said mark with a gentle look.

"You don't have to hide it. It adds beauty to what you already have."

"Talking about me again?" Jazmine's voice called from down the walkway. Naji and I stood from our seats as she neared. Her eyes were red and her hair looked like she had run her hands through it several times. There was a strained smile on her face as she walked up to us.

"He's gonna rest up and restore his energy for a couple weeks and we can visit again. And then we can discuss what he decides to do." Jazmine gestured to the trail. "We better hurry before nightfall otherwise Hunter won't allow you out again. And we should probably keep what happened a secret." She clapped me on the shoulder. "We need to get you trained some more. You got your ass handed to you."

I gaped at her in disbelief and spoke without thinking.

"I need more training? You're the one who got shish ka-bobbed by a table leg my dude," I said looking pointedly at her shoulder where her shirt was still torn even though there wasn't any blood.

Jazmine blushed slightly, pursed her lips, and crossed her arms over her chest.

"I've completed most of my training, I was just caught off guard," she stuck her tongue out at me. "You're the one that needs a special leash to make sure you don't wander off." Jazmine gestured towards Naji with a laugh. "Though I suppose that's to be expected since you kept trying to escape. Unsuccessfully I might add."

It was my turn to blush and look away and Naji burst out laughing at us and started to skip up the trail.

"We all need more training sillies. But in the meantime Seine and I can go back to the library and do some research to see if we can find any information on what Mr. Bradwell said about your mark. It might explain why he freaked out."

Jazmine and I followed after her, Jazmine giving my mark a quick frown before we went.

"Do you really think that I was reborn? You sure it's not just a regular mark? Cause I think I've had my fill with finding out I'm not human and all," I said while climbing over some twisted roots and vines.

Naji tripped over a partially covered rock and let out a strangled laugh as she recovered her balance.

"You know what, that's extremely fair… The last few months have been a lot for you. We should just forget it all and get something sweet to eat and watch a movie," Jazmine mused.

I looked at her sideways with a small smile and stepped over a line of ants. On one hand, I wanted nothing more than to stuff my face with chocolate and forget everything for a few days. But on the other hand, I wanted to look into it because it sounded interesting. Curiosity had always led to hours of researching basically for fun. Of course, the hyper fixation might have to do with my unmedicated ADHD. Researching marks and possible past lives sounded kind of appealing to me. If I were to ever go on a game show of random facts I would probably win. Unless there were math problems. I would most definitely lose horribly if there were math problems.

"I'm down for some sweets, maybe there's cheesecake or brownies or crêpes or ice cream or parfa-" Naji continued to list sweets, and Jazmine and I shared amused looks.

I would relax the rest of the day and watch movies while stuffing my face with ungodly amounts of sweets. Tomorrow I would worry about researching the possibility of having a past life. A past life that had gifted me with a mark that looked like poison…

TWELVE

I did not, in fact, get to stuff my face with sweets and watch movies for the rest of the night. When we got back and Hunter saw Jazmine's torn shirt, I was carted off to my room by him. Once there Hunter looked me over to be sure I wasn't in danger of dying. I had assured him I was perfectly fine and didn't have to worry so much. Of course, I was ignored and he poked and prodded me. He found a sore spot on my arm in the same spot Mr. Bradwell had grabbed it. When he had brushed across it, a low whimper had come from my lips.

He had pulled up my sleeve and sucked in a breath as he stared at my arm. I looked down as well and saw a bruise such a deep purple it looked black. Hunter had lifted my arm carefully to check if there was any serious damage and when I told him again that I was fine, he had scowled. He had dropped my arm suddenly and the bruise pulsed angrily. He had stormed back to my bedroom door and before slamming it shut, he snapped at me:

"You are lucky it is just a bruise and not a torn off limb. You will not be able to leave the premises again until Mr. Bradwell moves on. I hope you have escaping out of your system."

And then he was gone. And I was left to sit on my bed staring at the walls, thinking about how close I had been to being killed. Left to think about what Mr. Bradwell had said. During his… trance… He had said that I had killed before and that I would kill again. Of course, I had never killed anyone. But if what he said about marks was true, then whoever I was in a past life had killed someone. And from the way Mr. Bradwell had acted, whoever they had killed, it wasn't in self-defense.

After debating for what felt like forever, my room had turned dim as the sun started to set. I got up and showered off the sweat from the walk to and from the house in the woods. Stepping out of the shower I picked out a black tank top and a pair of mid-thigh pajama shorts. I pulled on a pair of thigh-high-toe socks with little pigs all over them.

I was going to be comfortable while I went to the library to find out more information. I left my still-wet hair tied up in a towel and opened the door to my room. Only instead of an open hallway two backs were blocking my way. Simultaneously they both turned to face me. Hunter looked wary as he looked down at me and Luke looked like he wanted to take the sword at his side and stab someone. That someone was probably me.

"Princess. What do you think you are doing?" Hunter asked, looking me over, his gaze pausing slightly at the exposed scars on my legs. He raised an eyebrow as he waited for my answer. Luke just turned back to face the hallway, completely dismissing me. Luke's mood from earlier had apparently followed him.

I crossed my arms over my chest and glared at him. Over the last six months not once did I have a guard outside my bedroom, let alone two of them.

"I could ask you the same thing. Why are the two of you lurking outside my bedroom door?" I asked in return. Hunter frowned at me, probably trying to think about what to tell me. I raised my eyebrow at him as he continued to stay silent. "Alrighty then. Keep your secrets. I'm going to the library. Please move."

Luke turned back to face me with a sneer on his face while Hunter's head tilted to the side in confusion.

"You can't just go to the library whenever the hell you feel like it. There are fucking rules you have to follow. Even a ditzy twat like you needs to follow the rules. Even if you are a spoiled bit-"

One second Luke was standing there throwing insults at me and the next second he was on his knees clutching his stomach. He was wheezing as if he couldn't suck in air. Hunter slowly sheathed his sword, his hand resting on the hilt. He picked at a piece of invisible lint off his lapel and dropped it over Luke. I watched as my lips parted in surprise as Hunter patted the hilt with one hand as he checked his nails on the other as if he was checking to see if he chipped one.

"You may be of an angelic bloodline, but do not forget who it is that you serve. Speak to her like that again and you will have more to worry about than a couple of cracked ribs." Hunter said before flicking his gaze down the hall. "Get out of my sight until tomorrow."

Luke glared up at Hunter, his blue eyes cold and mean. He struggled to his feet and looked me up and down in disgust with a sneer marring his face. He bowed deeply at the waist, one arm still wrapped across his stomach and the other stretched to the side. I heard him grit his teeth as he bowed and saw him swallow hard.

"Please excuse me Princess, I hope you have a great night." And with that Luke slowly walked away from us. I stared after him unsure what to do. I felt guilty even though I didn't do anything to him. Not that I remembered anyways. And even if I did do something he shouldn't hold it against me. Especially since he knew I didn't remember.

"Would you still like to head to the library Princess?"

I looked back at Hunter to see a surprisingly earnest expression on his face. It was odd in comparison to his usual stoic and slightly annoyed expressions. And if I was honest, it kind of bothered me that he was a few seconds away from being earnest to pity me. And pitying me was definitely worse than being annoyed at me. So I smiled wide at Hunter and gestured down the opposite hall that Luke went down.

"After you my big bad defender. If there's any dangerous books I'll make sure to let you handle them," I said while side-stepping around him.

Hunter's expression soured and rolled his eyes at me, but I could have sworn I saw a small twitch of a smile. He shook his head at me as he started down the hall. I smiled slightly before catching up to him so that I was walking alongside him.

By the time we were almost at the library door, there was absolutely zero doubt in my mind that Hunter regretted taking me. Between my random outbursts of random noises and bad jokes for the whole five-minute trip, I was only slightly surprised Hunter hadn't used his sword on me. But I guess being my personal guard and all he couldn't exactly stab me.

After another terrible joke, Hunter groaned and rubbed his face roughly.

"It is a wonder that you have made it this far into your life without being stabbed," Hunter grumbled under his breath.

I let out a strained chuckle and was surprised when he stumbled a step. He looked at me with wide eyes and his face was whiter than I had ever seen it. His cheeks were stained red in what I assumed was a blush. I did what Jazmine called the "white person smile" and rubbed the back of my neck.

"I am terribly sorry. That was insensitive of me and I deserve any punis-"

"I mean- technically I was never stabbed." To set him at ease I said, "Did you hear about the claustrophobic astronaut?" Hunter just stared at me, his eyebrows scrunched up in confusion. I chuckled and continued the joke. "The poor guy really needed some space."

Hunter closed his eyes while pinching the bridge of his nose. He inhaled long enough to make me wonder if he had abnormally huge lungs before he exhaled. He lowered his hand and opened the door to the library.

"I may be the one that ends up getting that honor if you make another joke like that," Hunter muttered as he held the door open for me and I smirked at him as I passed under his arm.

"Well doll, if you do get the honor, do me the favor and stab me in a badass standoff." At his incredulous look, I explained, "That way it'll be a cool-ass death."

Hunter let the door shut behind us with a loud thunk and rested his hand on the hilt of his sword and rolled his shoulders back.

"Go get the books you need before I give you a very uncool death," He fake threatened... At least I believed it was a fake threat.

I mock-saluted him and went off to wander the many bookshelves, having no idea where to start. But I wasn't about to tell Hunter that.

• • • • •

"Uuuuuuuuuugh," I moaned against the table. My cheek was against the cold wood of the table and my arms were stretched out in front of me. There were books piled around me in a cluttered order. The stack of books to my right was about marks and their potentially magical significance. To the left of me were science books about marks. In front of me between my arms, was a very large, very old book of the royal family holding portraits. I was only a quarter of the way through. Apparently, there were records all the way to the 1500s. And I was only in the 1620s. The sun had set and risen without me realizing it. Hunter was still standing in the same spot as when I started, about ten feet away occasionally looking back at me. At my latest outburst, he came over to me.

"Maybe it is time you give it a rest Princess. You have been at this all night. Perhaps get some food and go to sleep?" Hunter suggested as he looked down at me. I looked up at him without moving my head and saw that he looked even more exhausted than I felt. I slowly pushed myself up into a sitting position stretching my fingers out. I leaned back on the chair I was sitting in and it rocked back on its back legs. My spine cracked and I moaned as the tension eased. I gestured towards the mess in front of me while balancing on the back chair legs.

"I need to figure it out and this-" I picked up the big ass book in front of me and let it drop back to the table with a thunk- "this is the only way I can get an answer."

Hunter frowned down at the book and then at me. His eyebrows were scrunched together as he looked at me. I watched him as his eyes darted across my face, tracking my emotions before he looked me in the eyes. After a few seconds, I broke his stare and swallowed hard.

"They are not going to disappear. You can take a break." He reached across the table and went to close the book. I leaned forward and the chair slammed on the floor, the sound echoed through the library. I reached without thinking and grabbed his wrist. He flinched at my touch and withdrew his hand with a slight tug at my hold.

My face heated in embarrassment at my reaction. I had not planned on touching him and I definitely did not know him well enough to be touching him. Plus, I didn't know if there would be any consequences for my touching a royal guard. I withdrew my hand and moved the book away from him in case he tried to close it again. I looked over the many faces on the page, trying to find a connection between myself and one of them.

"Why is this so important to you?" Hunter asked, resting a hip against the table.

I traced the edge of the book while looking down at the page. A pale-faced woman with rosy cheeks, blue eyes, and copper hair stared back at me. Her eyes held no emotion even though her mouth was painted into a smile.

"I need to find out who I am," I whispered without looking up.

My chair was moved back slowly and my gaze moved to the floor. He tilted my chin up so that I had to look at him. Hunter had knelt down on one knee, his suit creased at his bent limbs, but he didn't seem to mind. One hand rested on the hilt of his sword, and the tip of his sword rested on the floor. His eyes were gentle as he held my gaze.

"What do you mean? How does looking through these old books help you find out who you are?" Hunter asked.

I didn't answer right away. I hadn't spoken to Naji or Jazmine about how I was feeling. Not since I woke up and found out the truth. Without looking away, I told him.

"I had my whole life planned out, you know. From the time I was in high school I knew what I wanted in life. Graduate high school with honors, go to college-any college- graduate college, get a job at a local art studio. From there I would teach kids that they didn't have to be alone in their feelings. That they could express it through art. That they make a difference in the world and are loved. But now- now-" I broke off as a tear rolled down my cheek. A sob broke free from my throat and I bit down on my lip before more could escape. I turned away from Hunter to hide my face.

Hunter swiped his thumb over my cheek, brushing the tear away at the same time he turned my face back at him. He had that look on his face again. Pity. Pity and what looked sad, understanding.

"And now?" he whispered, stroking my cheek in slow brushes.

I swallowed hard at his touch and took a breath that shook in my chest.

"And now all my plans mean nothing. Everything that I was- my very being- was a lie. I am not the daughter of a fallen Marine sergeant. None of my friends could be themselves around me. They all lied to me about who they are. About who I am. I am not human. I am not human and they all hid it from me." I sobbed the last part, tears flowing freely now. My chest hurt with heartache and my skin burned with angry embarrassment.

Hunter let go of my face and held my hands instead. His hands were rough, but soft at the same time. His hold was firm but gentle. His voice was rough when he spoke.

"Princess, that may all be true, but that does not change who you are on the inside. In the short time I have known you I know who you really are. You are naturally curious with a bright mind. You are incredibly stubborn when you are faced with a challenge. You are kind to everyone you meet. You fail, adapt, and try again. Here-" Hunter let go of my hands to press his fingers to my forehead, "-and here-" he laid a hand over my heart, "-have not changed. The world may have been made larger in your eyes, but who you are inside has not changed. Nor will it unless you allow it."

What he said made sense, but understanding and believing were two very different things. How was I to believe I hadn't changed when my very genetic makeup was that of a creature that was supposed to be fictitious. A thing from horror movies and scary stories. Learning that I was not human had shocked me to the core. I needed to find out who I was, since who I believed I was no longer existed.

Hunter's hand was warm even through the material of my shirt. His fingers on my forehead trailed to the side so that he was cradling my face. Hunter's orange eyes seemed to darken to a molten red as I continued to look at him. The ache in my chest changed to something warmer and spread to the spot behind my navel. Hunter's nostrils flared slightly in a deep inhale as he leaned closer to me. I licked my suddenly dry lips and Hunter's gaze dropped to them. He audibly swallowed as he watched my tongue slowly swipe across my lips. I leaned closer to him, our lips just inches apart. If one of us moved, our lips would brush the others. Hunter's breath mixed with mine. Slowly he raised his eyes to meet mine and whatever he saw on my face made him groan deep in his throat. The sound alone made my toes curl in my socks.

"Princess," Hunter whispered as his lips brushed the air right in front of mine. A small gasp left my lips as he pressed-

The library doors burst open banging the walls on either side. I jumped from my seat at the sudden intrusion. Hunter lurched away from me and took a protective stance in front of me. He pulled his sword from its scabbard and a flame erupted from the sword. I gasped as the flame circled us. There was an uncomfortable heat that emitted from it as it raged waist-high.

Jared strolled in with Yamka glued to his front and they were both making extremely lewd sounds as they tumbled in. Jared reached around blindly to close the doors behind them. I looked at Hunter and any softness that had been there before had vanished. The stern emotionless guard was back. He glared at the two that had come in and waved his sword above his head in a fast circle before sheathing it. As the sword was returned to the scabbard the fire that shone on it disappeared. The fire around us remained still and seemed to grow a few inches higher.

Jared and Yamka slammed into a table near the door and Yamka giggled as they fell to the floor. A shirt was thrown through the air as Hunter stalked through the fire. It parted for him then closed back as I took a step to follow him. When Hunter got over to them he reached down and yanked Jared up by the back of his shirt. Jared howled in anger and swore as he caught sight of who was holding him. I watched as Hunter leaned down to whisper something into Jared's ear. Jared's eyes went wide as he glanced up and saw me standing in my magical enclosure. I watched as the blood drained from his face and Hunter let him go with a hard push towards what I now knew was Yamka's shirt.

My eyes widened when Yamka stood up without any modesty -bare-chested- and ripped her shirt from Jared's hands. She glared at me around Hunter's shoulder and I could hear the warning growl he gave her before she bolted out the door. Jared ran a hand through his hair trying to straighten it out. He glanced back at me, his eyes lingering on the scars on my legs and arms before shaking his head and following Yamka out the door.

Hunter made his way back towards me and the remaining fire vanished, not leaving a single mark behind. Wordlessly I watched Hunter gather all the books I had been reading and they disappeared as well. I stared in disbelief as he gestured to the door of the library. Unsure of what to say I followed behind him as he walked me back to my room in a tense awkward silence. Once there, he waited for me to open the door before going in to check that no boogie men were hiding in any corners without a word to me. Once he believed it was clear, he turned back towards the door.

"Hunter-" I started but he cut me off.

"Get some rest, Princess. I will have someone bring you lunch in a few minutes. I will see you tomorrow when it is again my turn to watch over you." He bowed deeply, one hand across his chest and the other behind his back. Before I could say anything he shut my door cutting off anything I would have said. I threw myself on my bed to wallow only to be stabbed in the ribs by something hard. Rolling to the side I saw the books that I had been using. I stared at them for a minute before I looked back at the door. He brought the books here so I could continue on my own to find answers... But in return, he had also left me highly confused and wondering if I had imagined the whole thing in the library.

THIRTEEN

"Listen, it's easy. Just stop thinking about it," Naji said around a mouthful of bagel while gesturing with a butter knife still covered in cream cheese, raspberry jam, and Tajín. We were in the kitchen on the first floor eating breakfast at an island table big enough to seat eight people around it. Unlike the one on my floor, this kitchen was set up more like a commercial kitchen and not designed to actually have meals in. But Naji and I had gotten hungry and the one upstairs was crowded with soldiers this early in the morning. I wrinkled my nose at her and frowned at my plate of French toast. I didn't know how to stop thinking about what happened with Hunter. It had been two weeks and whenever I tried to bring it up he would start quizzing me on what lesson I had done for that day.

And whatever breakthrough we had made with him being more social was apparently over as well. He was strictly business only. Which was kind of annoying since he was with me every day. It was as if I had gained a very stoic, very there shadow at all times. Unlike when Luke was guarding me, I knew where Hunter was at all times even if I didn't have eyes on him. Luke simply disappeared into the background and I only ever noticed him when he'd make comments to himself.

I sighed and took a bite of my breakfast of champions. The maple syrup and butter-covered bite filled my mouth and I moaned quietly to myself. I wasn't sure what kind of magic it was, but any time I cooked something, it came out a thousand times better than when I was at home. Every flavor was perfectly balanced and it always tasted amazing. Even the burnt food. As soon as you plated the burnt mess it would turn into a perfect meal. It was great when trying out new recipes.

I heard Luke grumble something under his breath and I glared over my shoulder at him while I chewed another bite.

"You got something you want to say Mr. Opinionated?" I asked after swallowing.

Luke glared right back at me, not caring that he had already gotten in trouble once for being a dick.

"Oh no Princess, I just love to hear you two gossip about an unnamed person about an almost kiss that most definitely absolutely positively means fucking nothing," Luke said while rolling his eyes.

I turned fully around on the barstool the kitchen had conjured up and crossed my arms over my chest. For a guard that was supposed to be quiet, he sure as hell had a lot to say about conversations that didn't involve him.

"And I'm sure you have plenty of experience with almost kisses? With your lively personality?" I snapped at him.

"Oooooooooh," Naji whispered behind me, crunching on sliced apples.

Luke sneered at her before looking back at me with the same expression. He crossed his arms over his chest mimicking me.

The white around his eyes seemed to flash brighter as he looked me over.

"Oh sweetheart, I'm sure I'm more experienced than you are by a mile." He looked over me again and smiled smugly. "In more ways than one."

"Ew, nasty boy," Naji commented and an apple slice bounced off Luke's chest.

I blinked in surprise at the pure boldness of my friend. Luke looked down at his suit coat where a white glob of cream cheese slowly fell off. It hit the marble floor with a small wet sound and silence filled the kitchen. Rage radiated off of Luke as he continued to stare at the stain. I looked back at Naji and she sighed and set the next apple slice she had ready to fly back down on her plate.

"Good to know you're still as prickly as ever Lukiepoo," Naji said as she raised her hands. They started to glow purple and I turned back to Luke to see the cream cheese disappear. The copper taste filled my mouth again making an odd combination with the maple syrup. "You're no fun anymore," she muttered to herself.

Luke glared at her as he ran his hands over his suit coat straightening it out. His eyes still had that brighter white around the iris and he bared his teeth at her.

"Some of us had to grow up," he snarled at her.

"You say that yet you're here whining about a little cream cheese you big baby," Naji said as she got up to take care of her plate.

I swallowed hard and cleared my throat and went back to the topic at hand.

"So you think that if you were having an intimate conversation and you almost kissed someone you wouldn't at all be affected?" I asked, raising my eyebrows. Luke continued to glare at

Naji even while she blatantly ignored him. I waved my hands in front of his line of vision and he turned his glare on me.

"A kiss doesn't have to mean anything. Shit an almost kiss." Luke raised his hands to do air quotes before he continued, "means even less. People kiss strangers all the time and it doesn't mean shit." Luke rolled his eyes and scratched his nose, making his septum piercing flash in the lights. "You're making something out of nothing. Just like girls always do."

I frowned at him. On one hand, he had a point. People had one-night stands all the time and never thought anything about it afterward. Buuuut on the other hand Luke was a jerk and probably didn't know what he was talking about. I mean. How many people even have almost kisses anyways? He probably didn't even have any experience with them. I sure as hell didn't until this two weeks ago. I squinted at him as Naji walked towards him. Her sneakers squeaked slightly as she walked like she was set on a mission. Luke watched her approach him and stood his ground. A foot away from him Naji stopped and looked at him until he started to squirm where he stood. She took a step towards him and he took a step backward, bumping into the counter behind him. It was odd. This big bad macho man that had so much experience was backing away from my tiny friend. I mean. He simply towered over her by a good foot, yet he was cowering into the counter.

Naji placed her hands on either side of him on the counter and leaned forward so that he had to lean back to avoid touching her.

"What the fuck are you doing?" Luke whispered through his teeth.

She ignored him and looked up at him, putting on her best puppy dog eyes.

"Luke," she whispered. "Don't you think it would be better if you were nicer to our Princess? We all used to be friends, don't you think we can again?" Naji pitched her voice lower to sound more dejected. "I want to be friends again."

We all used to be friends? Did that mean I didn't meet her in freshman-year math class? And that I've known her from here? That didn't make any sense. I could distinctly remember meeting her in school though… Unless… Someone or something altered my memories…

Luke made a sound that drew me out of my musings and I saw that it looked like he was having a hard time breathing. His eyes had dimmed some from earlier and his mouth wasn't curled up in a nasty smile anymore. His eyes darted across Naji's face as if he was trying to figure out what she was thinking. I saw his throat bob as he swallowed even from where I sat. Naji placed one hand on top of his heart as the other reached up to hold onto his bicep through his suit. I wondered if it was soft to the touch and if she could feel his heart thundering in his chest under her other hand.

I watched as Luke's lips parted under Naji's gaze and a slight hitch in breathing led to a sharp exhale. The scent of cloves and lavender wafted across my cheekbones and I frowned. There was no possible way I could smell him from here. I looked back up at Luke's eyes to see him staring at Naji's lips as well. I fought a smile as Naji slowly peaked the tip of her tongue out from the corner of her mouth before bringing it back in. Luke leaned down almost as if it was against his will. His lips were centimeters from hers and just as I was about to make a snarky comment about being a third wheel, the kitchen swing door flew open as Jared walked in.

Luke practically threw Naji away from him and she danced back towards me. Her cheeks were flushed and her eyes were wide with mischief. Jared stopped midway through the doorway and the door bounced off his shoulder as he took in the atmosphere. His eyebrows disappeared into his hair as he looked over

Luke who was furiously blushing and straightening his suit coat. I was smirking at Luke and Naji was fanning herself with a dish towel.

Luke glared at us and stood up straight with his hand clinging to his sword hilt.

"Don't pull that fucking shit again," he hissed at Naji. She only smiled in response and blew him a kiss. Naji draped herself across the sink and sighed.

"That was actually kinda hot," she sighed and both Luke and I whipped our heads in her direction. She wiggled her eyebrows at Luke and grinned. "Too bad it means less than nothing," she mocked.

"What-?" Jared shook his head and propped himself up against the doorframe, keeping it open with his foot kicked to the side. "You know what? I don't even want to know." He looked at me again and I wiggled my fingers at him in a greeting. Jared blinked a few times and frowned at me. "I um. I came in here to get something to eat before I started my training. And to talk to you."

It took me a second to realize he was speaking to me. My eyebrows rose in surprise. Jared hadn't spoken to me since the day I was brought here. He had basically disappeared. And now he wanted to talk to me? Randomly? I didn't think so. Not after what happened in the library. I had a pretty good idea what it was about and I had a feeling I really didn't want to talk about it.

"Um. Okay," I said and looked at Naji to see her wagging her eyebrows at me. I pursed my lips before sticking my tongue out at her. She knew what had happened in the library so she knew what Jared wanted to talk about as well.

Jared pushed himself away from the door and made his way towards us at the island. No one spoke as he grabbed a plate and placed it on the island. Jared stood for a second and before my eyes, food appeared on the plate. What looked like an English muffin split in half covered in an egg with a slice of ham and some sort of yellow sauce, covered the whole thing. A small pile of small black stuff appeared next to the egg mess. I had seen enough TV to know that the black stuff was caviar and that it was expensive as Hell. A tall glass appeared next to the plate along with three oranges. One by one the oranges were squeezed by an invisible hand into the glass to make fresh squeezed orange juice.

"What in the actual fresh hell is that shit?" Luke asked.

I looked at him to see his face screwed up in disgust. I'm pretty sure my face looked similar. Jared sighed and I turned my attention back to him and his "breakfast." He was using a tiny spoon to spread the caviar over the eggs.

"This, you poor uncultured twit, is an English muffin with Canadian ham, two poached duck eggs, hollandaise sauce, topped with Strottarga Bianco caviar with a side of fresh squeezed orange juice. Gladys knows what I like to eat," Jared said, taking a bite of his food.

"That all sounds disgusting except for the orange juice," I said as I watched yoke drip onto the plate. "I'll stick with my French toast," I added, looking at my now cold food.

Naji made gagging noises while pretending to throw up. She suddenly stopped and looked over at Jared with a questioning gaze.

"Did you name the kitchen?" she asked.

I looked at her and then back at Jared. He was blushing slightly while sipping his orange juice. Heh. Big bad boy Jared was blushing because he was embarrassed. It was cute.

"You did, didn't you?" Luke laughed harshly. "What kind of idiot names a room?"

Jared glared at Luke and took another bite of his fancy pants breakfast.

"What kind of idiot questions the one person that could kill them?" Jared asked casually.

I gaped at him. At such a threat. I knew I had issues with Luke, it was refreshing to know it wasn't only me though. Though I wouldn't have gone as far as threatening his life. That seemed to be a bit much.

"You could try," Luke said looking over the three of us with a sneer, "but I'd take all three of you with me."

I blinked at him in surprise and looked at Naji out of the corner of my eyes. She was frowning at both of them but she didn't seem worried.

"Anyways," I said, drawing the word out. "What did you want to talk about?"

Jared finished off his orange juice before answering. The glass- and everything else on the island- disappeared. He brushed crumbs off of his hands and off his shirt.

"I was wondering if you'd like help with training?" Jared asked me.

"Um. What?" I responded brilliantly. Jared looked like he regretted asking. He rolled his eyes at me and sat on a barstool that magically appeared.

"Your academic training you can handle on your own. At least I hope you can. You'll have to start combat training eventually, so you might as well start sooner than later." Jared explained.

I looked at Naji and she shrugged at me.

"It wouldn't be a bad idea. Most of us transitioned when we hit puberty. You never did so it wouldn't hurt to have some physical training," Naji said as she threw an arm over Jared's shoulders. "Besides, who better to help you train then someone that can help patch you up?"

Jared grinned at her and unease grew in my stomach. That smile was too wide. Too toothy. His eyes were too bright. I frowned at him in suspicion and he tried to look innocent as he met my stare. I squinted at him and he grinned and batted his eyes at me.

"You're not the one that's going to be helping me train are you?" I asked, the ball of unease blooming into the beginning stages of panic.

Jared smirked and shrugged out of Naji's arm to lean forward on his elbows. His burgundy eyes seemed to brighten a shade as he smiled at me.

"Oh I'll be helping. Just not in the way you think," he responded cryptically.

FOURTEEN

"I hate you all," I gasped against the shiny pine floor. Sweat plastered my hair on my face and neck. The tank top and shorts I had changed into only allowed my sweat-slick body to stick to the floor. I couldn't feel my arms even as they lay out in front of me and my legs burned. A pair of black gym shoes stepped into my line of vision on the floor. They tapped against the gym floor in annoyance and I sighed. I rolled over onto my back and looked up. Over the black athletic pants, over the grey, skin-tight-sweat-resistant shirt. All the way up to the very stern, disgusted black eyes looking down on me.

"You're pathetic. You only ran for an hour. And you didn't even run! You did a pathetic jog-walk the entire time! How are you going to be able to protect yourself when you can't even do the basics!? If you can't fight, you run. And you can't even manage to do that," Damon ranted.

"Give her a break Damon. She probably hasn't had to run since high school. At least she's here and she's trying," Naji said, defending me.

I pushed myself up into a sitting position using my wet spaghetti arms. Jared was walking in a slow circle with a sword in each hand. He was doing some sort of exercise with them that included moving extremely slowly and pointing the swords in different ways. Sometimes he would swing them in arches, but mainly he kept them poised close to his body.

Damon growled deep in his throat and I looked back at him. He was glaring down at me like I was a nasty chewed-up piece of gum he'd stepped on. Despite my body screaming at me when I moved, I made myself stand up so that I wasn't looking up at him anymore. Wiping the sweat off my forehead with the back of my arm, I returned his glare.

"Well come on. Continue to teach me how to run properly." I lifted my right leg up behind me to grab my foot and stretched it by pulling up. I repeated the same step with my left leg then stretched out my shoulders. Once done I jumped up and down on the balls of my feet to shake away any tiredness I felt.

"Run for ten minutes. Actually run, then stop so I can tell you what you're doing wrong," Damon said with a flick of his wrist. Three black tendrils wrapped around his arm. They moved like snakes but at the same time, they also looked like they were made from smoke. Damon saw that I was still standing before him and scowled. "Get going or these will make sure you run," he threatened.

Before I could ask what they were, the tendrils dropped from his arm and pooled on the floor. Where they dropped were little puddles of black smoky goo. They spread out across the floor until it covered about five feet. Then they grew upwards. Black lean legs appeared four at a time, out of the smoke. Claws clicked at the floor as they each took a step in unison. Long bony tails swished across the floor in lazy sways. Muscled chests led to thick necks and muzzles that were wide open to show off very sharp very long canines. Three sets of blood-red eyes locked onto me as black drool dripped onto the floor like vapor.

"What the fu-" I let out a yelp as one of the black vapor beasts roared. I turned tail and ran. The beasts stayed by Damon, though I could feel them watching me, waiting for the okay to rip my throat out. I ran until my lungs burned for oxygen. My thighs screamed as the sweat started to cause chafing. My shoulders were on fire and the balls of my feet felt like they were going to break off from the rest of my body.

Just as black dots started to dance around the corners of my eyes, Damon called the time. I instantly stopped running and bent over with my hands on my knees. My breath was fast and loud, and I strongly felt like I was going to vomit my French toast all over the shiny floors.

"Well... You don't suck at running so there's a small ass blessing," Damon drawled sarcastically. "Apparently you just need your life threatened. Take a thirty-minute break and we'll start you on knives."

I felt warm hands on my shoulder and looked up through my mess of hair to see Naji looking down at me. Her usually chipper attitude was gone and in its place were tight eyes and pale skin. Her mouth was twisted up into a grimace as she glanced back at the beasts that were now sitting on their hindquarters.

"What. Are. Those?" I managed to gasp out.

"They're Damon's hell hounds. He created them years ago. One bite from them feels like you're burning alive," Naji shuddered and helped me sit on the floor.

I promptly laid down against the cold wood. It felt amazing against my hot skin even as goosebumps broke across my body. The scars on my body itched like it always did when it got sweaty. I ignored the itch because scratching it would only hurt.

I couldn't remember what had caused it from the attack, but the purple scar tissue never faded in color.

A bottle of ice-cold water was placed on my forehead, and I looked up past the water to see Luke holding onto the bottle. He wasn't looking at me but at Damon's beasts. The usual carelessness that he portrayed had disappeared. After balancing the bottle on my forehead, he straightened but didn't move away from me. He stood guard with his hand gripped onto the hilt of his sword.

"Drink that slowly. Too fast and you'll vomit," Luke said while keeping his eyes on the hellhounds.

I reached up for the bottle and sat up while crossing my legs. I didn't drink the water right away. I rubbed the cold condensation across my face and then let it rest against the side of my throat. It was an old cool-down trick I had learned from Dillion. Jared was still working with swords, though he was no longer going at a slow pace. The swords flew with small swooshes as they cut through the air. His moves were more aggressive and violent than they had been when he started. Apparently, he was unnerved by the hellhounds as well.

Before I knew it the thirty minutes were up, and Damon was snapping his fingers at me. I groaned and climbed up to my feet. Naji stayed on the floor while Luke followed me a few feet away. The hell hounds laid down on their stomachs while their eyes watched Luke and I approach. Damon waved his hands and a dark red wooden box plopped into his waiting hands. It looked old but it was polished so that the lights reflected off. There was a metal latch on the front that held it close.

"If you can't run, you'll have to fight. Since your arms barely have any muscle, you won't be able to hold a sword any time soon. So, you'll train with daggers." Damon popped the latch on the box and opened the lid. "Pick the one that calls out to you."

Inside laid five different blades. The first one had a handle about six inches long that led to a curved blade that reminded me of a claw. The second was a blade with a wooden handle that had grooves for a better grip. The blade was straight with a slight curve at the tip. The third had a shorter handle with an even longer blade that was smooth on one side but the other was serrated. The fourth was like the second, but the blade had a hook at the end of the blade. The last knife had a round handle with a double-sided blade. They all looked like military-grade combat daggers designed to kill.

I looked over the blades for a few minutes waiting for one of them to "call out" to me. I studied each knife, going over each detail. None of the knives called out though. I looked up at Damon and shrugged. His left eye twitched and he snapped the box shut, making me jump. The box disappeared only to be replaced by another. The new box was the opposite of the first. Whereas the first was bright in color and shiny, the new one was pale white with absolutely no varnish to make it shine. There was a metal keyhole on the front that was rusted.

Damon flipped open the top and tilted the box towards me so I could see inside. Inside lay a pale green fabric that looked like velvet. There was an empty inlay in the shape of a dagger. Above the empty inlay was another inlay except this one held a dagger. The handle was about five and a half inches long. It was thin and a light beige color with intricate designs. The hilt was small, only about two inches long. The blade itself was about six inches if not more. It started an inch and a half wide. It narrowed to a sharp point making a long narrow triangle. Engraved into the blade towards the hilt was a small delicate yet simple crescent waxing moon design.

My hand twitched at my side as a sense of familiarity washed over me. Well, not exactly over the one in the box. But I had a feeling that if I saw the sister of the dagger, the familiarity would be stronger. How I knew that, I didn't know.

"Well, if you're going to keep ogling the damn thing, take it," Damon snapped.

My hand reached out and wrapped around the cold handle and pulled slightly. The dagger left the box with little resistance. The blade was a little heavier than the handle, but it felt comfortable in my grip. The dagger looked older upon closer inspection, yet it hardly looked used. The ivory handle had brown stains in the designs and grooves. Damon clapped the lid shut, snapping me out of my observations. I lowered my hand which had drifted inches away from my face. The box disappeared and Damon clapped his hands together loudly.

"It's about damn time. I've been waiting for an excuse to kick your ass." Damon threw out a hand that connected with my shoulder and I stumbled back a couple steps.

"What the hell?" I glared at him. He grinned at me, but it wasn't kind. He stepped closer and shoved me back again. I glared at him, anger making my cheeks burn. "What're you doing?"

Damon laughed at me and reached behind his back with both hands. He pulled them back out and in each hand was one of the claw-shaped daggers. He spun them expertly in his hands and stalked towards me. Fear sparked in my belly as the light glinted on the blades.

"Stand down," Luke demanded, pulling his sword from its sheath.

"Damon, what the hell are you doing?" I looked over to see Jared approaching with his swords held to his side.

"I told you that you were going to regret telling me what to do," Damon said as he approached me.

"Damon, you can't train her like this," Naji tried to reason while walking towards us.

Damon whistled and the hellhounds stood from their spots and bounded away from Damon. I spun around to see where they went. One pushed its way between Luke and me. Luke instantly backed up away from it. The second one bared its teeth at Naji as they circled one another. The last one stood in front of Jared, its tail swishing back and forth like an angry cat. There was no way they could get to me without getting attacked by Damon's hellhounds.

A fist to the base of my spine made me cry out as I spun back around to face Damon. The dagger in my fist felt clammy as my grip tightened on it. Was he really about to risk maiming me with scary ass daggers because of the celebration? When that was months ago? Why wait when he could have hurt me any time he wanted?

"Well let's go girly. You wanted to train so put your hands up." Damon lifted his arms up, in front of his chest with a dagger facing out. The other arm was vertical in front of his face, partially hiding his smirking.

I shook my head as I backed away from him. There was no way I was going to be able to train while he was trying to hurt me. A growl behind me froze me in my retreat. I tried to swallow the large lump in my throat but failed.

Damon slashed forward suddenly, and I had to throw myself to the side to avoid his blades. He let out a loud laugh as I stumbled beside him. I spun on my heels as fast as I could so that he wasn't behind me. I looked desperately towards Naji, but the hell hounds had pushed all three back. Further away from me and further from being able to help. Damon spun his daggers again and approached me once more. I brandished the dagger in front of me, hopefully keeping him a few steps back. He only grinned and knocked my arm away with ease at the same time he slashed down again. Pain lit up the top of my sternum. I looked down to see my shirt cut open, revealing a long-raised scratch. With a shaky hand, I lightly touched it. He had really cut me.

"Are you going to use the dagger or are you going to let me give you another scar?" Damon taunted me by gesturing to my legs.

A different type of pain filled my chest; anger and embarrassment. He was enjoying this and making fun of me while I was scared out of my mind. Damon was just an asshole that thought he could hurt me. He spun again bringing both arms up to make a slash with both daggers. I fell back onto my ass, and a sharp shooting agony shot up my spine from my tailbone. The dagger fell out of my hand as I tried to catch my breath which seemed to have gotten stuck in my lungs.

Damon danced around me while I struggled to breathe. Every inhale I took in got stuck right behind each other. My throat felt oddly tight, and spots started to appear at the edges of my eyes. A sharp thump in the middle of my forehead made me focus on Damon as he bounced away. I was able to suck in a deep breath and my hand curled around the handle of my dagger.

"Poor little thing can't even stay on your feet," he taunted.

"Get up." His voice filled my head as Damon glared down at me with his smirk still in place. "Get up. The next time he lunges for you, smack his arm- cut at his chest."

I pushed up to my feet despite the pain in my back. I copied Damon's stance from when he first started. I braced my legs apart, anchoring myself to my spot. My left arm was held vertically in front of my chest. My right was held diagonally of my left forearm with my fist held tight around the dagger. I held the dagger away from me so that the blade was parallel to my right forearm.

"Oh, you think you're gonna be landing a blow huh?" Damon bounced back and forth on his feet and gestured with his hand for me to make a move.

"Stand your ground. Make him come to you."

When I didn't move, Damon let out a harsh laugh. He lunged forward, his left hand going forward. I started to move my left arm to counterattack, but I heard his voice again.

"Not yet. Wait until he's right in front of you… Now!"

Damon's arm was inches from mine when I lunged forward putting all my weight behind my arm to knock him aside. With his arm out of the way and him trying to find his footing from my counter, I had an opening. With my right hand, I sliced upwards with the dagger. Instead of connecting with Damon's chest, I connected with air. He whirled towards me, and I went to bring the dagger back down in a racing arc. And Damon was there. And that time, I connected with his dagger.

The blade sliced through his shirt and blood spread through the fabric at his throat. I pulled the dagger back and stepped away from Damon as he lifted a blade to the cut. He used the blunted side to scrape blood onto it. His eyebrows were furrowed, and the smirk dropped from his face. His eyes lifted from the blood on his dagger and stared at me over it. He lifted the blade to his mouth and licked it slowly while keeping eye contact with me.

I could only grimace in disgust as he smirked with blood-stained teeth. He was freaking insane. He had to be. He flicked the dagger at me, and I flinched away as the blood splattered across my face. He wiped the rest of the blood on his chest. He spun the knives and threw them at my feet. One of the knives stuck out of my right shoe just above my toes. The other stuck out of the floor.

My stomach jumped into my throat as I stared down at the knife in my shoe. He could have hit my foot. The amount of damage that would have been done to my tendons and bones. I looked back up to see Damon circling me and I could do nothing but stand guard. I could try to remove the knife from my shoe or even go for the other one. But that also meant taking my eyes off Damon. Which made my only choice to be to stand in one place and wait for Damon to make a move.

Minutes went by of him circling me and me keeping my front facing him at every possible moment. A chorus of growls to my right drew my attention away from Damon. The hell hounds hadn't moved from their positions. They were still standing in front of Jared, Luke, and Naji. Poised and ready to attack at any second. Damon made his move while I was distracted.

Damon kicked me in the back of my left knee, and I fell to the hard floor. The blade in my shoe ripped the cloth slightly as my right foot slid to keep balance. I was kneeling in front of him at his mercy. Damon gripped my loose bun tightly in his fist and forced my head back. My left hand reached up and grabbed his hand as hard as I could. My nails dug into his skin, and I felt his skin break as wetness coated my fingertips.

"This isn't usually how I like my hair pulled," I remarked through clenched teeth.

Damon hissed at me as he pulled the knife out of my shoe. He lifted the knife quickly at the same time I lifted my dagger. He held the point of his knife to my exposed throat. I held my dagger at his side, right below his ribs. He looked down and huffed out a laugh.

"Well looks like our Princess-"

"What the hell do you think you are doing?! Get your hands off her this instant!"

Damon didn't let go of me but twisted his hold on my hair as he forced me to my feet. He grabbed my wrist so I couldn't stab him as he stepped behind me. He pulled my arm behind my back tight enough to make my back arch. Hunter stood in the doorway of the training room with his sword drawn. Fire licked up the blade of the sword. As he walked towards us the hellhounds turned to him. They lowered themselves close to the ground as they stalked toward him. Hunter paid them little mind as his eyes locked with mine. His eyes searched my face and dropped for a second to my chest. When he saw the cut the fire flared brighter. One of the hellhounds pounced toward Hunter's chest. I cried out as the other two followed suit.

Hunter brought up his sword and slashed through the first hellhound as if it were butter. It let out a high-pitched howl that caused me to flinch back into Damon. The hellhound fell to the floor in two pieces that sank back into the vapor tendrils it was before. Hunter smashed his foot into the chest of the next hellhound, forcing his sword through its chest before yanking the sword to the side. It broke apart into its original state before it even hit the floor. The last hellhound circled behind him quietly. I opened my mouth to shout out a warning, but all that came out was a small squeak as Damon pulled my arm further behind my back.

Hunter's head shot up and glared at where Damon was touching me. The hellhound used his distraction and charged at Hunter's back. Hunter dropped to one knee and thrust his sword under his arm and up so that it pierced the throat of the hellhound. He spun on his knee, twisting the sword in its throat before decapitating it.

Hunter slowly stood up and stalked his way to us. His stare promised death to anyone and anything else that got in his way. I knew that it wasn't directed at me, and he was coming to help. Yet there was a small part of me clenched in fear at the fierceness of his anger. Another part of me clenched for a completely different reason that was definitely inappropriate considering the situation.

Hunter lifted his sword so that it rested next to Damon's throat. The heat from the flames warmed the skin of my face and chest. The fire dimmed and Hunter pressed closer.

"Release her and I may spare your life. Continue to hold her and I will end you where you stand," Hunter threatened.

Damon gripped my hair tight, tilting my head back further and I let out a low whine of pain. Hunter's eyes narrowed and he took a step forward just as Damon released me. He pushed me forward at Hunter with a laugh. Hunter caught me easily and quickly looked over me.

"Touch her again and I will mount your head in the woods for the animals to peck at," Hunter growled as Damon walked away.

Naji, Jared, and Luke rushed forward so that I had nowhere to turn. They all started to speak at once. Naji was trying to ask if I was okay. Luke was trying to explain why they couldn't do anything against the hellhounds. Jared was trying to excuse why they had Damon training me. I was still clenching the dagger in my hand, and I had started to shake now that I was no longer in any danger. Hunter put his sword away silently and pulled me under his arm. He pushed past them and walked us towards the door.

"I will deal with you three later. She needs to be taken care of," Hunter snapped as the door shut behind us.

He stopped further down the hall and stepped in front of me, putting his hands on my shoulders gently. I stared at his chest not wanting to look up and see that damn pity on his face. My eyes were burning, and my face felt incredibly hot. I bit the inside of my cheeks to keep the tears from spilling over. All I had to do was not think about it for a few minutes and I'd be fine. I would not cry in front of him.

Hunter tilted my head up gently and brushed my hair out of my face. I looked past him to the ceiling, and he moved in front of my gaze so that I was forced to close my eyes instead. Squeezing them shut forced the built-up tears to spill and I heard Hunter swear. A door opened and I was led inside. A light was flipped on, and it turned the back of my eyelids red. Opening them I was temporarily blinded by the overhead light.

Hunter had led me into someone's bedroom. A very bare bedroom at that. There was a simple queen-size bed pushed up against the wall with dark red covers folded back. A dark wood end table sat beside the head of the bed. There was a small lamp on the end table along with a book and pen. On the furthest end of the room was a dresser with three drawers on the left and right with a long drawer at the top. Piled on top of the dresser were a bunch of books.

Hunter led me to the neatly made bed and gently pushed onto my shoulder until I sat on the edge. I watched Hunter in confusion, which I guess was better than the fear I had been feeling. Hunter stood beside me; his hand clamped tightly around the hilt of his sword tight enough that his knuckles were white.

Taking a deep breath, I tried to smile reassuringly at him, but I think it came out more of a cringe. Hunter frowned at me, and his gaze dropped to my chest. I knew he wasn't looking at my breasts, but at the cut that Damon had left in my shirt. I lifted a hand to the scratch, and it felt raised, but it didn't hurt anymore. Hunter growled and I looked at him in surprise. The look of anger was back on his face as he looked at the cut Damon's dagger had given me.

"I should go back and kill him for even thinking about touching you," Hunter said in a scarily calm voice.

Not knowing what to say to that, I fiddled with the handle of the dagger. I traced the grooves and features. Something slick made the ivory slippery. Glancing down I saw that there was still some of Damon's blood on it. What felt like an air bubble rose through my esophagus and a gag fought its way out of my throat. I was able to hide the gag but not the shaking in my hands. Hunter's warm hands closed around mine and pulled the dagger from me and placed it on the end table. He unbuttoned his suit jacket so that I could see a light blue vest underneath. The vest had some boning on the sides and five metal clasps in the front. I blinked in shock as I realized that his vest was actually a male corset. And shit it did things to me. Hunter, unaware of my sudden inability to swallow, used his jacket to wipe off the blood on my hands. I was right- it was soft.

"Talk to me, it will help," Hunter whispered.

I looked up at him without saying anything. There were a bunch of thoughts flying through my mind. Everything that had happened in the gym. Jared training with swords. Luke being protective when I was in danger. Naji being actually afraid of something. The hell hounds. The way the dagger called to me. The fact that Damon could have killed me. But what I said had nothing to do with today.

"Why won't you talk about what happened between us?" I asked.

Hunter seemed to go still before sitting next to me on the bed. With both of us sitting, it seemed much smaller than when we first walked in.

"It should not have happened," Hunter responded as he placed his now-stained jacket beside the dagger.

"Why? Because I'm a 'princess?' Because you're a soldier?" I asked angrily.

Hunter shook his head and took my hands in his again. His engulfed mine and it brought me little comfort as he looked at me. The anger had vanished from his face and was replaced with worry.

"It does not matter what our status is. What matters is that I took advantage while you were in a vulnerable state."

"I- What?" Hunter chuckled quietly.

"You were in a vulnerable state. If I had kissed you that night, it would have been morally wrong."

"That… makes sense… I guess. But why were you ignoring me?" A small blush colored his cheeks and rubbed his thumbs over the back of my hands.

"I was ashamed of almost taking advantage of you. I was unsure of how to act around you without thinking about your lips." Hunter's eyes dropped to my lips before flicking back up to my eyes. I smiled a little bit at the image of Hunter being nervous around me. "I was also doing my own research to help you."

Surprise filled me. He was doing his own research when he wasn't with me. And here I thought I was doing it by myself. I was surrounded by people, but sometimes it felt like I was alone. Knowing that Hunter was helping me let me know I wasn't. The side of Hunter's mouth quirked up as a small smile slipped onto my face. I squeezed his hands gently as excitement coursed through my body. Hunter could get to places I couldn't. Which meant he could find more information than I could.

"Did you find anything?" I asked, resisting the urge to bounce on the bed in excitement.

"Not exactly," Hunter paused when my smile fell. "Not exactly, but I did find someone who could have some information. She is about three hours away. I was on my way to tell you when I found you in the gym." He frowned and looked at my cut again. "If you want to wait another day I will understand."

I gaped at him. Not only had he found more information. He had found someone. An actual person that could help me find out if my mark really meant anything. And he thought I wanted to wait? Ha. No way.

"No way José. I've waited this long; I don't want to wait any longer." Hunter smiled at my enthusiasm, but his eyes didn't seem that happy.

"We can wait until tomorrow, so that you have time to heal."

"There's nothing to heal! I promise I'm fine!" I stood up quickly pulling my hands from his. I tugged down the neck of my shirt revealing the cut to show him it wasn't bad. What I had forgotten was that the bra I was wearing wasn't exactly full coverage. Hunter's gaze dropped from the cut on my chest to my barely contained cleavage. He ripped his eyes away to look at the wall behind me. He cleared his throat, and it was my turn to blush. I let go of my shirt so that I was covered again. Hunter cleared his throat and quickly looked back at me.

"I know I said you will be unable to leave until Mr. Bradwell moves on, but I believe this makes the exception. It is still a six hour round trip though, you may want to rest up before we go. I will also need to speak with the others about what happened today."

I waved my hand dismissively.

"You can talk to them afterwards, it's not like they meant any harm." I grabbed my dagger off the end table and smirked at Hunter. "I'll need about twenty minutes to shower and change though."

Hunter shook his head at me and stood as well. He glanced at his jacket and frowned slightly. After a second's hesitation, he left it and opened the door for me. I practically skipped out the door with giddiness.

FIFTEEN

Hunter waited outside my bedroom while I showered and changed. I donned a pair of light faded jeans with false rips in the thighs. They hugged my hips and thighs deliciously, which I was sure Hunter would appreciate. I chose a light blue tank top that had a picture of a pink frosted donut with the text "I donut have time for this." Naji had given it to me a few days before and I loved it. I threw on a dark green military jacket to compliment the shirt. I debated on wearing the shoes I had worn to the gym, but the hole in it deterred me. I settled on a pair of black high-top sneakers. I slid my now clean dagger into the side of my right shoe. My hair was still wet, so I put it in a braid that hung to my mid-back.

I opened the door to see Hunter standing with Naji talking quietly. They both stopped talking when they saw me. Naji looked at my shirt and laughed whereas Hunter was looking at my hips with a slight frown. I shifted from foot to foot feeling slightly self-conscious. Hunter looked down at his hands and I followed his eyes.

He was holding a dark red leather belt of some kind that had a sheath in the middle of it and a metal ring about two feet down. The sheath was attached to the belt by two leather loops so that it was free to move around. The sheath had a thin piece of leather on either side of it held close with leather strings, almost like a corset. It was extremely pretty and that was saying something since I hated leather. Hunter gestured for me to step closer to him and I did so without question.

"Lift your jacket for me please," he asked and I did so with a questioning glance at Naji, who only smiled at me. Hunter's arms wrapped around my waist and I shivered slightly. I felt the heat of him through my shirt. His nose grazed the side of my neck as he wrapped the belt around my waist, leaving the sheath on my right hip. The metal ring sat on my left and Hunter wove the right end of the belt through it. He tied both ends together at the base of my spine. Hunter gave the belt a hefty pull at the front. I couldn't stop my gasp at the feeling of his fingers brushing my navel.

"Do you have your dagger on you?" Hunter asked me in a gruff voice. I nodded wordlessly, not trusting myself to speak. I lifted my knee up towards my chest and pulled my dagger out. Hunter's eyebrows shot up and Naji whistled.

"There are so many things wrong with that I don't even know where to begin," Naji said, shaking her head.

Shrugging, I placed the dagger in the sheath. It was a little loose, but Hunter used the leather strings to tighten the sheath around the blade. All I could think about was his hands on me and his corset. Hunter's gaze was heated as he locked eyes with me, but sadly he stepped away with a nod. I let my jacket drop down and it partially hid the dagger.

"Are you coming with us?" I asked Naji, begging with my eyes for her to say no. She smirked at me and opened her mouth no doubt to say something snarky, but Hunter answered for her.

"Najia will be remaining here with Jazmine to help prepare for the celebration at the end of the month. Samuel will be accompanying us."

"Unfortunately, some of us aren't royal and have to work to keep our well, keep," Naji rolled her eyes with a smile. "It's not anything we haven't done before."

"Oh," I felt bad that I was going out on an adventure, and they were stuck here doing work. I could wait until tomorrow and help out…

"Nuh-uh. Stop that. You two are gonna go on your super top secret field trip. Jaz and I have known about this celebration before you even came here. You being here isn't going to change anything," Naji said, crossing her arms and sticking her tongue out at me.

Scratching the back of my neck I looked at Hunter. He smiled encouragingly as if to let me know that whatever I decided he would be okay with my choice.

"If you're sure," I started.

"Oh, I'm sure as rain, get your ass out of here. It'll do you good after what happened with Damon." Naji's eyes flashed bright purple at the mention of Damon and her grin turned feral. "It'll also give me a chance to get even with him."

Hunter frowned at her and opened his mouth to say something, but Naji looped her arm through mine. She spun me away from him and dragged me towards the stairs giggling quietly to herself. After a minute, Hunter started to follow a few feet behind us and she whispered to me.

"Are you okay though? Honestly? Physically and mentally? We really didn't think Damon would be stupid enough to try to hurt you."

"I'm okay on both fronts. I always knew Damon was an ass-hole, I guess I never knew how much of one. I don't blame any of you except Damon," I whispered back to her.

She peered into my face trying to see if I was telling the truth or not. She nodded to herself and smiled suddenly.

"Any update on the almost kiss?" She asked.

A furious blush heated my face and I dared a glance behind us at Hunter. His face was stoic as he took in the surroundings, ensuring we were safe. He felt my gaze on him and his eyes latched onto mine. A small lift of his lips had me whipping my head back toward Naji. Her eyes were laughing at me and she smirked with a knowing grin.

"I guess we know that answer," she laughed. I shoved her gently making her dance away from me as she barked out an-other laugh.

When we got down the stairs, Samuel was waiting at the door practically jumping with excitement. Naji waved goodbye and jogged off toward the ballroom. Hunter and I continued to Samuel. The closer we got to the door the more excited I be-came. Sure, the last time I left I was almost killed, but I wasn't about to let that stop me from leaving again. Samuel smiled at me and opened the door. The sunlight streamed through the door momentarily blinding me. When I was able to see, there was a large four-door black truck parked at the bottom of the steps. I gave Hunter a sideways glance and saw him trying to hide a smile.

"There were cars here the whole time?" I asked.

Samuel walked down the steps ahead of us and opened the front passenger door and waited for us.

"Technically, that is a truck," Hunter remarked and Samuel coughed to hide a laugh.

My lips pressed into a tight line and "mmhmmed" at him, but ended up laughing quietly. I jumped into the seat. Samuel let out a low whistle as I rearranged the dagger at my hip.

"Now that looks like an old beauty. The handle alone looks like it has seen the world." At my confused look, he pointed at the stains in the crevices on the handle. "These show its age. There's only so much cleaning you can do without destroying the ivory. And these stains look decades if not centuries old."

I looked at the dagger with new eyes. It had served someone well enough to last this long. It was obviously a sturdy weapon.

"Oooo, I'll be gentle with it while I stab people," I told him sincerely. Hunter slid into the driver's seat and placed his unbuckled sword into my lap. I guess he couldn't drive with it buckled to his hip. It was still odd to be holding his weapon when I had never seen him without it.

"Get in Samuel, it is a long drive so we must be on our way," Hunter said as he turned the truck on. It was oddly quiet from what I was used to from trucks.

Samuel closed my door gently and swung himself into the backseat scooting into the middle. He leaned forward between the seats and I twisted in my seat to look at him. Both he and Hunter looked completely at ease. For Samuel it was normal, but for Hunter to look at ease was an unexpected surprise. I turned on the radio so that quiet alternative rock played and leaned against the door with a small smile. Hunter smiled as he put the truck in drive and steered the truck down the driveway with his left hand. His right rested on the console with his fingers grazing my thigh lightly every now and then sparking a fire within with each pass.

The first few hours of the trip Samuel chatted about anything and everything under the sun. The most interesting was the Academy of Soldiers. He talked about his time training at an academy. Hunter had apparently graduated years before

Samuel even started his first year. Depending on how well they did in the academy would decide where they would guard. If they did amazing, they had their pick and most choose to be a royal soldier. If they did horrible, the best they could guard was the mini-mart that was in a village on the other half of the island.

When I heard that there was a village Hunter had promised to take me. He smiled brightly as he spoke of the townspeople and their culture. They didn't speak much English so we would have to bring Luke since he was fluent. I wasn't so keen on going after hearing that, Luke was still an asshole. Then Samuel said it was probably dangerous going to the village because there could be spies. Enemies that had tried to kill me months before. So, Hunter decided it was probably best not to venture there until they found out who was behind my attack. He said even going out now was dangerous, but less so than going to the village. He also made sure to mention that neither he nor Samuel would ever let anything happen. After that, Samuel started to doze off in the back seat. At first, I thought Hunter would be upset about him sleeping on the job, but he smiled slightly and said that he needed the opportunity to sleep.

As Hunter drove down the dirt road and through the trees, we talked idly about what we liked and disliked. We both liked alternative rock which slightly surprised me since he was always so proper. Hunter preferred math classes and I preferred literature classes. I liked peanut butter chocolate ice cream and he liked strawberry. His favorite color was dark green and mine was peach. Where Hunter liked all things seafood, I only liked shrimp, scallops, and-

"Imitation crab is not real seafood," Hunter laughed.

"If they put it in sushi it counts," I defended.

"They put cucumber in it as well, that does not make the cucumber seafood," he pointed out.

"What about a sea cucumber? People eat those, are those considered seafood?" I bounced in my seat excitedly. "I know! I know! Let's go to the beach and throw a regular cucumber in and then it'll be seafood!"

Hunter stared at me in bewilderment as he slowed down the truck. I laughed at his expression and he shook his head at me with a laugh of his own. Hunter turned onto a side road that had trees overhanging the road. To the untrained eye, the road was completely invisible. The dirt road turned bumpy and Samuel's snores broke off. I turned to look at him just in time to see him wipe the drool from his mouth.

"Rise and shine Sammy, we're going off road," I told him.

Samuel sat up and looked out the window and I followed his line of sight. What sunlight was left couldn't make it through the leaves above. It was almost like it was night. A quick glance at the dashboard clock told me that it was seven-thirty at night. We probably had another fifteen minutes of sunlight. Hunter silently flicked on the headlights

"Rouse yourself Samuel, we will be there in twenty minutes," Hunter said.

Samuel stretched out with a bunch of groans. I faced forward when Hunter tapped my high. The road ahead was dark, the headlights almost making no difference. Samuel reached between the seats and turned the music off. His posture was straight and he looked serious. Hunter looked the same. I felt both giddy and nervous.

"Have you ever met her?" I asked fiddling with the sword on my lap.

"I have not. I only found vague information about her and I had to consult many books to find a location. She likes her privacy and has made it almost impossible to find her," Hunter told me.

"Who exactly are we going to see?" Samuel asked between the seats.

I opened my mouth to answer and realized I didn't actually know who we were going to see. All that I knew was that they were female. I glanced at Hunter to ask, just as the bumpy road evened out. We all seemed to lean forward at the same time. The trees stopped suddenly and the area opened to a clearing.

In front of us was a large, exquisite stone cottage at a side angle. Some parts of the outside walls were covered in vines. Almost all of it was covered in moss. There was a low cobblestone wall that was overgrown with grass and flowers that wrapped the front of the cottage. A large flower bush on the side had died and looked seconds away from blowing away.

A chimney was on the opposite side of the side facing us. White smoke wafted out of it and up into the night sky. From the amount of smoke in the air it looked like it had been going for a while. There were a few windows that I could see that had a lattice. The largest bay window was in front of us and as soon as the sun was completely set a light was flipped on. We were too far away to see inside the window, but I got a sense of comfort.

"Looks like the mystery lady is home," Samuel said, opening his door and sliding out.

Hunter and I looked at each other and I silently held out his sword to him. He took it, but not before wrapping his hand around mine for a few counts. I gave him an encouraging smile, but I had a feeling it was a little wobbly.

"You can do this. You are brave and determined. You were able to draw blood on a century old warlock," Hunter cradled my cheek in his hand. "You can do this as well," Hunter shut off the headlights and truck.

I nodded and Samuel opened my door. He held a hand out for me to help me down. I grabbed his hand and jumped down, my dagger bouncing against my hip. He shut the door softly and Hunter soon joined us, buckling his sword back around his waist. We stood beside the truck for a few minutes looking at the cottage. It seemed that I wasn't the only one feeling nervous. Whatever was on the other side of the front door may change my life.

The front door opened, streaming light onto the ground and illuminating the steps that led into the cottage. Someone stepped out but kept to the shadows so we couldn't see them in detail. I looked at Hunter and noticed his hand on his sword. I looked at Samuel and saw he also had his hand on his sword. I placed my hand on the handle of the dagger, ready to fight alongside them.

"Get your fucking asses in here before my damn tea gets cold," the figure yelled out.

When a mysterious voice yelled at you to get in the house like your mother does when it's time to come in as a kid, you did it.

SIXTEEN

The delicate teacup warmed my palms as I sipped it carefully. Even being careful the tea still burned the tip of my tongue. With a small grimace, I set it down on the saucer with a slight clatter.

"Be careful with that, they have sentimental value."

I looked up at the wary voice that belonged to the person that sat across from me. I was sitting at a round table while Hunter and Samuel loomed behind me. Leaving me alone at the table with her.

She had young sharp features that looked like she hadn't seen the sun in years. She had large eyes and a small nose that was slightly upturned. Across each cheek were pale pink marks that looked like bird wings. Her hair was such a light shade of blonde it could have been mistaken for as white. It was loose with a section braided with purple iris flowers woven in.

A fine gold headpiece made of small chains rested on her hair and over her forehead. At the center of the chain that rested between her eyebrows lay a small crescent moon. The dress she was wearing was a bold contrast to her skin as it was pitch black. It was sleeveless and showed off quite a bit of her chest. The torso of the dress had boning and was made of lace so that her pale skin shone through. She looked about my age, but there was an air about her that suggested that she was a lot older than me. Her pale blue eyes locked onto mine and she raised an eyebrow.

"If you keep staring at me, I may have to take you to my bed," she said with a smile and sipped her own tea.

Samuel let out a small chuckle before cutting it off. I turned in my chair and glared at him. I knew for a fact that he had been staring as well. Turning back to the woman before me I smiled in apology.

"I'm sorry, you just look like something out of a story," I apologized.

"Well, that's a new one," she mused.

"Who are you exactly?" I asked, leaning back in my chair.

"You were able to track me down, but unable to discover who I am. How interesting," She mused as she set her teacup down soundlessly. "I am the Oracle Odette Dubois and who the fuck are you?"

She, Odette, didn't say it with venom, but with genuine curiosity. Back in school, we had learned of the Greek oracles, but I also thought they were wise old, wrinkled ladies. Not young flawlessly skinned, vulgar ladies.

"If you are an oracle, should you not already know who we are?" Hunter asked and I could hear the skepticism in his voice.

"Is that how you knew we were here?" Samuel asked next.

Odette steepled her fingers in front of her chest and leaned back in her chair as well resting her elbows on the armrests. She nodded her head slightly and pursed her lips.

"Yes. My visions showed me that you lot were coming."

"Really?" Samuel sounded both impressed and unnerved.

Odette rolled her eyes and let her hands dangle in her lap.

"No, you fool. You shone your damn headlights into my home, that kind of gives you away." I snorted out a laugh and I even heard Hunter laughing quietly.

"My name is Seine Rudi. These are my soldiers and friends, Hunter and Samuel." I introduced us and the two men at my back muttered hellos. "We came for you to tell me who I am. Or was I guess."

Odette hummed quietly and looked me over. Her eyes lingered on my mark before taking another sip of her tea.

"Seine Rudi," she repeated. "Daughter of the Crowned Head, younger sister of Dillion Rudi. Unfortunately, that's not how my powers work. I told your brother that same thing almost four years ago. I could not help him on his quest then and I highly doubt I can help you now."

Shock coursed through me at the mention of him. Dillion had come here? He had traveled to this secret island filled with the unimaginable? He was able to hunt down the mystery woman? That didn't make any sense. He would have told me.

Wait. Four years ago? I gripped my armrests as pain spread through my chest. If Dillion was here almost four years ago, that meant he hadn't died shortly after leaving us. Dillion had left to fight in the army, but he somehow found himself here before he died? What was so important that he risked being a deserter?

"Hmm. You didn't know he'd been here. Where is the young Prince anyhow? I would've thought he'd try to swoon me again," Odette laughed.

"He um," I had to clear my throat of the lump that had lodged itself there. "He died," I whispered.

"Huh. Well, that's unfortunate," Odette stood from the table to grab something from a cabinet behind her. She pulled out a bottle of wine and pulled the cork out before taking a swig of it. She tipped the wine bottle towards me in an offer and I shook my head. She shrugged and took another sip before putting the bottle back.

"How do your powers work then?" Hunter questioned.

Odette sat back down in her chair and dropped a sugar cube in her tea. She stirred it before answering.

"I can see your future in small snippets. I can't tell you who you are, but only who you will be. I can only see the past of those I knew in my first life." She looked me over again and snorted loudly. "And you definitely don't look like you're three hundred years old."

I raised an eyebrow at her and made a show of looking her over. From what she said that would mean she was born in the eighteenth century. She didn't even look like she was in her thirties, let alone three hundred years old.

"Right back at you," I said and crossed my arms over my chest. "Someone told me that marks were a reminder of what killed them in the past. Obviously, I have a very distinct mark. You're saying you can't help me?"

Odette kicked her feet up on the table revealing fuzzy cat slippers.

"Just because you have a mark doesn't mean shit." She brushed her dress away from her knee revealing a black mark that looked eerily like mine. "I got this running away from riots during the French Revolution. I lived as a servant of a noble person and there were many people that wanted the bread we had. After three hundred years I still have it." She covered her knee again and gave my mark a disdained look. "You'd have better odds of winning the American jackpot than of you even being reincarnated."

I scratched my own mark and frowned at her. The odds of us having the same types of marks should have been impossible. The fact that she was alive during the French Revolution was hard to wrap my head around. To be alive during such an important part of history. That had to have been absolutely terrifying.

"It would not hurt to try since we have come all this way," Hunter said behind me.

Odette rolled her head on her shoulders and rolled her eyes again. She dropped her feet to the floor and sat up straight in her chair. She pushed her teacup and saucer to the side. Odette stretched her arms across the table holding her hands out.

"Well, Princess let's take a look at your future, shall we?"

Nervousness filled me as I placed my hand in hers. Her hand was chilly and her grip tightened on mine. Her nails were shaped into long ovals and painted matte black. They lightly scraped across my skin as she placed her hands on top of mine. A chill worked its way up my spine and I fought off a shiver. Odette's eyes went from pale blue to completely white. Even her pupils had turned white. The wings on her cheeks turned a darker pink the longer she held my hand.

After a few seconds, bloody tears rolled down her cheeks and dripped onto the table. I looked over my shoulder to look at Hunter. His eyes were wide as he watched us. He didn't look concerned thankfully, so I turned back to Odette whose hands were starting to shake. Her mouth opened and a raspy echoing voice came out.

"*Five lives lived and lost, ended before being awoken.*

Ended unfairly, with sickness, by strife, in birth, by greed.

The sixth different from the last.

A sacrifice to be made when the earth bleeds red and the moon turns black.

Him or her."

I stared at her as Odette basically repeated the same thing Mr. Bradwell had said two weeks ago. Odette let go of my hand with a gasp and slouched in her seat. Her eyes returned to normal and the wings faded back to pink. The bloody tears remained on her cheeks. She lifted her teacup to her lips and took a sip before putting it down with a clatter. Odette looked at me and rubbed her temple.

"Well… Fuck," was all she said.

I slowly pulled my hand back to me and cradled it to my chest; it was freezing. Hunter and Samuel moved to either side of me. Samuel had his sword drawn but held it to his side. Hunter placed a hand on my shoulder and I looked up at him. His jaw was tense and his shoulders were straight as he kept his eyes on Odette.

"Explain." Hunter's voice was hard and left no room for arguing.

Odette looked at him from her slouched position. After a second, she slowly raised both her hands with her palms facing her. I watched her carefully. I didn't know what all an oracle could do. For all I knew she could vaporize us at a single thought. Just as my mind started to make up a bunch of wild ideas, Odette flipped off Hunter with both hands.

My mouth dropped open in disbelief. Hunter's hand on my shoulder tightened slightly and I glanced up at him. His throat was slightly red and his jaw was moving slightly as he ground his teeth together.

"I don't have to explain shit," Odette said casually and wiped the tears from her face. The tear-stained slightly, giving her a rosy complexion.

Samuel raised his sword quicker than I could blink and held it so that the tip was under Odette's chin. She merely glanced at it before snatching the blade in her hand. Blood ran down the blade as she squeezed it in her grip. She smiled wildly at Samuel before flinging his sword away from her. He stumbled back a step and put his sword back to his side with a hard swallow.

"I am over three hundred years old, boy. Do you think you'd be able to kill me?" She raised her hand and showed us her palm.

A sound of amazement left me as I saw her wound stitch itself shut right before my eyes. She kicked her legs up on the table again and ran a hand through the loose part of her hair. She leaned her head back against her chair. Odette peered at me through squinted eyes. I smiled meekly at her and lowered my hands from my chest. I took a sip of my tea which was now cold.

"Can you please explain what you said means?" I asked, putting down the teacup gently. Odette huffed at me and rolled her eyes yet again.

"That's not how it works. Did you not learn about oracles in school? I know the American education system isn't the greatest, but shit. I give the prophecies; you figure out what it means. The most I can tell you is that I have never told a prophecy that was both past and future. That was weird as fuck."

"Can you tell me which part was past and which was future?" I asked.

"Nope," Odette said with a hard "p."

I shook my head disbelieving that she wouldn't be more forthcoming. I had come all this way looking for answers and all I had was more questions.

"Wait. Does that mean the Princess did have a past life if you saw the past as well? That you knew her?" Samuel asked.

"It does, doesn't? That's what that means? Mr. Bradwell was right then? My mark was how I died in the past?" My mind was whirling at the fact that I was reincarnated. Yes, I had known it was a possibility and had been researching it for the last two weeks. But in the back of my mind, I had always known that I was trying to distract myself. I couldn't spiral into a depressive state if I didn't have time to think.

"Give them a prize, they can connect the dots." Odette waved a hand in the air. "You've been reborn, congrats. What does it mean? I don't fucking know. The most I can tell you is that it looks like vines."

I stared at her for a minute. She was definitely not what I thought an oracle would be. She was really starting to piss me off. And if she rolled her eyes at me one more time, I was going to stab her. She would obviously heal so I doubt I would feel bad about it.

"Yes, thank you. I'm fucking aware what it looks like. I've only stared and analyzed it every fucking day since it appeared. You can make an educated guess using your three hundred years of experience and tell me what caused it."

Odette slowly put her feet down and stood up pushing her chair back with a soft scratch against the floor. Samuel raised his sword again and Hunter let go of my shoulder. He drew his sword and moved in front of me the best he could. Odette sneered at them as she walked around the table and poured herself more tea. She leaned against her counters and peered over the cup at me.

"You're feisty. I like you more than your brother. You were either poisoned or struck by lightning. Or," she took another sip of her tea.

"Or?" I asked.

She smirked around her cup and lowered it slightly in front of her chest. The crescent moon on her forehead glinted in the light and there was something familiar about it.

"Or you went all slasher and that's someone else's blood that left its mark on you."

"So, my only two choices are being murdered or being a murderer. Awesome. You've been a great help. I think it's best we leave now."

I stood up and placed a hand on Hunter's bicep. He lowered his sword and bowed slightly to Odette. He put his sword away and stepped to the side so that I could squeeze past him. He placed a hand only lower back as I walked to the front door. She didn't seem to have any more information for me. Hunter stayed at my side while Samuel waited until we were past him before he moved. As I opened the front door, I paused and looked back at Odette. From where she stood, she looked like a goddess with the light above her. I brushed my jacket aside to put my hand on my hip.

"I really do appreciate your help, if you need anything I'm sure you know where to find me," I told her.

Odette didn't respond because she was busy staring at the dagger on my hip. She had a weird look on her face. She shook her head a little and grinned at me.

"If I need you Princess, I'll come see you in your tower. Now get the fuck out, I need my damn sleep."

The ride back was silent. The only sounds were the tires on the road. Samuel stayed awake this time and the music stayed off. Hunter had me hold his sword again and this time he held my hand. I had a lot to think about and didn't know what to say. So, I stayed quiet. I needed to talk to Naji to get another opinion on what Odette had said.

SEVENTEEN

Naji gaped at me from her buried position in her purple bean bag chair, her spoon frozen in front of her mouth. Ice cream dropped off the spoon and fell back into her bowl. She looked slightly like an owl with her eyes wide open. It would have been funny if it wasn't in response to what I had just told her. I sighed and took a hefty bite of my peanut butter swirl ice cream. After the night I had, the creamy peanut butter goodness was exactly what I needed.

"So, what you're telling me is that Mr. Bradwell was right. You did have a past life. And that you have a prophecy about you. But no one knows what it means… Goddess you've got a busy life" Naji took a bite of her ice cream and kicked her cold feet up so that they rested on my bare thighs.

I slouched further into my own beanbag chair and stirred my ice cream into a smooth mush. For whatever reason the mush that was ice cream always made me feel better. If I was honest with myself, it made me feel like a kid and made me feel safe. Of course, the ice cream always melted faster in that state, but ice cream never lasted that long with me in the first place.

"I feel like it's one thing after another and I just keep getting bombarded by crazy ass shit you only read about." Even I could hear the whine in my voice.

Naji scrunched her toes, pinching my skin between her toes. I smacked the top of her foot lightly with my spoon which made her yelp and let go. I took another bite of my ice cream making Naji fake gag.

"You so nasty, you don't know where my feet have been. But fair. Most of us were raised knowing what we are from birth. The Crowned Head had your mom take you to the States after an attack hurt both of you…" She trailed off and eyed her ice cream as my brain whirled both with brain freeze and confusion.

I had already pieced together that I hadn't always lived in America, but it was the first time I had heard anything about any kind of attack on Mom. If what Naji was saying was true, then whoever attacked me at the dance had done it before. Knowing what they did to a grown adult I didn't want to know what they did to a kid. But since that kid was me, I had to know.

"Was it as bad the first time?" I whispered.

Naji placed her now empty bowl on the coffee table next to us with a clink and sighed.

"The scars on your palm? The one you have no memory about? The one that hurts from time to time? That's from falling through the floor in the greenhouse. The Crowned Head thought it was best to take those memories from you… Which ended up erasing your memory of me and Luke which sucked."

"So, when we met freshman year you already knew who I was," I stated with a sigh. "At this point I shouldn't be surprised."

I frowned into my ice cream and set it down next to Naji's bowl, no longer hungry. I had already suspected that Naji knew me from what she said to Luke. But having her confirm it still hurt my heart. A friendship built on a lie. But after all the years we spent together I thought of her as more of a sister. And after a decade of being together, I have learned to forgive her quite easily.

"Well, not at first. When you first asked me to draw the wolf for you, I had no idea who you were. I just thought you were amazed by my awesome drawing skills. But in my defense, you didn't tell me your name until after I drew it. And then we went on the scavenger hunt for your crystal ball... And even then, how was I supposed to tell you? You had no memory. You would have thought I was crazy... well crazier."

"I... that's extremely fair, I definitely would've thought you were crazy if you even tried to explain," I reasoned. I suppose any normal person would have thought all that I've gone through was crazy. It happened to me and I thought it was crazy.

"You're not mad at me, are you?" Naji asked, picking at her lip like she did when she was stressed.

"Nah I'm not mad." I reached out and wiggled her big toe playfully.

"Okay phew, that would really suck since we're supposed to be getting fitted for dresses at the end of the week and you being mad would be awko taco."

"Dress fitting? For the celebration? I thought it was just a regular party type of thing?" I sat up as much as I could in a beanbag chair and gawked at her.

Naji returned my look with one similar to mine. She pulled her feet off of my thighs and let them drop so that they dangled over the floor. She pushed herself up on her arms and struggled to sit up fully.

"Hunter didn't tell you what the celebration was for? Did no one tell you?" She asked.

"Um. No." I said a bit unnerved at her reaction.

Naji fell back in her beanbag chair and ran her hands over her face roughly. After a moment of silence, she groaned and looked at me gingerly. I steeled myself for whatever was about to come out of her mouth. I was tired of surprises.

"The celebration is for you, 'the lost princess' coming home," Naji said slowly.

My eyebrows scrunched up in confusion. I had been "home" for months, why wait until now? I asked Naji just that and she picked at her lip again.

"Well… They wanted to wait until the Crowned Head came back so they could have a double celebration at once."

The Crowned Head? As in my supposed father? A man I had never met before and apparently the man who erased my memories. The ice cream in my stomach turned sour and I slouched in my beanbag chair.

"Woo," I said, closing my eyes and rubbing my temples. "The last one ended so well."

EIGHTEEN

A few days later Jared found me in the library reading from my lesson book. After months, I was finally more than halfway through the thing. It was no longer about lady etiquette. Instead, the pages were filled with drawings of step-by-step fighting stances. It was a vast improvement and the drawings were beautiful. To the average person, they would look rushed and rough sketches, but to me they were perfect. They showed blocking techniques using swords and shields. Some drawings even had paragraphs explaining what a fighter did wrong and how to avoid making the same mistakes. I practiced what was on the page until the library thought it was perfect and flipped to the next technique.

When Jared walked in, the library said hello using the chalkboard and I straightened out of my stance. Sweat beaded on my forehead, chest, and thighs. A glass of ice water appeared on the desk beside me. I tipped it towards the chalkboard in thanks. I sipped it slowly while I watched Jared walk around the library, taking everything in.

"I haven't been in here since I was sixteen," he murmured while lightly touching a pile of books put to the side.

I continued to sip my water in silence. Jared had apologized for the situation with Damon. He had offered to train me himself if I wanted, but Hunter had beat him to it. I had started training with him every day after lunch. At first, it was only stretching and running, but we had recently started hand-to-hand and dagger training.

I had forgiven Jared, but Hunter had not been so forgiving. In fact, I was surprised Hunter had even allowed Jared up the steps alone. We were making progress apparently, since he was standing before me. Hunter would have been in the room with me, but after I read the same sentence for the fifth time the library kicked him out. Hunter had argued with the library, which was funny just remembering it. When Hunter left, I could have sworn I felt the library roll its eyes. That meant the library must have considered Jared not to be a distraction to allow him in the room.

"How're your lessons going?" Jared asked, turning to face me.

I drained the rest of the water and the glass disappeared.

"They're great now that I'm not reading misogynistic outdated shit." The room got slightly colder and I smiled apologetically to the library. "No offense."

"What're you reading now?" Jared came up next to me and looked down at the book. "I don't remember this part of my lessons." He frowned and looked around the library. "Seems likes someone's breaking the rules to teach you." The book slammed shut and disappeared from the desk. I chuckled when Jared jumped at the sudden movement. He put his hands in his pockets and grinned. "I wasn't going to tell Gladys, she's your princess too," he said and the room warmed up. He turned his grin on me though I noticed it faded a little. "So, I actually came up here to see if you were up for a field trip?"

My eyebrows raised in surprise. Two field trips in one week? Surprising, since they all knew that I wasn't allowed to leave the premises.

"A field trip where? I thought I was confined to the premises?" I wasn't gonna tell him I'd already left with Hunter and Samuel though.

Jared leaned up against the bookcase and grinned wider.

"I mean, technically the Royal Crown owns most of the island so by those standards those parts of the island are part of the premises." Jared shrugged and ran a hand through his hair. "Shit technically when he isn't here, you're in charge. So, technically you own most of the island at the moment."

At first, I didn't understand what he was saying. But slowly the words made it through my tired mind. When it did click, I gaped at him. He was saying I own the island. Because my… Father owned the island. I could go anywhere on the island on a technicality. Jared was apparently more than a smart-ass who made out in libraries.

"What were you going to college for?" Causing Jared to raise an eyebrow at my question.

"That's random as hell, but my cover was studying to become a lawyer. It was fun stuff, lots of laws to learn. It was great training for an ambassador-to-be." Jared smiled. "It turned out to be useful from time to time."

"A lawyer… I would have guessed something sporty," I started, "But the way you talk definitely has lawyer vibes"

"I don't know if I should take offense to that or not," Jared mused.

I shrugged and frowned at the door, in the direction Hunter was no doubt standing guard. I looked back at Jared who was flipping through books. I couldn't tell if he was doing it to look busy or if he was actually looking for something. After a few minutes, I knew my answer. He flipped his book around so that it was facing me.

It was a map of the island. It looked as if a glob had decided to become an island since it had rounded corners that had been stretched out in random directions. In some parts, it was obvious that there had once been more of the island, but it had been eroded away by the ocean over the years. There were smaller unmarked pieces of land scattered around the main island. In the bottom center of the territory marked as L.M.C, it showed the manor a few miles away from what was labeled "Death Drop cliffs" which seemed a bit on the nose for me.

To the left of the L.M.C. was a large part of the map covered in trees and trails. It was cleverly labeled as "The Wood." I knew Mr. Bradwell's home was somewhere on the edge of it. On the opposite side of the L.M.C. was a smaller territory marked with mountains and a large river starting from the bottom of the map to halfway through the mountain regions. It was called "Taoxin Summit."

Just above that was an unnamed territory with rivers criss-crossing all over it. It was more river than land. I would have been severely surprised if it was safe to build anything there. The very top of the map was black and grey. Just looking at it made my skin crawl. It too was unnamed. Possibly for a good reason. Naming things tended to give them powers. Gave them life. Made them real.

The majority of the middle of the map was taken up by a large territory labeled "The Wild." It touched every territory, some more than others. The space was completely barren except for a few drawn-in boxes and triangles. Jared pointed at a small area within the L.M.C territory on the border of The Wild and the Taoxin Summit.

"There's a small village here that we can go to. We're not able to use magic to get there so it's about a day's travel by vehicle. There are a few items we need for the celebration and this way you can look around. They usually have a street market; you'd probably like that."

I probably would, especially if they had fresh vegetables, books, or local art. I looked back at the map and frowned slightly. It was a technicality, so there was a very real possibility Hunter wouldn't allow it.

"Does Hunter know about this field trip?"

"I do," Hunter's deep voice rumbled from the doorway.

Jared snapped the book shut in his hands and tossed it on the shelf haphazardly. The book floated, smacked Jared upside the head, and placed itself correctly on the shelf. He had the gall to scowl at the library for his laziness. Hunter rolled his eyes at Jared and locked eyes with me. He had the intense look he normally did when he was on duty, but added to it was a slight sparkle. He looked excited but was keeping it in check.

"Normally I would not agree to this, but I am the only head soldier permitted to the village. And I know that if I were to leave without you it would only cause more trouble. Do you remember the village I spoke of before?" Hunter asked me.

"I- the one that you said was too dangerous for me to go to? Because if that's the one you're talking about, I do. I also remember you saying there could be spies. You know, wanting to kill me."

"Sounds right to me," Jared laughed. "Though since no one knows what you look like we should be fine."

I looked over at Hunter in his uniform. His close-fitting, fancy, sticks-out-in-a-crowd uniform. I glanced at Hunter's sword strapped at his side. At his very sexy corset that would most definitely sick out in a village. The villagers wouldn't think we were

merely tourists. Not with someone who clearly looked like a soldier. He alone would draw attention to us.

"Yes, because we won't stick out at all with soldiers marching
down the market square," I quipped and Hunter grinned at me.

NINETEEN

If I thought Hunter in his uniform was sexy, I was ill-prepared to see him in casual clothes. Well… Casual for him. He, Samuel, Jared, and sadly Luke, had all changed into grey polo shirts and black cargo pants. Out of the four of them, Hunter was the only one who hadn't traded his sword for a sleek black gun. His reasoning was that the others had guns to get threats from afar. If they were to fail it was up to him to use his sword to protect me. He smiled when I asked about it sticking out and informed me that it was glamoured outside the walls of the manor. Those who didn't know he was carrying a sword would see a gun matching the others.

For once I was wearing pants and not shorts. Samuel had been kind enough to inform me that we'd be doing a lot of walking once we got to the village. There wasn't enough room to drive on the roads since there would be stalls everywhere. And the last thing I needed was to experience chub rub.

"So, what you're telling me is that someone created a magical way to keep cars running on the same tank of gas for a MONTH, and you haven't shared this with anyone else?"

"I don't see why you're having trouble understanding this," Luke sighed as he followed Hunter around a tight turn. I had been stuck in the truck with Luke and Jared since Hunter and Samuel were driving the military-grade cargo truck. None of us were happy about the seating arrangements.

"Think of it this way, humans go to war over the drop of a hat. What do you think would happen if they found out we had not only magic but a way to replicate fuel from thin air?" Jared flipped a page of the book that he had brought with him.

I leaned back in my seat with a frown. He was right of course. If anyone found out about what they had discovered, the secret island would be overrun with war. I couldn't remember a time when there wasn't a war happening somewhere in the world. All for land, resources, religion, and race. My eighth-grade teacher made sure to drill that into us. And now having a world of magical and mythological creatures, opened the possibility of even more war.

"Fair enough," I mumbled.

"Why don't you read your book or something? I'm tired of answering your questions." Luke snipped.

"I would, but you refuse to turn the radio on and I can't concentrate in the quiet."

"What kind of backwards kind of shi-" Luke was cut off by the radio blaring to life and I gave Jared a grateful smile.

I pulled my bag across the seat and pulled out the book the library had packed for me. The first one it tried to pack was too obvious about being smut by the cover, so I asked for a different one. When the new one plopped into my hands, the naked male cover was replaced with a bright fire. The title was scrawled across the book in gold font, The Burning Fires of His Highness.

It was about fallen angels and demons being... Romantically involved with each other. It was good until I got distracted by how quiet it was in the truck.

"You're just jealous that you're the only one not reading."

Luke locked eyes with me in the rearview mirror and his blue eyes were cold.

"I have no interest in reading that disgusting shit." Jared gave him a dirty face which he ignored. "We still have three more hours of driving, read your book or I'm throwing it out the fucking window."

Well okay then.

•••••

By the time we got to the village, I was seconds away from stabbing Luke with my dagger. Nobody would know. Well... Jared would... I could kill him too. Get rid of witnesses. Of course, I would have to give myself some wounds to throw off suspicion. They came out of nowhere, I did the best I could, I could say. Heh. I could totally get away with it. I was the frail princess that needed protecting.

I was really getting into the idea when my door was opened and there stood Hunter. He looked as ragged as I felt, which was saying something since I was contemplating murder. Hunter silently held out his hand for me to help me out of the truck. I grabbed my bag before sliding out of my seat with his help. Rocks shifted beneath my feet and with my stiff limbs, I stumbled into Hunter's chest. He was warm and smelled of woodsy citrus with spice that tickled my nose but also made my mouth water. I clearly needed a good night's rest because the scent was awakening parts of me that normally only books did.

"Careful, we won't have a flat road for another ten minutes," Hunter said in a gruff voice.

I pulled away, my face hot, and saw Hunter glance at my book with a slightly raised eyebrow. I murmured my thanks and stepped back from him to stretch and look around. Over his shoulder, I saw buildings lit by dim lights that barely touched the ground. It was also eerily quiet compared to the constant manor's quiet hum. It was too dark to make out any of the details of the buildings, but they were single stories.

It was odd being in a village when no one else was walking about. It was probably weird as hell for the villagers to see us strolling through in the dead of night. It felt weird to me. We should have planned it better so that we arrived during the day, but we were short on time with the celebration being so soon. None of us spoke as we made our way down the road. Hunter was on one side of me holding both our bags, Samuel was on the other carrying his bags, and Jared and Luke took up the ranks behind us. The atmosphere was tense and cautious and made me uncomfortable. All I wanted to do was fall face-first into a bed and sleep.

After forever had passed we finally came to a stop at a large building that had several floors. It was the odd one out amongst the other buildings. There was a large wood-burned sign above the door that said something in an unknown language. Luke pushed past us and opened the door, momentarily blinding me with the light from within. I felt a hand at my shoulder edging me forward while I squinted against the harsh light.

Inside was surprisingly modern despite the old feel of everything outside. There was a large sitting area on the left and the right had a small dining area. Straight ahead was a large desk that took up much of the wall. Behind the desk was an older man sitting in a chair watching old reruns on a computer. He looked up as we approached and didn't look surprised to see five strangers before him. Luke and the man conversed for several minutes quietly, though at the end Luke seemed irritated.

He handed the man foreign currency and snatched something off the desk before he made his way back to us.

"There's only three rooms available. Apparently, there was an infestation in multiple homes so most of the rooms are occupied. I will not be sharing a room with any of you," Luke dropped two old school keys in Hunter's open palm. "You can figure out the rooms. I'm going to bed." And with that, he left us standing in the lobby of what now I gathered was an inn.

The remaining four of us looked down at the keys in silence. I did not want to share a room with Jared. I knew that much. I also knew that rooming with Samuel would lead to nonstop talking on his end. Rooming with Hunter would be awkward, but a lot better choice than the other two. Hunter handed Jared a key and told Samuel to go with him. Jared frowned slightly but didn't press an issue with it. I wordlessly followed Hunter to our room. It was the bare necessitates: bathroom, dresser, end table, lamp, and one. Singular. Bed. It was going to be a lot more awkward than I thought.

"I will go see if the other rooms have two beds." Hunter started to walk back out the door but I waved dismissively.

"It'll be fine. We don't have to bother them when we've just got here. If you don't kick in your sleep, we should be fine."

I kicked off my shoes, which had developed a thin layer of dirt, and threw myself on the bed. I let out a groan as I snuggled my face deeper into the pillow. In comparison to the hard truck seats for six hours, the bed was heaven.

"I promise to stay on my half of the bed as long as you promise not to steal the covers."

I lifted my head from the pillow high enough to peek at Hunter through my hair. He was smiling at me as he slipped his sword from his side. And I watched his hands as he undid the belt of his sword. And it shouldn't have been sexy. But it was. Hunter propped his sword up against the wall closest to the bed.

I watched as he untied his boots and slid them off. He turned on the lamp before turning off the overhead light. He slid into the bed next to me and we watched each other without saying anything. I was wrong. It wasn't uncomfortable or awkward, it was nice. His scent filled the small space between us and my mouth watered slightly again. There was just something that his scent did to me. Whatever he saw on my face made his eyes darken a shade and he swallowed hard.

"We should get some rest Princess, we have much to do tomorrow," he whispered gently.

I pulled the blanket up to my ears to hide my blush and nodded. I thought about turning onto my side, but if I turned away from him, he'd probably think I was upset. If I faced him, I'd probably be engulfed by his smell. Laying flat on my back would just be awkward. So, I stayed face down on my pillow. Considering how tired I was, I'd be asleep in no time, and what position I was in after that was out of my control.

"Okie, goodnight, Hunter," I whispered. I was drifting off when I heard Hunter's soft voice say,

"Goodnight Seine."

• • • • •

It was hot. Too hot. There was sweat covering my chest and my arms were clammy. I was laying on my back with an arm over my eyes and there was a heavy weight on my torso. I had read enough books to know that if I opened my eyes, I would see Hunter's arm wrapped around me. If there was an air conditioner in the room, I would have welcomed the added heat from his body. But it was hot as hell in the room and I was dying. I moved my arm slightly to look down.

Instead of seeing Hunter's arm on me, there was a pair of eyes staring at me inches from my face. They were completely black except for a small ring of yellow. When it saw that my eyes were open it reached out with a paw and tapped my nose gently. I let out a squeal and it jumped away from me.

Hunter appeared out of nowhere with his sword drawn. Despite sleeping in his clothes there wasn't a single wrinkle and he looked wide awake. I quickly sat up in time to see a black tail disappear over the side of the bed. Hunter slowly walked around the foot of the bed while I leaned over the side. Sitting on the floor looking back at me was a small black cat. Hunter lowered his sword and looked at me in confusion. I shrugged at him and slid out of the bed and onto the floor.

"Here kitty, kitty," I pspspst at it and it looked at me like I was a dumbass; a true cat. It sauntered over to my held-out hand and rubbed its cheeks against my fingers. "Such a good kitty," I crooned.

"Such a bad kitty," Hunter countered and I raised my head to scowl at him. "There is no possible way that cat should have been able to get in this room without me knowing," Hunter explained.

"The kitty is just better at going undetected than you are at detecting," I teased.

Hunter frowned slightly at me petting the kitty with such ease. The kitty had started purring as I rubbed the bridge of its nose gently. Its eyes squinted and I could just barely see canines as it rubbed against my fingers harder. It was freaking adorable. Black cats were my favorite. They were one of the friendliest and the cuddliest. Not to mention they got a bad rap for being bad luck. I had read years ago that animal shelters wouldn't let anyone adopt black cats the week of Halloween because cruel terrible people would kill them.

"Perhaps you should not touch it since we do not know if it is diseased."

"Diseased or not, you don't deny kitties pets," I said and scratched the base of the kitty's spine and it arched but didn't pull away. "Maybe you should try petting them, they're super soft."

"Cats do not like me," was his only response.

"Hmm. I wonder who it belongs to," I wondered as I stood up. I would have continued to pet the kitty, but its ears flattened in what I called "airplane ears." It was a sure way to know when a cat was done being affectionate. I turned to face Hunter just as someone knocked on the door in a specific rhythm, scaring the kitty. It hissed and hid under the bed.

Hunter opened the door and there stood the others. They all looked tired except for Samuel, who was bouncing on his feet in excitement.

"We need to get going if we're to get what we need before night falls," Jared told us. "Plus, Samuel here can apparently smell fresh kettle corn and is dying to buy some."

Samuel smiled and pushed in between Hunter and me to sling an arm over my shoulder.

"If you've never had fresh kettle corn you're missing out in life." He spun us back towards the bed and picked up my shoes from the floor. Just as I was about to tell him that I could put my own shoes on, the cat bolted out from under the bed. It jumped over Samuel and ran out of the room, startling Luke and Jared. Samuel fell back but managed to catch himself before falling to the floor.

"Awww bye kitty!" I called after it and the men looked back at me like they'd never seen me before. I shrugged as I slipped on my shoes and popped off the bed. Maybe if there was one cat there would be more in the village. "Well let's go boyos! We got things to do!" I skipped past them into the hall, letting them follow behind me.

• • • • •

The streets were a complete one-eighty from last night. I couldn't see the dirt road with the amount of people out. Though when they saw our group, they made room for us to walk through. We stuck out in the crowd still, but not as much as we would have if they were wearing their uniforms. Stalls had been erected throughout and those without a stall had large tables. None of the stalls were selling the same products and many of the villagers seemed familiar with Luke.

We had already visited several stalls, one being the freshly cooked kettle corn. Samuel was correct, I was missing out in life. The villager in charge of that stall only had a table which made sense considering the contraption he had to make the kettle corn. It looked like a large metal box with a large bowl above a fire pit. The man was stirring kernels in the bowl with a large spoon. Samuel informed me that the stuff he had added to the kernels was sugar, salt, and oil. When it was fully cooked, he gave us two bags and Luke handed him money in return. My bag was already gone by the time we hit the next stall.

After a few hours both my arms were full of bags and baskets. I had grains, citrus, and baking ingredients. Luke had told us that we would have quail, lamb, squid, oysters, snails, and other livestock would be delivered later that night to load into our cargo truck. When I questioned Hunter about the sea life making the six-hour trip, Hunter told me that each individual tank was spelled to keep the animals alive. My favorite haul was in a box Jared was carrying. We had found a stall selling farm-grown cucumbers and tomatoes for cucumber tomato sandwiches. There were also a couple of books, handmade bracelets, and small wooden figurines.

Soon none of us could carry anymore and it was a good thing because my arms had just started to burn. Training with Hunter had helped a lot because otherwise I would have collapsed hours ago. Sadly, I hadn't seen any other cats, but Hunter said it was probably because there were so many people out. After we had loaded all of our purchases into the cargo truck, we went into the inn to eat before leaving. We sat at a table and the innkeeper came over to us and dropped a single wooden menu on the table. Luke picked it up and looked it over.

"There's kebabs, meatloaf, stew with lamb, and fish," he told us.

I ordered the stew, Samuel and Jared got the fish, Luke ordered the kebabs, and Hunter ordered the meatloaf. When the food arrived, it was steaming from heat and the smell made my mouth water. We didn't talk as we ate; the only sounds were clinking dishes and other people dining. Before I had placed my spoon in my empty bowl, a young boy came over and took the dirty dishes away. As Luke was paying for our meal, the innkeeper came back and whispered to him.

"Apparently there's an issue with one of the stall orders we put in. They won't be able to gather the quail until late, so we won't be able to leave until tonight." Luke looked over at me and nodded toward the innkeeper. "There's a large pond behind the inn that you can swim in if you want, he says you're more than welcome."

I hadn't gone swimming in forever and I kind of missed it. I smiled at the innkeeper.

"Can you tell him that I appreciate it, but I don't have anything to swim in?" I asked Luke. He relayed the message and he tilted his head slightly at what the innkeeper said in response.

"He says that each room have bathing suits in the bathroom cupboards."

My mouth dropped open slightly in excitement. I looked at Hunter though to confirm it would be okay. He was the one in charge of our trip. He would have to decide if it was safe or not. He shrugged slightly with a smile.

"I do not see why not. We have what we need for the most part. I will have to put a protection circle around the pond first," Hunter told me.

"Does anyone want to join me?" I offered. I hoped they would say no so that I didn't have to be self-conscious about my body, but still felt the need to ask. Out of politeness.

"Samuel is going to stand guard by the pond as a precaution while the rest of us are going to see what the delay is with the livestock," Hunter explained.

I looked at Samuel as he frowned at Hunter. I had the feeling we were thinking the same thing. I didn't want to say anything to hurt Samuel's feelings. But Samuel wasn't fully trained yet and we were in foreign lands. If something were to happen, I wasn't fully sure he'd be able to protect me. Not by himself anyways.

"What if something were to happen? I don't think I'm fully capable of protecting her by myself yet," Samuel hedged quietly.

"You have almost completed your training, I have full faith in you being able to protect the Princess." Hunter smiled warmly at Samuel before continuing, "Besides, with the protection circle no one else will be able to approach."

Samuel looked relieved and I gave him a reassuring smile even as a pit of unease formed in my stomach.

TWENTY

Hunter had cast the protection circle around the pond while I changed into the bathing suit provided by the innkeeper. When I emerged from the back door the heat wasn't as bad. It was probably due to the ring of trees around the pond. Though in my opinion, the pond was actually more of a lake. There was high grass around the outskirts of the water with the occasional cattail. There was a clearing off to the side with a singular weeping willow whose branches swayed in the slight breeze. Samuel was stationed not far from the edge of the water, but far enough to give me privacy.

I slipped my shoes off, dropped my towel, and welcomed the cool air on my skin. Soon I came to the edge of the trees, and I could hear the water above the sounds of hiding critters. After walking for a few more minutes, I came to the weeping willow tree with rocks laid around its base. I stepped over the rocks and up to the tree. My hand trailed across the bark as I looked up through the branches. A soft wind was slightly moving the branches causing a low "whoosh" sound. My brother and I used to sit under a similar tree back home and eat the lunches our mom had packed for us.

Stepping away from the tree, I looked across the water. The sun became tiny sparkling diamonds on the surface of the water. Reflections from the trees were disfigured as the water moved. Now and then dragonflies would land on the water before taking off again. To my right was a pier, fifteen feet long at least. It was so similar to the pier my brother and I used to visit back home. My feet slapped the wood as I jogged and memories bombarded me. I could see him standing on the end straining to reel in a fish. I could hear him swearing as the fish got away. I could feel him tickling my sides as I laughed at him. The smell of rubber lures filled my nose as I threw them at him.

The taste of water, as he threw me into the lake, filled my mouth as I jumped off the pier. The cold lake water engulfed me. Bubbles floated up toward the sky, trying to escape. The further down I went, the warmer the water seemed to get. My lungs started to burn and I kicked off the bottom. In no hurry, I watched the bottom grow darker. I broke the surface and floated on my back. Clouds drifted across the sky. My hands lazily drifted through the water. It was the most relaxed I had been in a while.

When goosebumps decorated my skin, I swam to the pier. I pulled myself up like I've done hundreds of times back home. Except the plank of wood lifted away from the nails that held it in place. Frantically I reached for the next plank, but I was too late. I fell back into the water, my back slapping the water first. The heavy wood sank fast and I was dragged with it. A twisted nail had caught on my bathing suit and I fought to get free of the wood. I succeeded in tearing my bathing suit, leaving me topless. In a panic, I swam to the surface. My heart thudded in my chest in despair. I sucked in a few quick breaths before diving back down.

I searched the bottom for my top, but my quick movements caused muck to rise and swirl around my hands. Unlike the warm water, the muck was cold and felt like slime. I dug through it in circles, hoping that the fabric would catch on to my fingers. The only things I found were rocks and lake weed. Seconds passed and I still hadn't found it. My lungs were on fire and my movements were becoming sluggish.

Where was it? Come on, come on, where was it? I was so stupid! I shouldn't have tried to get out of the water using the pier! I was so stupid. Where was it?! Then by some miracle, I saw the bright blue fabric. I swam over and wrapped my hand around it. I pulled it near me and there was a "clisssh" sound through the water. A bunch of muck floated up revealing a branch the top had been snagged on. The fabric had snapped when I had pulled on it. I pushed myself through the water, leaving the top behind. Even if I managed to get it free, the top wouldn't have covered my chest anymore. Emerging from the water, I sucked in deep breaths of air. The once bright sky was now dark and storm clouds were drifting in. Rain started to fall, causing ripples in the water and thunder crashed above me.

"Shit," I cried.

I was at least twenty feet away from the shore. My arms and my legs cut through the choppy water as fast as I could. It was an odd sensation swimming with my breasts free. The water was angry though. With every foot I gained, it dragged me back a couple of inches. By the time I pulled myself onto the shore the wind was whipping everything around. My hair was blown every which way. The grass was plastered to the ground. I looked around wildly for Samuel but didn't see him. The pit that had formed earlier had turned into full-blown panic as I covered my chest with both arms. The branches on the weeping willow were tangled as I ran through the grass, slipping every now and then. I needed to get the hell away from the trees. Light flashed behind me followed by thunder. The ground shook as the weeping willow split in half as it was struck by lightning beside me.

"Shit, shit, shit."

I neared the back door and I sprinted, stretching a hand out to fling it open. Only to hit an invisible force shield. I bounced off it and landed in a painful heap. Tears sprung from my eyes as I looked around. I was supposed to be safe. I was supposed to be safe with the protection circle and Samuel. But Samuel had left me. He left me! And the protection circle had backfired. I couldn't get to safety. I was alone as the storm raged on behind me. I tried to punch, push, kick, and claw at the force shield until I was spent. There was no way to get out on my own.

I curled into a ball against the force shield. My body shook with fear and the cold of the storm. I wasn't sure how long I stayed in that position. It could have been minutes; it could have been hours. I had stopped feeling the rain pelting my skin. I was numb. Both to the temperature and emotions. I lifted my head and watched the storm rage. The willow tree was smoking despite being drenched in rain. It was a shame that it had been destroyed.

"What the hell?" I jumped at the sound of Luke's voice.

I fell back as the force shield disappeared behind me. Luke caught me in his arms as Hunter covered me with my towel. I blinked up at them, not quite understanding the expressions on their faces. Luke looked more concerned than I've ever seen him, Jared looked embarrassed, and Hunter… Hunter looked downright murderous.

"Where is Samuel?" Hunter demanded.

"I-I'm not sure," I stuttered. "H-he was here, then the s-storm started, and he was g-gone." The three of them stared at me then back towards the water and I followed their gazes.

The sky was no longer dark and gloomy with a raging storm, but quiet as night had descended. It looked like hours had passed… It was as if there was never a storm in the first place. It was as if I had imagined it all. But that was impossible… right? I looked at the willow tree still smoking as it slowly died. Proof that I hadn't imagined it. I was about to point it out when a low groan drifted from the cattails.

Hunter drew his sword and stalked over to the noise while I huddled in the safety Luke and Jared now provided. When Hunter was at the spot the sound originated from, he sheathed his sword and yelled for Luke. Luke lifted me and placed me in Jared's arms somewhat awkwardly. For me being on more of the curvy side, they both handled me like I weighed nothing.

Luke ran to Hunter and together they pulled a limp-soaked Samuel from the water.

"Oh, my gods!" I whispered in shock, and I slightly felt Jared's arms tighten around me.

They carried Samuel closer to us and I could see a large bruise forming on Samuel's forehead. His gun was gone from its holster and his polo was stained red on his side. Even through my dazed state, I knew he'd been shot and tossed in the water.

"Is he alive?" Jared asked and I clutched my towel tighter.

"He is. It is a through and through wound, Luke should be able to heal him." Hunter said with his face tight. "It is a good thing he is not awake."

Luke laid his hands over Samuel's body and a light blue glowed. Samuel groaned and tried to turn away. Hunter forced him still by holding him down and I watched helplessly as more blood spilled from the wound.

"Why can't Hunter heal him if he has magic?" I whispered to Jared.

Without taking his eyes from the scene in front of us he responded.

"Hunter's magic is limited to protection or destruction. I can only heal the human way; bandages and such. Because Luke is of angelic blood, he has the best magic for healing."

Jared seemed to want to say more but another cry of agony came from Samuel, and I cringed. Who would do that to him? Samuel was the sweetest person I had met on the island. He hadn't deserved this! We would find out who hurt him and who tried to hurt me.

After Luke had healed Samuel enough for him to walk on his own, everything happened fast. Jared gave me to Hunter, and I was whisked away to our room. After assuring him I was fine he left me to shower. I had assumed it was to investigate, but when he came back not a minute after I got dressed, he had our bags packed and in his hands. We were soon in the cargo truck and the others were together in the other. Hunter told me Samuel needed the room to lie down to heal more. I believed the true reasoning was that Hunter didn't want me out of his sight. I was okay with that. Hunter had cast protection circles on both vehicles, and we left without the livestock. When I asked about it, Hunter said it was a problem for another day. Soon we were far away from the village and the closer we got to the manor the easier it was to shake the feeling of being watched.

TWENTY-ONE

illion watched as the trucks flew out of the village like a bat out of hell. He thought back to what had just transpired, and his jaw clenched.

When Seine had looked up, he had thought that Seine had seen him. Much to his disappointment and relief, she hadn't. Dillion looked at the now ruined weeping willow tree. As the storm had died down, Seine had drifted away inside her mind, and he was worried that she was lost.

Rocks on the road crunched and it alerted Dillion to the presence of the person behind him. Dillion watched as the dust settled from the trucks. He wished he could ignore the man, but he couldn't. It was the same person that had caused the storm. Someone who was made of ash and smoke. Dillion turned away from the road to face the most dangerous person he knew.

"Was it necessary to have lightning?" Dillion had asked.

"Not really, but she pissed me off," the other man responded.

"And how exactly did she do that?" Dillion asked and the other man smiled.

"She was born," he answered.

"Let me get this straight. Seine was born- something she has zero control over- so you almost hit her with lightning?" Dillion gave a bitter laugh. "You're such an asshole." The other man only shrugged his shoulders.

"I don't see your point," he responded. They stood in silence for a few minutes.

"What was the time bubble for?" Dillion asked.

"That was just an experiment. I wanted to see how it would affect someone as powerful as her," the other man said.

"What was the point? It's not as if it'll change anything," he said glumly.

"That you know of. Only time will tell," the other man said, crossing his arms and looking up at the blue sky.

"I don't like this. You know that right?" Dillion asked as the other man started to walk away.

"Ya, well, then you shouldn't have gotten yourself killed, Dillion," the other man called back.

It was becoming increasingly difficult to keep his sister alive and he wasn't sure if he'd be able to intervene again.

TWENTY-TWO

Wincing, I tried not to move on the pedestal as the seamstress pulled yet another pin out of my thigh. It was the fifth time in the last two hours that I had been pricked. Naji chuckled next to me on her own pedestal in a green slip. We had shown up to the ballroom expecting to pick out our dresses and then have them fitted. Only to find out that wasn't the case. The seamstress had already designed our dresses and just needed to get our measurements. Hence why I had been stabbed with the pins.

"Sorry My Lady, it has been an awfully long time since I had to make a dress from scratch," the seamstress apologized, with a slight European accent.

She was an older lady with a soft voice. Her brown and grey hair was pulled back into a soft bun. If I had to guess she was in her fifties and her hands were light except for the occasional pin. It was a good thing that she had chosen a maroon color for me otherwise the blood would have surely stained the cloth,

"It's okay Ms. Anne," I said with another wince.

"I am almost done and then we can start on your brooding man over there," Ms. Anne said, nodding her head towards Hunter. He was standing several yards away with his signature stoic expression.

After we had returned from the village the men had disappeared to figure out what had happened. I had headed straight for my bed because sleeping in the truck next to Hunter had proved difficult. After that, Hunter tried to be more soldier and less friend. One step forward, eight steps back it seemed. Or at least, until I sat him down and told him I was okay. That he didn't need to stop being friendly because of the mishap. It had taken a lot of convincing, but eventually, we went back to normal. It took me a few beats to hear part of what she said.

"He's not my- we're not like- I don't know what you're talking about," I finished lamely. Both Naji and Ms. Anne laughed at me and I ducked my head to hide my blush.

"Not that she doesn't want him to be." Naji wiggled her eyebrows at me and giggled.

"Sir Wight would be an excellent choice for My Lady," Ms. Anne said and stood back while circling around me. "Alright My Lady we're all finished with you, put your arms up and we'll wiggle this off you."

"Right here?" I glanced at Hunter who in turn returned my look.

"You can't take it off alone dear, and Ms. Najia is pinned herself." Ms. Anne turned toward Hunter and gestured for him to turn around.

Hunter waited for a beat before doing as he was directed. Ms. Anne had me lift my arms and carefully inched the slip off. After what felt like forever, I was free of the pin-filled slip and I was left standing in just my panties and slippers. Ms. Anne laid the slip on a table and handed me a robe to put on. She helped me off the pedestal and I sat on a fluffy chair facing the same pedestal.

"How come I'm still wearing my porcupine outfit?" Naji asked.

"Because despite what you believe Ms. Naji, you are not a princess," Ms. Anne quipped but helped Naji out of her slip as well. "Alright Sir Wight your turn. Get on up here."

Hunter turned back to face us and frowned at Ms. Anne. He looked conflicted about coming over to us for whatever reason. Maybe it was a conflict between doing his duty of standing guard and listening to his elders. To be fair Ms. Anne did seem to be a no-nonsense kind of woman from the number of times she corrected my posture.

"It will have to wait until I am off duty ma'am," Hunter told her and she scowled at him.

"Boy, I don't have all day to wait. Get your ass up here so I can take measurements. It won't take but a few minutes. You can even keep your damn sword on." Ms. Anne pointed to the pedestal and snapped her fingers at him.

Hunter dragged his hand down his face and sighed as he walked over to us. He gave a pleading look at Ms. Anne, but she only pointed again. He crossed his arms and stood beside my chair. I smiled slightly behind my hand at his discomfort. I glanced at Naji and saw that she too was smiling.

"Ma'am, my measurements have not changed since I was indeed a boy," Hunter said with a surprising amount of sass I hadn't heard from him before.

"Are you copping an attitude with me boy? You're not too old to be spanked."

Naji and I shared a wide-eyed glance. Ms. Anne was about half the size of Hunter and he definitely outmuscled her. Not to mention he had a sword and the most she had was some pins.

But to my surprise, Hunter got on the pedestal and Ms. Anne brought out a stepladder as he towered over her even more.

"I would never give you attitude ma'am," Hunter said and I could have sworn I saw him roll his eyes. Ms. Anne must have thought so too because Hunter let out a hiss of pain when she stabbed him with a pin.

"You best watch it boy, I'll bend you over my knee in front of your Princess."

Ms. Anne was true to her word as Hunter's measurements only took a few minutes. When she was done, unlike with Naji and me, she didn't use pins on him. She only used a measuring tape and wrote down his measurements. When she was done she prodded him in the ribs and he stepped down with an annoyed expression.

"Call your Lord Cedric when you get the chance, he wants to discuss you training a new boy," Ms. Anne told him as she gathered her materials.

"Another one? Do we not have enough? Does he think we need extra for the celebration?"

Ms. Anne shrugged and bowed to me which in turn made me feel extremely uncomfortable. I had told her when we first met that she didn't have to bow or curtsy, but she went off about showing respect to royalty. I didn't try to tell her again and instead nodded to her to show my gratitude.

"How would I know what he thinks? Thirty-two years with that man and I never know what's going through your father's mind," she huffed.

I felt my mouth drop open finally connecting the dots. The reason Hunter hadn't reached for his sword and why Hunter spoke casually with her. If Ms. Anne was with Hunter's father of thirty-two years that would make her his-

"Ma, you and I both know that there are only ever two things in Pa's head. The first being training soldiers and the second being his love for you," Hunter said and leaned down to kiss his mother on the top of her head.

Ms. Anne blushed slightly and pushed Hunter away from her with a small laugh.

"Go on and get My Lady in some proper clothes. She's got just her unmentionables on and that's unbecoming of a princess," Ms. Anne said, making me blush a furious red as Hunter turned to look at me.

His eyes were darker and heated as they slowly trailed over my body. I fought the urge to cross my arms over my breasts because I knew that would only draw attention to them. Instead, I smiled at him and stuck my tongue out, even as my stomach twisted at the smile he gave me. It was filled with wicked secrets and I desperately wanted to know all of them.

"I will make sure she returns to her room swiftly." His voice was deeper with a bit of a husky undertone that made my toes curl in my slippers.

He held out a hand to help me up from my chair and I willed my hand not to shake. There was no need to fully reveal the way Hunter affected me. Though our nightly chats in the theater room got intimate at times. Purely conversational, we talked until the early hours of the morning. Besides hand-holding and light snuggling we never went further. Neither one of us was in any rush to go further. But if Hunter kept looking at me with a heated look hot enough to melt glass, I would change my mind soon.

"Hey, what about me?" Naji asked with her hands on her hips.

Ms. Anne only looked at her and walked out of the ballroom with her arms full of fabric. As she walked past, she was muttering about cuts and trims and frills, already in her own world.

"Well let's get going buckaroos." Naji clapped her hands. "Apparently this was a prime time to take our clothes to wash them."

I pursed my lips together. It did seem a bit odd that the housekeeper came to the ballroom only minutes after I mentioned to Naji that I had to do laundry. I hadn't let the housekeepers clean my clothes before because it made me uncomfortable. Yes, I knew it was part of their job, but that didn't mean I couldn't make their job easier. And because the housekeeper hadn't come back with our clothes, it meant we had to walk to our rooms in the robes Ms. Anne gave us.

Hunter smiled slightly before sweeping his arm to the side indicating for us to go first. Walking past I trailed my hand down his arm in a small attempt at flirting.

"Your shift ends in a couple of hours. Do you want to get changed and come back to my room?" I smiled suggestively.

Hunter's eyes widened and he looked at Naji warily as she whistled. I had talked to Naji about what I had planned tonight and she was on board.

"I will change and come back with food for the both of us," he blushed slightly before asking, "Did you want me to make more of my lasagna and garlic knots?"

My stomach growled at just the thought of tasting his food again. If he was born in another life, I would have bet that he was a world-class chef.

"Gods yes please," I moaned, and the look Hunter gave me made me hungry for more than food.

● ● ● ● ●

Hunter's shift was about to start in an hour and he needed to head back to his room to shower and change. We had gone to sleep around three which made me feel a little guilty since Hunter's alarm went off five hours later. He had rolled over on the bed with a sleepy moan that made me smile from my curled-up spot on the beanbag chair. I had insisted that he take the bed since he was too tall to sleep comfortably in the beanbag chair. And my bed was too small to fit the both of us sadly. I stayed curled up as he sat up with his hair twisted in every direction. It was adorable to see him so disheveled.

"You look like a kitten curled up for warmth," Hunter told me with a small smile.

"Meow," I smiled sleepily at him as I stretched out my slightly stiff muscles. My shirt rode up and I saw Hunter's eyes linger on my stomach.

"You managed to get paint on your stomach as well, you messy girl."

"Just a casualty of creating a masterpiece." I laughed with a glance at the still tacky canvas laying on the end table. I had spent the night painting a portrait of Hunter. I had painted him standing alone with his sword drawn in dark woods. I had used almost all cool colors, even the flames on the sword were dull and almost faded into the background. The real focus of the painting was Hunter's face. The fierceness as he looked off into the woods. The only place I had used warm colors was for his eyes. The orange and red burned bright, making them stand out against the rest of the canvas. When I had finished it, Hunter was quiet for a long time. When I was worried he didn't like it, he hugged me tight and then laughed when he saw paint on my cheek.

"Well, Miss. Kitten, I must go shower and you may want to as well to get the rest of the paint off," Hunter said while he got out of bed. At the new nickname, little butterflies fluttered in my stomach.

"I guess I'll take a shower," I playfully whined.

Hunter laughed quietly and opened the door to Luke's back. The door opening made Luke turn to face us. Luke eyed me in the beanbag chair, his gaze lingering on the paint on me. I gave him a small wave and he ignored me like usual. He leaned in close to Hunter and whispered something in his ear that I couldn't hear. Hunter's relaxed posture slowly stiffened at whatever Luke was saying. The happy carefree atmosphere disappeared when Luke pulled away and glared at me.

"I will handle it," Hunter growled with enough venom that the hair on my arms stood on end.

"Make sure you do, he's killed for less," Luke said and Hunter pushed past him and left without another word.

I stared after him then turned my stare on Luke, who returned it. He was silent as he looked at me, though his jaw kept moving like he wanted to say something. I was curious about what they were talking about. The reaction Hunter had made me a little scared to ask. Then there was a good chance Luke wouldn't tell me anyhow.

"Are you gonna-"

"No. Shower you look like a mess," he said and slammed my door shut making me jump.

I pursed my lips and rolled onto the floor with a heavy sigh. When I was younger, I would lie on the floor at least twice a week. The scratch of the carpet would clear my head. Unfortunately, the carpet in my room was extremely plush and didn't have the same effect. I stood up and went to shower before the paint started to make me itch.

TWENTY-THREE

"**T**oxucondendron radicans." Luke drawled while he stood with his back to the study room's door. It was around noon the next day and apparently Luke was still in a mood. He had taken it as his personal assignment to grill me about plants that could kill me. Even though I had just started the lesson today he expected me to know them already. Or he was just being an ass and wanted to make me feel stupid while giving himself an ego boost... It was definitely the second one. He also took great joy in hearing that the flowers outside of Jazmine's house back in home caused me to have a reaction. Apparently, it was wolfsbane and it only reacted to those of a werewolf family. He was a real jerk.

"I don't know. A toxic radish?" I rolled my eyes at him which in turn made him glower at me.

"Obviously the human education system failed you more than I thought. It's poison ivy you twit. The most common plant and you don't know it." I got the feeling that if Luke wasn't standing as my guard, he would have facepalmed.

"In case you haven't noticed, I'm not exactly the outdoors type. So, there wasn't any reason for me to worry about plants that may or may not kill me. And in case you didn't know, poison ivy can't kill," I crossed my arms over my chest and leaned back in my chair.

"No Princess, unless you're deadly allergic to it like your father. Perhaps we should take you outside and test if you are." Luke looked like he rather liked that idea and I slid further down into my seat. "Nerium oleander."

"Ugggggh," I let my head fall back and I glared at the ceiling. "Oleander? I don't freaking know."

Silence. I turned my head to look at Luke expecting him to belittle me again. His lips were pursed together tightly and he looked slightly annoyed. Well, more than he did normally.

"You guessed it, didn't you?"

"No." Yes. One hundred percent guessed it.

"Alright then what's so dangerous about it?"

"It kills you, obviously."

"Obviously," he mocked. "What color is it?" He challenged.

"Um. Blue?"

Luke smirked at me and I knew I had guessed wrong. He was taking too much joy out of the whole lesson. Too much joy in making me feel dumb. In being an ass.

"And you're dead. Atropa belladonna."

I tried to hold in my reaction. I was actually familiar with that one from a book I had read as a child. Of course, in the book it was called a different name, but I knew what it was based on. It was a dark berry that could be mistaken for a blueberry if one had never picked blueberries before. I made myself look upset as if I didn't know the answer and scowled at Luke.

"Obviously I don't know," I paused for effect before continuing, "that Atropa belladonna is deadly nightshade,"

The bewildered expression on Luke's face was better than I imagined. His mouth opened and closed like a fish while his eyes bugged out. I smiled smugly and gave him a mocking wave. His mouth snapped shut and he slowly smiled in a way that made my stomach twist.

"If you answer this one correct, I'll end the lesson."

"And if I get it wrong?"

"Then we'll go and get up and personal with the plants."

I swallowed hard and my earlier triumph faded away leaving me feeling hollow inside. I sighed, already accepting my fate. It was only a coincidence that he had picked nightshade. I wouldn't know another plant.

"Aconitum napellus."

I didn't bother to answer him. Luke's stoic face slowly changed into a smirking condescending grin. I frowned at him, which made him smile wider and I wanted to punch him in the face. With the lessons I'd been taking with Hunter, I'd probably be able to do some kind of damage.

"Let's go, Princess," Luke turned and walked out of the study room without waiting for me.

I rolled my eyes and the chalkboard wrote out a message. I snorted out a laugh as the board erased itself and I followed behind Luke. The board had called Luke a narcissistic know-it-all and wouldn't know the difference between Hemlock and Queen Anne's lace.

I followed Luke who, like a psycho, was going down the rickety old spiral staircase two at a time making it groan in protest. I waited for him to get to the bottom, before going down holding onto both handrails and taking one step at a time. Like a sane person. Luke looked at me in disgust and motioned me to follow him. He led us out of the library and down the hall. I had no clue where he was taking me until we came to a stop in front of the glass door that led to the greenhouse.

I balked and instinctively stepped back. There was no damned way I was going to step foot on the glass floor. There was nothing Luke could say to change my mind. Luke stood behind me and placed a vice-like grip on my elbow.

"If you can correctly identify three plants, I'll tell the library you passed this portion of your lessons."

I hesitated in my retreat. If Luke was able to do that, I'd be grateful because the herbology lessons were almost as boring as the etiquette lessons. But that also meant I would have to get over the heart-wrenching feeling I had every time I looked at the floor. There was no way I could force my body.

"I can't," I tried to pull my arm from his grip, but he held strong.

"I have seen you go head-to-head with Damon, but you can't enter a simple room?" Luke scoffed.

"My body remembers what happened here as a child even if my mind does not."

Luke dropped his grip on me and walked into the green-house. A quiet grinding sound came from the room. Before my eyes, a wooden floor slowly appeared beneath the glass. It was as if it had been pushed to the side and was getting stuck in some parts. Once the floor was fully transformed, Luke came to the doorway.

"It's solid Australian Buloke; one of the strongest woods and it's been enforced with magic on top of that," Luke told me.

"Why not just have the wooden floor to begin with?" I inched forward tentatively. Why go through having a second floor in-stalled when you could've just had the one?

"The Crowned Head enjoys his aesthetics," Luke replied and it looked like he tried not to roll his eyes.

"Of course," I muttered and quickly crossed the threshold before I lost my nerve. When I didn't immediately fall through the floor I smiled slightly. Not so bad, I could do this. I'd show Luke I knew my plants and I'd never have to set foot in here again.

I looked around the large room. There was a clear path across the floor, which was good considering everywhere else was covered in plants. Enormous leaves waved in a slight breeze, palm trees stood tall, and bright flowers were everywhere. There was a slight mist in the air that felt rather nice since it was warm.

"See, not so scary now that you're not worried about plummeting to your death."

I stopped my hand from touching a large leaf next to me and glared at Luke. He only smiled in return.

"You're kind of a jerk, you know that?"

"I'm quite aware. We need to go in further for you to identify the plants." Luke walked away from me and I soon lost him behind some overgrown bushes.

I hurried after him, keeping my eye on the floor with each step. I passed by a small cart covered in gardening tools, seeds, and glass vials. The deeper we went the wetter it became. Apparently, they had a rainforest growing in the manor. I rolled my eyes to myself. I shouldn't have been surprised; most of the rooms in the manor were over the top.

Luke stopped in front of a section of raised flower beds. The one he was standing in front of had herbs of all sorts. The next flower bed had a bushel of leaves and a familiar orange spade-shaped plant. I knew that if you peeled the outer orange layer off, inside was a small berry. I used to peel these apart back home to make "potions" in a bucket. When I told Luke that, he just stared at me wide-eyed.

"Seine, it is out of pure luck that you've been alive this long." Luke rubbed his face and looked back at the plant. "This is poisonous, but it also has medical properties. If you can identify it, I'll count it as one of your three."

"Easy, it's a Chinese Lantern," I answered smugly and Luke shook his head at me.

"Not the scientific name, but I'll accept it. What about this?" Luke pointed at a small section of white flowers with a yellow center. I looked back at him and then back at the flowers. Surely, he was joking. It was too easy, it had to be a trick.

"A daisy?" I asked, confused.

Luke's answering grin was all I needed to know I was wrong.

"Matricaria chamomilla, also known as chamomile. Similar to daisies, but chamomile only has one row of petals while daisies have several. Chamomile also doesn't have leaves- daisies do." Luke crossed the pathway to a new flower bed. "Last chance, I'll even be nice and change it to two out of three."

I walked up to the new plant and frowned. They were tall stems without any flowers at the top. Upon closer inspection, they looked freshly cut off. How was I supposed to figure out what kind of plant it was if it didn't have its most telling part? I leaned in to smell it to see if its scent could clue me in. Luke grabbed the back of my neck, freezing me in my descent.

"Perhaps you shouldn't smell unidentified plants that may or may not kill you."

I shook his grip off and straightened with a frown at the plant. It didn't seem poisonous. But what did I know, it didn't have anything that could tell me what it was. All I knew was that it kind of reminded me of the time I tried to grow my own garlic. The stems of the garlic looked similar to what I was looking at now.

"It looks like garlic," I guessed with a shrug. "Not much to guess since most of its gone."

"What?" Luke nudged me aside and crouched down to look at the plant. "They're not supposed to look like this, there's supposed to be a flower."

He pulled out his sword and used it to gently inspect the plant. When he did, I heard a soft sound further down. I left Luke while he inspected the apparently beheaded plants to investigate. I heard the sound again in what I knew was just regular spider grass. The grass moved slightly and I parted it, unsure what to find.

I definitely wasn't expecting to see the black cat from the inn to be laying in the dirt of the flower bed. Its side was moving up and down fast and its eyes locked on mine. It looked scared and it was panting like a dog.

"Luke!" I called, fear sinking in my heart. How the hell did the cat get here in the manor, let alone into the greenhouse?

Luke hurried over and he leaned over my shoulder to see the obviously sick cat.

"That explains where the daffodils went," he mused. He walked away from me and searched through the cart before pulling out a large container. He walked back and frowned down at the cat. "I need you to gently force the mouth open so I can put this in."

I frowned at the unlabeled container but did as I was instructed. The cat tried to resist but was too weak to fight me. I gently opened its mouth and Luke dumped a scoop of fine black powder into its mouth. The cat instantly tried shaking its head and I let go so that it didn't get hurt. The cat struggled to its feet and threw up chewed-up daffodils and mucus. Afterward, it still looked a bit sick, but its tail swished and its eyes didn't look fearful. I reached out a hand and it rubbed up against it with a quiet purr.

"I suggest you hide that cat from the Crowned Head, he despises cats. I'm not even going to ask where it came from.

You should be able to get supplies from the kitchen for it." He picked up the cat despite its yowling protest. He turned it this way and that way before putting it in my arms. "Congratulations it's a boy."

I scratched under the cat's chin and it- he started to purr again. I grinned down at him. He was so cute and soft even with his fur covered in dirt and water. I grinned up at Luke and he blinked for whatever reason.

"I'm going to name him Hades," I smiled down at Hades.

The room glowed slightly around us and I looked around in surprise. Several flowers had started to glow. Some glowed pink, others yellow, but most glowed a blueish white.

"They're night flowers, they glow around six at night once a month…" Luke drifted off and looked at me weirdly. "Though I thought they had already this month…"

I shrugged carefully with Hades in my arms. I had more important things to worry about than glowing flowers. I had to get the sweet baby everything he needed. Luke and I walked out of the greenhouse and he nudged me gently.

"By the way, you only got one right."

I glared at him and Hades hissed quietly.

"You're definitely not a jerk, you're an asshole," I told him and he barked out a laugh. It was the first time I'd heard him laugh. It was nice. He should do it more often. I smiled back at him and we made our way back to my room.

TWENTY-FOUR

The hallway was surprisingly well-lit even though it was absolutely pitch black outside the windows. I could look out of the windows with someone on the other side and I wouldn't even know. The thought made me shudder and I hurried my steps while also trying to be quiet. The training with Hunter had allowed me to be nearly silent when I walked. It was three in the morning and I didn't want to wake anyone up.

A loud crash and a string of curses filled the hallway. I turned around to see Samuel trying to right himself from the rug he tripped on. His sword scraped and clanged against the uncovered wood floor as he climbed to his feet. Even from where I stood, I could see the blush on his face. I raised an eyebrow and the well-trained soldier straightened his suit. He had fully healed after a day and was back to guarding the front door. The soldiers that went to investigate the pond found traces of magic. They weren't able to find who was behind it and had returned with the livestock.

"How the fu- How can you see? I can't even see a foot in front of my face!" Samuel whisper yelled.

I shrugged and turned back around to continue down the hall. I had always been able to see well in the dark, especially after waking up. It was a benefit of having blue eyes. Being able to see well at night and being overly sensitive to the sunlight.

"Maybe you should do some training at night," I whispered back.

Samuel appeared beside me and let out an exasperated sigh.

"It's not my fault you decided you needed fruit before dawn even broke," he muttered.

"Yes… Fruit… That's what I told you we were getting…" I trailed off hiding my smile.

"I may not be able to see your face, but I've gotten to know you well Princess. You are up to something. Something Hunter won't approve of which is why you're taking me and not him."

I smirked at him and he shook his head but followed me into the kitchen.

Before the door swung shut a basket appeared on the counter. I knew that what I needed would already be inside as it was the night before. Samuel frowned at the basket and then at me as I shouldered it with a small grunt. It was heavier than it was last night which was odd. But I wasn't going to open it in front of Samuel in case he figured out what I was doing. I glanced back at Samuel to see him staring at me with a calculated gaze. I grinned at him and walked back out of the kitchen, letting him trail after me.

"You're going to get us into trouble, aren't you Princess?" He muttered behind me and I grinned to myself. Yes, Samuel was a soldier. Yes, he was "my" soldier. But he was fun to mess with and have around since he wasn't as serious as Hunter or mean like Luke. He was my friend. And I hadn't had any new friends in a while.

"I would definitely never get you into any trouble... on purpose..."

Samuel bumped my shoulder with his and took the basket from me with a small frown at the weight. I only smiled at him and looped my arm through his to continue our way down the hall. We walked in silence and with my arm in his, Samuel didn't trip again. Eventually, we made it to the once-empty bedroom down the hall from my bedroom. Samuel gave me a questioning look, but I merely smiled and ushered him inside.

The room was dark and I didn't flip the light switch until the door was fully closed. When I turned on the lights there was a quiet mew from Hades. The room was quite large; it could have fit a coffee shop in the space. The walls were covered in various wall mounts for Hades to perch and lay on. There was a small sitting area off to the side and on the other was the cat box. I had gone to clean it the night before, but the manor had done it for me, which was nice. There were a couple of windows that I could open for fresh air. They were spelled like all the other windows. That way nothing could get out or in them and they could be left open for hours at a time.

Hades trotted up to me and rubbed up against my calves. Luke had told me that the black powder he had used was activated charcoal. It induced vomiting and helped get the toxins out of Hades' system. I was warned to only use it in extreme measures. It had definitely helped since Hades had been acting like a kitten again.

"That-that's a cat," Samuel said.

Laughing I picked up Hades and he rubbed his head under my chin. He was such a cuddle bug. I carried Hades over to one of his many carpeted wall mounts. They had appeared the night after Luke and I had discovered Hades. I was under the impression that the manor had conjured the supplies, but then Hunter caught me sneaking out of my room one night. Hunter revealed that he had gotten the supplies. I had thought that he would tell me to get rid of Hades, but after Hades cradled in his lap Hunter was won over quite easily.

"Where did the cat come from?" Samuel asked as he sat the bag down on the wooden coffee table. Hades instantly jumped down from his perch to inspect the bag.

"He stowed away in one of the trucks when we came back from the village. He apparently decided that village life wasn't for him and needed to live the life of royalty."

I pulled out jars of meat baby food, dry kitten food, a water fountain, a whisker-friendly bowl, some felt balls, plastic bottle caps, and lastly, a small catnip fish. Samuel raised his eyebrows when I pulled out the bottle caps and I chuckled. With cats, it was the simpler things that they enjoyed. Hunter and I had discovered that Hades liked to play fetch with them. I guessed the kitchen knew that and packed some.

Samuel reached out to pet Hades on the head and his ears went flat. I opened my mouth to warn Samuel but wasn't fast enough. Hades swiped at Samuel's hand and left behind four bloody stripes. With a hiss, Hades bounded up his scratching post where he watched Samuel with a puffed-up tail and canines on display.

"I'm so sorry!" I apologized.

I turned to see how badly Hades had scratched Samuel in time to see a look disappear from his face. I wasn't sure what the look it was, but I got the feeling that bringing him to meet Hades was a bad idea. I swallowed past the lump of uncertainty and reached for Samuel's hand. The scratch didn't look deep, but cleaning it was a priority.

I turned on a lamp for Hades and turned off the overhead lights. I pulled Samuel out of the room and the door closed with a quiet click. The uneasiness didn't leave my body even after I cleaned Samuel's wound in the kitchen. It stayed with me as I stared up at my bedroom ceiling. It wasn't until I started to fall asleep that I was able to put a name to the look Samuel had made.

It was absolute hatred.

TWENTY-FIVE

Hunter and I walked down the hall without talking. The silence I had grown used to was replaced by the hustle and bustle of people preparing for the celebration tonight. It made me feel unnerved having so many people around. I had never liked crowds and with so many people rushing around, it made the feeling worse. Some were running with white tablecloths that were the whitest I had ever seen before. A couple of ladies hustled past with their arms filled with flowers. Several new soldiers had stalked by us, silent and lethal.

Hunter had changed shifts with Luke early so that we could go to our final fitting together. Luke had rolled his eyes and muttered something, but left. Naji would be down in the ballroom already since she oversaw the flower arrangements. We wouldn't be seeing our dresses until tonight, right before the celebration. Which meant we wouldn't be in the ballroom for long. Which also meant Hunter could fit in a dagger session. We had been training every other day and I was getting better at handling my dagger. I had been able to make the dagger stick into the bal-listic gel dummy in superficial wounds. Despite that, according to Hunter, I was a natural at dagger throwing. But I was a little upset that I still hadn't made a killing blow. The dummy was as realistic as an actual person which-

A shoulder rammed into the back of mine as we walked down the stairs. I would have fallen down them if Hunter hadn't grabbed onto my dagger belt. Hunter pulled me back onto the safety of the step. I looked down the stairs and saw a woman running down the steps. Her arms were filled with a huge metal box with flowing white ribbons. I glanced at Hunter and saw him frowning down at the woman. I shrugged at him and continued down the stairs. With so many people running around, it was bound that someone would bump into us.

The ballroom was completely decked out which was a com-plete one-eighty from what it was a month ago. A black and white patterned rug outlined the room that left what looked like a forty-foot circle. There were a dozen tables covered in the white cloths I had seen earlier. They were spread out across the rug with nine chairs and full table settings. Vases sat on each table, some with flowers already. Naji was at a long table at the far end of the ballroom filling one of the three vases sitting on it. Instead of chairs, there were two thrones sitting behind the table. The left was shorter than the throne centered in the middle of it.

Ms. Anne gestured for me to come over to her. She had a measuring tape and a small notepad clasped in her hand as she waited for us. She had a pencil stuck behind her ear and her hair was a mess.

"Come now My Lady, I don't have all night."

"Ope, sorry," I hurried over to her and she helped me onto the pedestal. Hunter laughed quietly behind me and I turned to stick my tongue out at him. He grinned and tapped his imagi-nary watch on his wrist.

Ms. Anne's light touch tickled while she measured me again. She made little noises as she wrote in her notepad. She pursed her lips as she measured me for the third time, her face screwing up more each time. It was an excellent self-esteem booster.

"Is uh, everything okay?" I asked her, fidgeting slightly while she wrote more in her notepad.

Ms. Anne sighed and thumped the notepad in the palm of her hand. She shook her head and "tsked" at me.

"You're lucky that the celebration is tonight. After another week I'd have to make a whole new dress with the amount of muscle you've gained," she mused.

I blinked at her, unsure if I should feel bad or not. Had she said it was because of food I would've definitely felt bad. But since it was muscle gain it meant I was actually making a difference with the training. Yes, I had a mirror in my room and bathroom, but past years of hating what I looked like made it a habit to avoid them. So, it made sense I hadn't seen the progress Ms. Anne did. I looked up to see Hunter beaming in what looked a lot like pride.

"Do not worry Ma, you are the best seamstress on the island. If anyone could make a dress fit for a princess and warrior, it is you," Hunter smirked. Ms. Anne beamed at her son and tucked her pen in her bun.

"Alright you sweet talker, take Our Lady to lunch and take a break from training," she chastised after my stomach growled loudly.

Hunter grinned and bowed to his mother and helped me off the pedestal. I fluttered my eyelashes at him playfully and Hunter rolled his eyes at me with a sigh. But he couldn't hide the small smile that twitched at the corner of his lips. I eyed the corners of his lips thinking about how they tasted like warmed sugar. I looked up to see his eyes warming red and I smiled at the effect I had on him.

"Let us head to the kitchen and then we will make our way to the library for a study session, Princess," Hunter smirked because he knew I hated studying.

My lips pursed and grinned up at him; two could play that game.

"Oh, goody. The library wants to go over what types of tea a princess should drink and what they mean in different settings," I made up while trotting alongside him.

"You are lucky my mother is here otherwise I would run you ragged practicing drills."

"And because you're a good boy you're gonna do what mommy tells you?" I laughed.

"Aye, she may seem sweet now, but she is the one that taught me half of what I know."

My mouth dropped open in shock and I looked back at Ms. Anne in a new light as the doors shut behind us. If she taught Hunter, that meant she was a badass warrior and that there was hope for me yet.

• • • • •

"The gonadotropin-releasing hormone is controlled by the hypothalamus and it makes its way through the body. Once there is enough of the hormone in the body, it begins to change. The once slumbering magic awakens and transforms the body. Within one to three years the transformation will be complete and the male will come into their full power. The luteinizing hormone and follicle-stimulating hormone in the female body causes the ovaries to enlarge and they begin to produce estrogen. After one to two years the power will go dormant. At this time of the transition, the female will be unable to reproduce until their second transition at the age of twenty-five. The second transition allows the female to bear children and come into their full power…"

I stopped reading with an apple slice dangling from my lips. I felt like a cartoon from the way I was staring at the pages of the old book; bugged-eyed and slack-jawed. From what I just read I had gone through my "first transition" when I went through puberty fifteen years ago. But I had no memory of anything abnormal happening when I did. Just the usual pain and embarrassment that came with bleeding every month. But I guess it went dormant before I could even get used to menstruating. It would make sense I wouldn't have known abnormal even if it hit me with a bat. I wouldn't notice anything until I turned twenty-f…

The apple slice fell onto the plate with a small thud and I looked at Hunter with wide eyes. Hunter looked up from his own plate with his eyebrows quirked as he chewed. The celebration at school was in February. I woke up six and a half months ago. Before that, I was in a coma for two and a half months. I planned the celebration for almost three months…

"What's today's date?" I asked Hunter, my brain was struggling to believe what the math was adding up to.

Hunter frowned and looked out the window beside us with a clear look of concentration. It was oddly reassuring that I wasn't the only one who didn't remember the date.

"I believe it is the twenty-eighth of November," he finally said and it felt like my heart exploded and froze at the same time.

My eyes unfocused from Hunter's face as my emotions were shoved into the far back of my mind. Just another day of the year. Unimportant. Just like last year. Emotions were hard. It was better to go numb at the moment and deal with them alone. Better to hurt in private than with witnesses. A warm touch on my hand caused me to refocus on Hunter's worried face.

"My darling Kitten, what makes you look so forlorn?" Hunter asked.

His eyes were open, unguarded, and completely willing to listen to whatever I had to say. It was… different. Usually, I was the therapist friend. I listen to others' problems, not the other way around. Perhaps that was why I told him the truth.

"According to this-" I trailed off to swallow against the lump in my throat. I jabbed a finger against the page I just read. "-This says that I'll be starting my second transition and will be coming into my powers." I laughed harshly. "And to top it all off, I turned twenty-five. Almost two weeks ago. What makes it worse," I lowered my eyes as tears gathered in them. "I didn't even remember my own birthday."

Hunter's hand went slightly lax on mine before tightening again. I looked up to see a burning heat blazing a bright red in his eyes. It was intense- the fierce protectiveness that he had for me. Not just as a soldier protecting his princess. But as a man protecting his… Whatever I was to him…

"My darling Kitten, your bringing into this world is a cause to celebrate. I wish I had known when your birthday was. We would have celebrated long into the night. After the celebration we shall go watch movies and play with Hades as long as you want." Hunter nodded to himself and squeezed my hand again. The heat in his eyes lightened from a blazing fire to a simmer. He also looked slightly confused as he looked at me.

"If this is true that you are twenty-five, then you should have been experiencing your powers awakening. Have you noticed anything out of the ordinary?"

I laughed sadly and ran my hands over my face. Out of the ordinary? Everything here was out of the ordinary. It was easier to tell him what was normal. I thought back trying to remember anything odd. When I came up with nothing I sighed.

"What exactly would be out of the ordinary?" I asked Hunter.

"From what I have seen other werewolves go through you would experience a number of differences. Increased strength and speed being the most common to appear." Hunter frowned at me and seemed to be staring at my eyes. "Correction, usually the first to happen to signify that you were coming into your powers would be the change of your eye color."

I blinked at him in stunned silence. I had forgotten about that aspect of being part of the supernatural. After being around so many people with abnormal eye colors I had gotten used to it. Hell, I was the odd one out for having my normal ass blue eyes. I was stronger and faster from my training not from magic.

"Maybe I'm just a really late bloomer?" I offered up and Hunter nodded slowly although I didn't think he accepted the answer.

"Yes. Perhaps that is it," he murmured.

The book closed with a soft thump and I looked up at the board in confusion. I had only been reading for an hour. More often than not, the library had me read for at least two. Scrawled across the board was the message:

"*It is 2:30 pm. It is time to get ready for the celebration.*"

I looked at the clock by the door and sure enough, the library was right. But I was told that I didn't have to be at the ballroom until five. There was no possible way that it was going to take two and a half hours to get ready. Or at least I hoped it wouldn't. I gave Hunter an exasperated look which he returned with a smile.

"It will be your first appearance to most of the court, you may even be a few minutes late."

"What could I possibly have done to me that'll take that long?!"

The library door opened and a new message appeared on the board.

"*Only one way to find out Princess.*"

I glowered at the board.

TWENTY-SIX

Two hours later I had been bathed, waxed, moisturized, and plucked. My body was the smoothest it had ever been. Ms. Anne had brought a team of five handmaidens to help her in getting me ready. They had told me their names, but I had promptly forgotten. In my defense though, they told me their names and then told me to get naked. I had been more worried about them seeing my naked body. Thankfully though after they had gotten rid of every stray hair on my body, they reintroduced themselves.

The older lady with black hair greying, tanned skin, and yellow eyes was Marianna. She reminded me of a grandmother with her quiet voice. There was Zuri who had the darkest skin I had ever seen. It wasn't dark like African skin, it was as if she had been born from the night sky. With her teal eyes, it made her skin look darker. Then there was Emily, a quiet girl who didn't talk like the others. She had red eyes like Jared. The last two handmaidens were… Odd. Linette and Posy were twins with matching green skin and beady black eyes. They were able to communicate with each other without saying anything.

After being turned into a plucked chicken, I was given a plush robe and sat in a barber chair that the group had brought with them. Zuri was on my right hand, Emily was on my left, and the twins were at my feet. They were applying a light coat of nail polish with a French tip to my nails. I knew that the first training lesson I had with Hunter would chip the polish. Marianna was brushing and drying my hair while Ms. Anne did something behind us. She refused to let me look in the mirror until I was fully done. Even without being able to see what Marianna was doing behind me, I could feel what she was doing to my hair. She had separated my hair at the crown of my head and split it into two even sections. Marianna braided each part so that they were tight on my scalp part down then hung loose. By the time the rubber bands were added at the ends, my nails were done. Marianna slid two objects into the top of my hair which piqued my curiosity. When Emily was done painting my nails, she grabbed a large makeup bag and got started. Her touches were light and delicate. After only a minute or so she was done and MS. Anne stepped up.

She held out her hand for me to take and lifted me from the barber chair and led me to the center of the room. There was a large garment bag hanging on a portable rack. It was unzipped and beside it on the rack was my dress. The skirt of the dress was large with its dark red lace that flowed down in delicate waves. At the waist, there were a few silver chains in the shape of small circles that fell at different lengths. The bodice of the dress was of a corset style with lace off-the-shoulder sleeves. Ms. Anne and Zuri helped me step into the dress so that I didn't mess up the makeup. After some maneuvering, the dress was in place and Ms. Anne started to lace up the back of the bodice.

"Shit," I gasped in surprise at a particularly strong pull.

"My apologies My Lady, sometimes I forget how much strength is left in my old bones." She gave another pull, but not as hard. "I am almost done and then the twins can help you into your shoes."

"They're not high heels, are they?" I asked nervously. Despite all my training with Hunter, I was still clumsy on my feet at times. Plus, heels hurt after a while and I doubted I'd be allowed to take them off. With it being a royal party and all.

"No dear, I was under strict orders not to give you heels," she chuckled quietly. "Falling over your feet at your debutante ball would not go over well."

I knew from my historical romance book readings that debutante balls were used to introduce coming-of-age girls into society. It was also a way for the girls to find a husband, which is why the traditional dress was white. To symbolize a wedding dress. I peeked down at my red dress in gratitude. I was not looking for a husband so why would I wear white?

"All done. Emily, help me hold up her skirts."

As Ms. Anne and Emily held up several layers of my dress, the twins approached with strappy shoes with flat bottoms. I slipped them on and they wound the straps around my calves. On my right, something cold and hard pressed into my skin. Without a mirror, I had no way of knowing what it was.

Fully dressed, I was escorted to a full-length mirror where I stared at a familiar stranger. It was both me and not. My features were more pronounced and as Jazmine would say, "my waist was snatched." My eyes left my body and drifted to my hair. The items Marianna had placed in my hair were two silver crescent moon hairpins. The way they sat in each braid almost made them look like horns. I turned my head from side to side to get a better look at them and nodded my approval. I hiked up my skirts to see the silver gladiator-style shoes. Twisting my leg to the side, my eyes widened in surprise to see my dagger in a metal sheath.

The straps of the shoes kept it secure and I got the impression that no matter what I did, it wouldn't come loose.

"That was Sir Wight's request. He said you can never be too careful." I locked eyes with Ms. Anne in the mirror and she smiled. "Such a worrier my son is."

I swallowed past the sudden emotion in my throat and fought back tears so I wouldn't ruin the makeup. Hunter was thinking of my safety even now. I nodded at her with a grateful smile.

"Thank you all so much, this is more than I could have hoped for. For once I look the part of a princess." I said.

"You've always looked the part My Lady, it is only now that you look like a queen," Ms. Anne beamed at me. "You better get going now otherwise you'll be late."

The handmaidens walked with me to the bedroom door and Ms. Anne opened it for me. Luke turned from his post and his bored eyes sharpened as he took me in. A hot blush spread across my cheeks at his reaction. If that was how someone who hated me looked at me, I was ready to see Hunter's reaction. Luke bowed to me though it seemed a bit stiff. He straightened and gave me a bitter smile and held out his elbow for me to take.

"I'm here to escort you to the ballroom doors Princess."

I wrapped my arm through his, smiled, and waved goodbye to the ladies. We made our way down the hall in a comfortable silence. The only sound was the quiet taps of my shoes and the clack of Luke's. Ever since the greenhouse he had been a lot nicer towards me. I wasn't sure if it was due to our herbology lesson or if it was because he had a soft spot for cats. Whatever the reason, I was glad.

As we neared the grand staircase instrumental music drifted up towards us. It was mainly piano and violin that rocked between soft and haunting. I had no idea what song it was supposed to be, but it made my heart ache. Such a sad song to be playing at what was supposed to be a celebration.

Luke stopped us just before the first step; out of sight of any-one that could have been in the lobby. With a tap on my hand, he withdrew his arm. He turned to face me head-on and his usu-ally hard eyes were gentle as he locked eyes with me.

"After today everything will change for you. There's going to be several people that are going to test your abilities as a mem-ber of the royal family. Keep your head on your shoulders and keep your chin high. You belong here just as much as anyone else, if not more. Once you walk through the doors, you'll be sit-ting at the grand dining table at the far end of the ballroom. Sit there, relax, watch, listen." Luke trailed off as the music faded and a new perkier song began. "Most importantly, if someone asks you to dance, you cannot refuse. Dance for a few minutes then excuse yourself. It's going to be the only way to save your feet from dancing for hours."

I blinked at Luke in shock. He could have let me walk in there and made a fool of myself. He didn't have to look out for me, but he was. It was completely out of the norm for him... Though he did watch out for me in the training room with the hell hounds...

"Why are you telling me all this?" I asked.

"I promised I'd look after you, that hasn't changed now that we're adults. I should've been nicer to you when you first came back. I'm sorry," he smiled slightly. "I think I kept you long enough, time to make one out of two of your grand entrances." He tapped a finger under my chin in a reminder and stepped back.

Taking a deep breath, I squared my shoulders and ap-proached the stairs. There were several people in the lobby that turned at the sound of my steps. I gathered my skirts in my hands and began my descent down the steps. It was odd having eyes on me in such an obvious way. There were a pair of fiery orange eyes missing though.

I scanned the lobby looking for him. The furthest away from me, at the ballroom doors, were Hunter and Samuel. He was dressed in his usual uniform style, but tonight it was a dark emerald green. His uniform was offset by his signature corset being jet black. And as usual, Hunter's sword rested against his hip. He was my complete contrast in color. He stood with his back facing the stairs but turned as the hush fell amongst the lobby. My breath caught in my chest as I watched his eyes slowly climb up the steps until they met mine.

I could have sworn I felt the burning heat of his eyes trail every bit of my body. When our eyes finally met, I gave him a small smile and the look he gave in return had my body heat up. Slowly he gave an answering smile and subtly tapped his calve with the end of his sword. I dipped my head to signify that I was in fact wearing the dagger. Hunter's grin widened and I could see his plans to explore my body later to ensure that it was in fact there. By the time I stepped off the final step and released my skirts, I was in dire need of a shower to damper my needs. I would most definitely have to thank Ms. Anne and the hand-maidens again.

I was approached by one of the men loitering in the lobby and he escorted me to a small line at the ballroom doors. I was told to stay behind a woman in a pale green dress and wait for my name to be announced. There were several women and men in front of her and one by one they disappeared through the door as their names were called. Hunter and Samuel opened the doors for each one. Every time Hunter opened the door, I could see the muscles under his uniform. Training me was also apparently training him. His muscles didn't normally flex that much in his uniform. He was wrong in saying his measurements hadn't changed.

"He's quite handsome, isn't he?" A deep male voice asked directly in my ear.

I jumped and moved away from the man beside me that was standing inches away. Frowning I looked him over, barely hiding my disgust at a stranger standing so damn close to me. He straightened from whispering in my ear and he was tall, at least a foot taller than me. He was middle-aged with dark brown hair, almost black that was peppered with grey. His beard was closed-shaved and was greyer than his hair. His golden yellow eyes stared at me, searching for something in mine.

"Excuse me?"

The man tilted his head towards Hunter and he grinned a mocking smile.

"He's a good-looking individual despite being tainted by his bloodline. It's a shame honestly. He could have been much more if he wasn't damned. He'll be here until he dies and no one will miss him because he hasn't made a difference in the world." He nodded towards Samuel. "Though that boy will surpass his teacher due to his lineage alone."

With each word, the arrogant, opinionated, pretentious asshole said the angrier I became. For someone who hadn't introduced himself, he sure was ballsy to talk shit about Hunter. Hunter who could kill this excuse of a man without thinking twice about it. And by what I was feeling, I might have helped Hunter.

"And who are you to say such bold shit about a man that has kept the oh so important princess safe? While you were what? Sitting back in your fancy ass home judging those in your home while they fed you?" I challenged him.

His head fell back as he howled with laughter. I felt the gazes of those in the lobby on us, Hunter's heaviest of them all. The man's face showed a wide smile, but his eyes as he looked back at me were hard. The man was a threat, that much I could tell.

"Well Princess, you are not what I expected. You are much more… lively." He didn't say it like it was a good thing. He held out his arm much like Luke had done. "Name's Maxwell Anthony, I'm your escort into the ballroom."

I gaped in disgust at the arm he offered me. There was no way in hell I was going to walk in with him. I opened my mouth to refuse when the name announcer spoke.

"Now entering Princess Seine Isabella Rudi, escorted by Maxwell Anthony Rudi; The Crowned Head."

My eyes widened and the man- Maxwell- the Crowned Head- grinned at me. He took my limp arm and folded it in his with a light pat on my hand.

"Well daughter, shall we?"

TWENTY-SEVEN

Before I had the chance to protest being escorted into the ballroom by Maxwell- I was not going to call him dad- Hunter and Samuel opened the ballroom doors. Maxwell tightened his arm around mine and tugged me along aside him. As I passed Hunter, he gave me a reassuring smile, but it seemed off.

The ballroom was like a fairytale. What was done this morning had been multiplied tenfold. As Maxwell and I made our way across the floor, soft music began to play from a harp. I looked around for the orchestra but didn't see one. Perhaps there wasn't a live band, but instead, music coming from hidden speakers. What I did see was the eyes on us. The people that made up the kingdom were gathered around the edges of the ballroom. They ranged in age, the youngest looking to be around sixteen and the oldest looking to be in their nineties. Through the crowd, I saw Aurora, Jazmine, and Naji standing in similar dresses to each other. Yamka was standing near them but was sanding with her own group. Yamka locked eyes on what I was wearing and whispered amongst her group. I started to lower my head but remembered what Luke had told me. My shoulders straightened and I kept my eyes ahead.

We neared the large dining table I had seen at the fitting and saw that a third throne had been added. And Jared was standing next to a throne on the right wearing a tie the same color as my dress. I struggled to keep the confusion off my face. Why would he be standing at the table? I was under the impression that the table was going to be for the "Crowned Head" and myself. You know, "royalty." But… When I thought about it, I hadn't seen Jared wear the standard soldier uniform. He always wore T-shirts and black slacks. I had just assumed that because he was under-cover while in America, he had gotten used to wearing more lax clothing. Was I wrong? Was he actually royalty? Was he Maxwell's son? Did that mean he was my brother? I fought the urge to throw up. If he was in fact my brother and we had flirted... I turned away from Jared as Maxwell let go of my arm. We were at the throne on the left and he stood in front of the last throne in the middle. I folded my hands in front of my waist and waited.

"Welcome esteemed guests and friends, please dance, talk as we have a bit before the food will be served." Maxwell projected his voice across the ballroom.

The music started up in the Waltz and the floor was soon filled with couples. Maxwell sat on his throne and motioned for Jared and me to sit as well. We sat there in silence for several minutes while those around us conversed. I saw Naji and Jazmine give Jared confused glances before giving me small smiles. Well, Jazmine gave me a small smile. Naji waved her arm wildly at me and Maxwell snorted softly. I looked at him quickly just as he rolled his eyes. He picked an invisible piece of lint off of the sleeve of his tuxedo coat.

"I see she's just as animated now as when she was a preteen," was all he said.

Bitterness crawled its way through my heart. He was there for Naji growing up, but for me, he was a ghost. Sure, Naji said that he sent me away to protect me, but what sense did that make? I was on an island only those with deep connections knew about and it was spelled to keep intruders out. How was America safer than an island that didn't exist? It was safe for the other children growing up here obviously.

"She's my best friend," was all I said.

Maxwell looked me over and looked back at Naji. I could feel the judgment radiating off him. I raised an eyebrow at him, daring him to say something about our friendship. Let him. I'd love an excuse to tear into him. He only tapped his fingers on the arm of his throne.

"How's your mother?" He asked after a beat and it was my turn to snort. He stiffened in his seat as a few eavesdroppers snickered. He glared at them and they scattered across the floor. "Is it wrong to ask about my once beloved?"

"Considering you had over a decade to get in touch, it seems to be a bit late to care." My voice was an empty void of emotion.

"It's a two-way street, your mother could have reached out as well. The one time I reached out to your mother she told me to take a hike."

Probably for good reason if our interactions so far were anything like their marriage.

"I thought there wasn't any outside communication?" If I could have been talking to my mom all this time, I was going to lose my shit.

Maxwell reached inside his tuxedo coat, into the pocket on his lapel. He pulled out a slim cell phone in a black case. He flashed the screen at me and I could see that the phone had full bars. As I watched he dialed the number to the local pizza place down the street from my mom's house. It rang and rang and someone on the other end picked up. Maxwell told them he had the wrong number and hung up.

"I have a way to communicate outside of the island. No one else does." Maxwell slid his phone back into its hiding spot. "Anyone that has my personal number can get through the spells."

I didn't know what to say to that. My mom could have contacted Maxwell at any time while I was growing up. But from the thirty minutes I had known him, I could understand why she didn't. He was a boiling pot of sunshine. I opened my mouth to say something, but an older man approached the table. He bowed to Maxwell and turned his gaze to me.

"Greetings Crowned Head, I was wondering if I could ask the Princess for her first dance of the night?" He asked Maxwell and it bothered me that he asked Maxwell for permission.

Maxwell steepled his hands as he looked down at the man, who was still bowing. After a few beats, Maxwell flicked his wrist and the man stood straight.

"I'm sure the Princess would be delighted to join you for the first dance of the night, Duke Ashton." I frowned at Maxwell when he gestured for me to join Duke Ashton. Apparently being the daughter of the Crowned Head meant being spoken for. How fun.

I turned my attention back to the Duke and used the customer service smile I had long mastered. The Duke flushed slightly and his hands fluttered at his sides.

"It would be a pleasure to join you, Duke. You'll have to forgive me if I step on your toes though, I'm sure that I'm not as graceful as the other women."

Rising from my seat, I walked around the table and took the Duke's hand. It was clammy and I fought the urge to pull my hand away. When we walked through the crowd, they parted for us. I tried to ignore their hushed whispers and stares as we neared the center of the floor. The music shifted once again to a medium pace with the violin, cello, and harp. It sounded like the earlier song, but a bit altered.

I followed his lead and held my hand up in front of his palm, about an inch apart. We circled each other without talking and it was kind of awkward. We changed directions suddenly and I did in fact, step on the Duke's foot. He grimaced but assured me he was okay. After the third time I stepped on him, he excused himself from the dance and I heard the snickers from a group of ladies behind me.

Before I could retreat back to the throne in shame, another man approached to ask to finish the song with me. He introduced himself as Count Pierce. He was younger than the Duke and unlike the Duke's yellow eyes, my new dance partner had teal eyes like Luke. He was more forgiving than the Duke when I stepped on him. Also, unlike the Duke, the Count talked. Quite a bit.

"A what?" The Count had been musing to himself out loud about why I hadn't transitioned into a werewolf yet. He had suggested that I was "hors de combat."

"Damaged in a way. Not even your eyes have turned yet. Curious. Anyhow, we've all been eager to meet you since the news about your arrival." We walked away from each other then back as part of the dance and spun in a circle. "I do have to say, you're more developed since the last time I saw you. It is surprising since you came from that prole of a woman."

My body stiffened at his words, both in disgust and anger. The last time I was here I was a literal child. Which meant that the Count had been looking at me sexually when I was a child. I would have to talk to Maxwell about getting him registered and investigated. As for his remark about my mother, he was zero for two. "Prole" was a derogatory slang term I learned about in social history freshman year of college. He had basically called my mom a peasant and if I was correct, a count wasn't far off from being a "prole" himself.

I excused myself and stepped away from him only to be swept up into another dance. By the time I was paired up with my tenth dance partner, I was stepping on toes on purpose. Some men didn't say much, just welcoming me back. Some wanted to hear gossip and were disappointed when I didn't tell them any. And the rare ones tried to cop a feel and learned quickly that their advances weren't reciprocated. The tenth partner excused himself and I started my way back to the throne.

"I hope you have room for one more on your dance card Princess."

I turned at Hunter's voice to see him standing a few feet away from me. He bowed to me and I smiled the first real one since walking through the ballroom doors. I gave him a small curtsy and bow in return. From my etiquette lessons, I learned that the deeper the bow, the more respect the person has for you. My bowing in return showed that I had high respect for Hunter. The gasps I heard came from more than just the women watching. Hunter held out his hand and when I took it, he spun me in a fast circle in time with the music. He pulled me back close and whispered in my ear.

"How is your first ball going, Kitten?" The combination of his warm breath and his use of his nickname for me caused a shiver to work its way up my spine. I knew Hunter felt it when he smiled against the shell of my ear.

"You're the first dance partner I won't purposely step on," I whispered back to him.

Hunter pulled back with a chuckle and we swayed in time with the music. Even if I tried to step on Hunter's toes, the slow pace and easy dance moves Hunter used would make it difficult. Unlike the other men Hunter led at a pace I could follow.

"Ah yes. With the expression on your face after your discussion with Count Pierce, I was expecting you to show off your new sheath."

Hunter twirled us around the edge of the dance floor as the music reached a crescendo. The song ended with drawn-out notes of a violin bow drawn across the strings of the cello. Hunter raised his eyebrows at me in question when notes from a new song started. This time I held my hand out for him to take. He took it with a smile and led me into a new dance. I leaned into his chest, pressing closer to him than I needed to, and whispered into his throat.

"You just wanted to see my calves tied up in the shoes you picked, with the dagger that I know how to use." I was sure that the flush in my cheeks and the warmth in my stomach weren't from the dancing alone. Being pressed up against Hunter and then spun away was teasing my body over and over. He pulled me into a particularly sensual dance movement that had me blushing. Once again Hunter leaned in to whisper into my ears.

"Trust me sweet Kitten, if I wanted to see you tied up, it wouldn't be just your calves."

And wow. What those words did to me. Not only did it make me imagine Hunter tying me up, or his hands on parts of my unexplored skin. But it had me imagining everything that came with it.

"Careful there Sir Wight, don't start anything you can't finish," I whispered in a shockingly husky voice.

"Call me sir again, and we'll have to do something else for your birthday celebration." Hunter's teeth lightly grazed my ear, emitting a small gasp from me.

"Shall I say it aga-" I was interrupted by a hand pulling Hunter back a step.

The sudden cool air on my front in Hunter's absence had me feeling cold. I looked to see who the hand belonged to and saw

Maxwell's irritated face looking back at me. My eyes narrowed as I recalled what he said about Hunter in the lobby. Surely, he came over here to stop us since he had such high thoughts of Hunter.

"Well don't hog the Princess to yourself all night, leave some dances for the rest of us." He gave a hearty laugh for the room to hear and they laughed with him. What they couldn't see though was the warning in his eyes as he stared me down. Nor did they see the barely concealed disgust he directed at Hunter. "Come, let's have a chat."

Maxwell's grip tightened on Hunter's shoulder as they walked away. I watched as they stopped in a corner of the room. Any partygoers that were nearby quickly found something else to do on the other side of the room. Had it been anyone else Maxwell was talking to it would have seemed like a normal relaxed conversation. But I knew Hunter. I knew that the rigid straight back he had meant it was taking everything in him not to fight. I knew that Hunter's feet were braced apart in a fighting stance even while he tried to look casual. I knew that the tick in his jaw meant that he was trying to hold back his words. He looked at me over Maxwell's shoulder with a lingering look before he left the ballroom.

What the hell did Maxwell say to Hunter?

"Care for a talk Princess?" A woman asked beside me.

I turned to see Odette standing beside me in a dress that looked like it belonged to a goddess. It was long and flowed with layers and layers of creamy lace. The bottom of her skirt had teal ruffles and her bodice was enhanced by teal and rose gold lines of sparkles. What tied it together was the rose gold chain harness she wore over it. She looked more like a princess than I did at that moment.

"Odette? What're you doing here, I thought you had to be hidden?"

Odette rolled her eyes and interlocked her arm around mine and she steered us to a dark corner away from everyone else. No one looked at us as we went by. In fact, it was as if we had vanished from sight. It was both welcoming and a bit concerning how easy it was for Odette to manipulate what others saw. In the safety of our canopy of darkness, Odette pulled out an object wrapped in silk from her long flowing sleeves. Unwrapping it she revealed a dagger that was in a thin sheath. The hilt of the dagger was a twin copy of the one strapped to my calve. I knew instantly that it was the sister blade to mine. The only difference was that ivory was stained. It had seen more battles than mine. Odette held it out for me to take and rolled her eyes when I hesitated.

"I didn't search around my house for a fucking month for you not to take the bloody thing." I had forgotten how colorful her language was.

"Well Odette, as much as I love being gifted random ass daggers, what do you expect me to do with it? In case you haven't noticed, I don't have anywhere to put it." I crossed my arms over my chest in exasperation. "For an oracle you don't seem to look into the future," I sassed her, knowing she wouldn't mind. That she most likely welcomed the back talk.

Odette raised her eyebrows at me and glanced at my chest with a pointed look. Before I could slap her hands away, she darted forward and slipped the dagger in between my breasts. A cold tingling lightning zapped through my body and I felt more awake. I gaped at her and she frowned slightly before adjusting me so that the dagger was out of sight. Besides Naji, no one else had touched me so brashly. Looking down at my chest I could hardly see the hilt. Which meant no one else would be able to see it as well.

I looked back up to ask what the fuck was wrong with her, but she was gone. I looked around the ballroom and locked eyes with Naji and Jazmine. They hurried towards me, dipping and weaving around dancers. I met them halfway and grinned when Naji danced in a circle around me.

"Damn Seine, leave some sexy for the rest of us," she teased.

"You're one to talk Naji. You're looking mighty fine yourself," I smiled at Jazmine and hugged her close. "I haven't seen you in forever. How was your grandfather's farewell party?"

Jazmine returned the hug tightly before pulling back. She looked a bit sad, but her smile was real.

"It was really good. I was still a little sad to see him go but I was glad for the extra time. After tonight I'll be glad to sit down and relax for a while."

"Yooooo we should all go on vacation together! The cabin will be perfect for us to use. Mr. Bradwell had added a saltwater pool before he left too! Jazmine we could have a weeklong slumber party!" Naji suggested as she swung her arms over Jazmine's and my shoulders.

Naji's sudden burst of energy reminded me of what Maxwell had said about her. My mood soured as my eyes found him lounging on his throne. What a dick.

"Well, that's a dark and scary face. Who pissed you off?" Jazmine asked.

I looked around to see if anyone was listening and huddled us closer together. I didn't want anyone to hear what I had to say in case it got back to Maxwell. Naji glanced around with wide eyes and pressed us even closer.

"Secret time!" Naji whispered.

"He's a big bag of dicks. I didn't expect him to be such an asshole," I confided.

Jazmine nodded, understanding who I was talking about, but Naji tilted her head in confusion.

"Who?" Naji went to look around again, but Jazmine and I grabbed her shoulders to stop her. She was going to make it obvious we were talking about someone here.

"My father," I hissed.

Naji's eyes widened and nodded quickly.

"Oh yeah, he's a barrel of snakes," she whispered back.

"You should have seen him years ago. He was an absolute-" Jazmine was cut off as Maxwell's voice boomed over the chatter and music.

"Attention friends! Dinner is about to be served, please find your seats."

The girls and I looked at each other in silent communication. We would have to continue this conversation later. Jazmine and Naji went to a table on the far side of the room where Aurora was already sitting with Damon. I quickly made my way over to my spot, ignoring the heavy stare coming from Jared. Once everyone was seated, Maxwell stood up.

"I hope you have worked up an appetite for the meal that has been prepared. The Princess traveled far to gather the main course," Maxwell paused as they clapped unfairly. I wasn't the only one who went and I was just a tagalong. "Tonight, we are here to celebrate the return of the Princess-" more hoots and hollering- "as well as my return after years away trying to negotiate with the other kingdom." Maxwell paused for dramatic effect and boos filled the room. I glanced up to see him the slight curve of a smile and I frowned. "Not only were we able to come to an agreement, but we were also able to unite our forces."

Confusion filled the air and I got the impression that it was not his original goal. Many of the partygoers were looking around and whispering. They were trying to see if anyone else knew what the Crowned Head was talking about. He gestured for them to settle down and gestured to Jared and then to me.

"In the coming months, the Swigaroian Kingdom and the Rudianda Kingdom will be united through the marriage of Prince Jared Niklaus Swig and our own Princess Seine Isabella Rudi."

There was no fucking way.

TWENTY-EIGHT

The ballroom erupted in chaos while my brain was trying to understand what was happening. I could see Naji and Jazmine sitting in their seats even through the crowd. Jazmine was gesturing wildly around while speaking with Naji. Naji on the other hand was staring at Jared with her mouth open in shock. I knew how she felt. There were many shouts directed at Maxwell.

"How can she marry him?! She doesn't even have her powers!"

"Is this why the Princess came back?"

"This won't fix the war!"

"How could have a prince from the Swigaroian Kingdom been allowed inside our walls?! He could be a spy!"

I leaned around Maxwell to look at Jared to see his reaction. He was staring straight ahead, his face blank of any expression. He must have felt my gaze on him because he turned his head. When he caught my eyes, he shuttered and guilt filled his eyes for a second before it disappeared. So, he had known. I thought we had become friends, but I guess not. Friends didn't keep life-altering secrets from you.

I pushed my throne back and it screeched across the floor making the room fall silent. I stood and surveyed the faces of everyone. Many had the same shocked expression as Naji, some had confused expressions, but most of them were angry. In the very back stood Ms. Anne, her face the picture of sympathy.

"If you'll excuse me," I said, a void of emotion. I bowed the barest of inches to Maxwell which elicited gasps. I walked away without waiting for a response.

Without a destination in mind, I ended up at the front doors where two soldiers were. I had never seen them before. They took one glance at me as I approached and frowned at one another. They were not about to stop me. Not tonight, not now. I needed to get out. Needed to think. Because what the actual fuck?

"Princess, we're sorry but we can't allow you to leave," one soldier said.

I merely glanced at him and he flinched at whatever he saw on my face. He and the other guard shared a look and their hands tightened on their swords. I gave a tired chuckle and smiled.

"Go ahead. But be warned that I've been trained by Sir Wight himself. You'll both end up on the floor and I'll still get outside. So, make it easier on yourselves and fucking move." I growled out the last word and they practically jumped out of the way.

I rolled my eyes at them and pushed the door open where the night air welcomed me. I took a few deep breaths to try and center myself. I thought it would have worked if it wasn't for the presence that soon joined me. Neither one of us said anything for a few beats. I tried to ignore him, hoping he'd just leave me alone. But of course not. I pinched the bridge of my nose and sighed.

"What do you want Jared?" I asked.

"I need you to know that I didn't know. Not until today. And when I did, I tried to figure a way out of it. I tried until they called my name. We'll figure it out, there must be-" I cut him off.

"Can you just, leave me be? Just for an hour or two. I need time alone to think."

Jared looked utterly defeated as he ran his hands through his hair. I almost changed my mind and told him to stay. That we'd work it out together. But I held my tongue. The fact was that he wasn't even from the same kingdom and was just another lie.

"I'll… I'll go find Hunter and send him out here to be with you."

Jared slouched back into the manor, leaving me alone with my thoughts, the stars, and the moon. The more I thought about how Maxwell made an arranged marriage the angrier I became. The man didn't even know me! And the fact that he announced it in front of the entire kingdom. The freaking audacity.

I started making my way through the woods, not paying attention to the branches that caught on my dress. The trees were quiet except for the occasional hoot from an unseen owl. Even with the trees covering the sky from view, the moonlight found paths through the leaves. I followed the moonbeams, grateful that Hunter had picked out flat shoes. I paused on a fallen tree overgrown with moss and mushrooms. Pleurotus ostreatus, oyster mushrooms. Resting on a branch reaching towards the sky was a Luna moth. Its wings glowed a delicate green that fluttered in the light breeze.

"Fucking shit tits in my ass."

The moth flew away at the sound of Naji falling through the trees and vines. I blinked in surprise. How long had I been staring at the moth? It had to have been a while since it was a tad darker and the temperature had dropped lower. Wrapping my arms around myself I turned to watch Naji pick herself up from the dirt. Fallen leaves stuck to her dress and she brushed them off while swearing.

"I don't understand how the fuck you're able to see at night. I would understand if you'd transitioned but you haven't yet and that's the weird part. I mean you've always been able to see in the dark better than the regular human, but this is ridiculous. How are you able to see better at night than in broad damn daylight? You were eating dirt on the way to Mr. Bradwell's cabin for crying out loud." I huffed out a faint laugh. Leave it to Naji to make me laugh. "Whoo girl, someone didn't get the memo about not wearing heels to trample through the woods, let's sit."

Shaking my head, I stepped off the log and sat next to her. I looked down at my dress and cringed at the rips and tears. After Ms. Anne had spent so much time on the dress I'd gone and ruined it. I'd have to thank her and apologize profusely when I saw her again. Naji kicked her heels against the log and looked up at the sky.

"You know... You don't have to marry him. You're a grown woman, you can't be forced to do anything you don't want to do. In my opinion, I think the Crowned Head is trying to make a power grab," Naji told me, but I didn't think she fully believed it herself.

I leaned back on my hands, the soft moss pressing into my palms. It was nice of her to try, except we both knew I didn't have any power over Maxwell. I knew I could fight him tooth and nail. I could even leave the island. But I would have to put others in danger to help me. Then there was no way to guarantee that Maxwell wouldn't come after me. There was nowhere that I could go that he wouldn't find me. Not if it meant more power for himself. Even in my short time with him, I knew that about him.

"Do you think that was why I was brought here? Was I born to end the war? Simply a tool?" I asked quietly. I had grown up thinking my mom and dad loved each other deeply. But I couldn't think of any possible way for my mom to have loved Maxwell.

A deep rumbling noise came from Naji's chest, and I glanced at her in surprise. The coals on her skin burned bright enough to warm my side. Her pupils had turned into slits, almost identical to a cat's. Claws appeared from the tips of the fingers and dug into the log. Wisps of smoke wafted out of her mouth as she spoke.

"Your mom loved him; it was the truest love when we were kids. I can't tell you if the Crowned Head loved her... I think when he sent the three of you to America, something that was cracked in him broke entirely. And when Dillion died, he became worse."

"Do you think that when Dillion died, it forced Maxwell into forming a union with me and Jared? Considering Dillion was the first born?" I mused. Even as I said it, I knew that wasn't the case. When we were young Dillion was his own person and couldn't be controlled. Maxwell had obviously thought I'd be the easy one. "How come no one told me Jared was from another kingdom?"

Naji retracted her claws and picked off a mushroom only to rip it into pieces.

"Honestly? None of us knew." There was sadness in her voice, sadness, and betrayal.

"You don't think that he was the one that attacked me, do you?" After all, he had been lying about who he was to everyone for years. Perhaps even before high school. It was highly possible.

Naji was already shaking her head before I had finished asking the question.

"There's no way! Jared has always been looking out for you since he transferred to our high school. He wasn't allowed to interfere directly, but he did what he could. Of course, he wouldn't do anything to hurt you." She trailed off, her eyes unfocused. She faded deep into her thoughts while I tried to stay out of mine. "Do you think this is why Yamka changed?" She asked suddenly.

"Do I think what was why Yamka changed?" My lips pursed in confusion as I was unsure what leaps she made in her head.

"Why she suddenly started hating you. Because she knew about Maxwell's plans somehow?" Naji's eyes were wide as she talked.

My mouth dropped open. It made sense. But how could she have known when Jared hadn't even known until tonight? Could she have been from the other kingdom as well? She was a werewolf, so I had just assumed that she had to have been from this one...

"But how did she know?" I asked her and Naji shrugged. A new thought came to me. "How would my marrying Jared make Maxwell more powerful?"

An owl shrieked above us, and we both jumped at the sudden sound in the surrounding darkness. Naji rubbed her hands over her arms as if she was trying to rub her fear away. I scooted closer to her, hoping it would help her feel more relaxed. She gave a smile of gratitude and took my hand in hers with our fingers intertwined.

"Politically. The kingdoms have been separated and at war for over two-hundred years. If you and Jared got married, your powers would combine. You'd both become hybrids- half werewolf, half vampire. And if you were to have an heir-"

I cut her off by squeezing her hand. She turned to face me fully and I could see that she was trying not to cry. Her eyes had returned to normal, but they were watery with tears. The coals on her still burned brightly enough to warm the air around us.

"I don't have any powers though. I'm nothing. I don't have any powers so I'm a useless powerless dud." I kicked my legs up and the moss softened the sound of my heels against the log. Naji's coals flared at my words, and she smacked my thigh.

"You're not a dud. You're just a late bloomer. Any day you'll get your powers. You'll be able to heal super-fast, be insanely strong, fast as shit, and heightened senses... Although you already see crazy good at night... Not to mention you'll get your pretty yellow eyes." Naji smiled at me warmly, trying to reassure me. Her eyes looked worried though, which was understandable. It was apparently extremely rare to be a late bloomer.

"Have I ever told you that I hate the color yellow? It's too... Happy."

Naji didn't say anything for a few seconds then burst out laughing. I grinned back at her. It was loud but was nice to hear after the day I had. Even if what I said was true and I really didn't like yellow.

"Have I ever told you that I love you?"

"I love you too, Naj-"

Something warm splattered across my face and neck. The scent of iron filled the air and my mouth, just like when magic was used near me. I wiped my eyes and blinked away whatever the substance was. In the moonlight, I was able to see a dark liquid covering my hands. It looked black, but as clouds moved away from the moon, my hands turned red. Looking up, I was going to ask Naji what it was but paused. I didn't understand what I was seeing.

Something was sticking out of the base of Naji's throat. The same liquid that was on me was trickling down her neck. Her mouth opened and closed like a fish out of water. I reached out to her, and she fell forward. I tried to catch her and we both fell to the ground. Rocks and sticks dug into my legs from the added weight of holding Naji in my lap.

"Naji what're you doing? It's dirty down here and there might be bugs."

Naji ignored me and grasped my hands tightly, smearing the red stuff on both of us. Didn't she know that she'd get her dress dirty? The thing in her throat bobbed as she tried to swallow. I watched as more of the strange liquid came out of the object. I leaned down to see what was causing Naji to act so silly.

There was a small four-pronged metal object. It was sharp and was made up of triangular shapes welded together. If I hadn't known any better, I would have thought it was a heavy-duty metal arrowhead. But I couldn't be right. Because if I was right then Naji would die. And if Naji died, I would lose my best friend.

My heart seemed to have stopped beating and my body turned cold. There was no way this could be happening. Not to Naji. Not the purest person on earth. I wouldn't allow it.

"Don't worry. Hunter will come and he'll heal you. Well not him exactly, but I'm sure he'll have Luke with him. And he'll heal you. You'll be okay," I said in between sobs.

Naji had tears rolling down her cheeks as she looked up at me. She was afraid, it was clear in her eyes. I had never seen her look afraid before. I didn't like it. I'd kill whoever made her feel this way. How dare they harm her.

A branch snapped off to the side of us, further in the trees. My head snapped up and I squinted toward the sound. It was darker in the trees than it was where Naji and I were. Seconds ticked by and slowly a figure stepped out of the trees. The moonlight bounced off coppery red hair. My heart lifted in hope.

"Samuel! Hurry, Naji's hurt!" I called out to him.

Samuel didn't come closer. Instead, he stayed far enough in the shadows that I couldn't see him well. Confusion raced over me. Why wouldn't he help? What the hell was he doing? Naji was dying and he was just standing there!

Naji's hands tightened on mine and I turned my attention back to her. Her eyes were wide, and she kept looking between Samuel and our clasped hands. I shook my head; I wasn't sure what she was trying to tell me. There was the sound of a metal clink and scuffing sound. I glanced back up at Samuel and saw he was doing something with his hands. It almost looked as if he was dancing... Badly. When he lifted his arms, the moon illuminated what was in his hands. I understood what Naji was trying to tell me. Trying to warn me. In Samuel's hands was a crossbow.

"For a defective prole, you're harder to kill than I would have thought."

I heard the click of the arrow locking into place and leaned over Naji squeezing my eyes shut. I had to protect her. There was a ringing sound of metal on metal. I was still alive. I opened my eyes to see our surroundings lit up by the flames from Hunter's sword. I didn't need to see his face to know his eyes would reflect his weapon. They would be a burning orange. He stood in a fighting stance on the other side of the log, protecting us. His sword was a stark contrast against everything else. Warm colors against cool... It looked so familiar...

TWENTY-NINE

"Put the bow down Samuel," Hunter ordered, and I snapped out of my thoughts.

Samuel pointed the bow at Hunter with a soured expression. It was almost as if he had hoped Hunter wouldn't show up. So, it was okay to attack us, but when it came to Hunter, he drew the line? Thank gods for small miracles. Maybe it meant Samuel wouldn't hurt Hunter.

"You should have stayed in the manor. I didn't come alone," Samuel warned.

Hunter made a hand gesture and Damon popped into existence next to Hunter. A body dropped down from the trees and when they straightened, I saw that it was Luke.

"Neither did I," was all Hunter said.

Samuel snapped his fingers and his backup appeared from the trees. Flaming red hair. Familiar piercings. Katja and Alice. What the hell were they doing here? They were supposed to be at a prestigious boarding school in Europe. What were they doing on a secret island that humans weren't supposed to know about? And what the hell were they doing with Samuel?

I was too far away for them to see me behind both the log and Hunter. But I could see them. Katja's hair was pulled back into tight double French braids. She was tanner and leaner with muscle. She was holding blades much like the ones Damon had used when he "trained" me. Alice had gotten rid of her long hair and had gotten an undercut with line designs. She too had gained muscle. Alice was brandishing a katana held high. They were both wearing all black, tight fighting wear. They had obviously been training much as I had.

Luke walked backward away from the others to kneel at my side. The others didn't pay attention to him. He laid his hands over Naji's throat and his hands glowed teal. He was trying to heal her like he did Samuel... He should have let Samuel die back in the village. As Luke worked, I noticed that Naji wasn't as warm as she had been moments before. Her coals were dimming, and the night felt colder. Luke sat back on his heels and sighed. He was pale and there were tears in his eyes. I had never seen him look so emotional.

"Why are you stopping?" I questioned him. Naji wasn't waking up and the arrowhead was still in her throat. "You have to save her! You have to save her!" I sobbed.

"I can't. The arrow has been spelled so that it can't be removed or healed," Luke whispered. "There's nothing I can do."

I was shaking. There's no way this was it. I had known Naji for most of my life, but I wasn't ready to say goodbye. But as I held her, her grip was starting to go limp. I instinctively gripped them tighter. Naji looked at me before sliding past the sky. The purple in her eyes dulled to a dark brown. And just like that, she was gone. My shaking got worse as I looked down at the body that was once my best friend. It was odd, I didn't feel anything. Just a whirling buzz in my head and a burning sensation in my chest.

I lifted my head in what felt like slow motion. Hunter and Damon were standing back-to-back while facing the others. Damon was facing off with Katja and Alice with glowing orbs in his hands that transformed into blades. I heard him say that his magic wasn't working over the buzzing. Samuel and Hunter were staring each other down, teacher and student. Samuel had ditched his crossbow for his usual sword. All five of them looked roughed up. They had been fighting hard for a while.

I felt Luke's hands on my shoulders, talking to me, but not loud enough for me to hear over the buzzing. I gently removed Naji's body from my lap as I stood, ignoring Luke. My bones groaned in protest after staying still for so long. The movement caused Katja and Alice to turn their heads toward me. Their faces changed from emotionless to shocked as they saw me.

"Seine? What- what're you doing here?" Katja asked, her weapons lowering slightly.

"You attack, but have no idea who you're attacking? Typical," Damon snapped.

"They didn't need to know. The huntresses are just hired help," Samuel said in a mocking tone.

"You hired the Princess's friends to kill her? That's fucked up," replied Damon.

"Princess? Seine's a princess? Since when?" Katja questioned.

"The Princess? As in the princess of the Rudianda Kingdom?" Alice turned to face Samuel. "You told us we were hunting a threat to all of mankind."

Both Katja and Alice backed away from Damon and faced off with Samuel. They apparently didn't like being lied to. Samuel looked at those surrounding him and saw that he was outnumbered. He shifted into his wolf form and before I could blink, he was at Hunter's throat. Hunter grunted in pain but slashed out with his sword. Samuel fell to the ground and circled Katja and Alice while blood poured out of his side. Hunter pressed a hand to his throat and fell to one knee. Blood spilled out between his fingers. I was watching Hunter die before me, just like Naji. I wouldn't- couldn't- lose them both. I'd save him. And I would kill anyone who got in my way.

My shaking became worse, and I realized that everyone else was shaking as well. The ground was shaking, not me. Samuel lunged for Katja, and a growl came from between my bared teeth. Samuel's wolf head whipped around towards the sound. My eyes burned, but not from tears, from anger. I barely noticed when the moon no longer lit up the area. I only saw Hunter fall to his back and his sword's flames extinguished.

I pulled my blade from my shoe straps and the blade from between my breasts. I flung the sheath of the dagger Odette gave me and stood in one of the fighting stances I learned from the library. One of the hilts burned hot in my hand, the other cold. Before Samuel could get his groundings, I attacked. I swiped up with one hand while the other swiped down. The daggers cut through Samuel's fur and skin easier than I expected. His eyes flashed in pain, and I had to remind myself what he had done. He was no longer the goofy kid I had grown to know and love. He was a murderer and traitor. He had killed Naji. He had hurt Hunter. He had to be stopped.

Samuel shifted back into his human form, and I saw that the wounds I had given him were already healing. He somersaulted diagonally and picked up his dropped sword. He lurched forward with his sword aimed at my chest. I parried the tip of his sword away and dodged to the side. Samuel stumbled forward before spinning around to face me again. We continued the dance for several minutes. It was difficult to get an advantage when we were both trained by the same person.

Finally, Samuel made a desperate attempt at landing a deadly blow. He swung too hard, too wide and I was able to disarm him.

I advanced until his back was pressed against a tree. He snarled at me, and I held the point of a dagger at his throat.

"Why? Why would you do this? You were my friend," I pleaded for an answer.

"You should have never lived this long." Samuel leaned forward enough into my dagger that he drew a bead of blood. He grinned manically, causing my skin to crawl. "The Temnaya Koroleva says hello."

I flinched back from him. Those were the same words my attacker had said. Which meant Samuel and my attacker were connected. Samuel used my distraction and pulled out a small dagger that was hidden in the boning of his corset. His hand shot out before I could block it and pain shot through my chest. I staggered back and watched in horror as Samuel used his own blade to slit his throat.

I collapsed to my knees and fell to my side. I hadn't been able to save Hunter after all. I had failed. I hadn't been able to get any answers either. Before my eyes drifted shut, I could have sworn I saw a small purple dragon flying across the sky.

THIRTY

When I opened my eyes again, I was sitting in the front seat of Dillion's truck. I was in the passenger seat and sitting behind the wheel was Dillion. He looked the same as he did when I had hallucinated him. He looked more tangible now like he was really there.

I threw myself at him and he caught me easily in his arms. He squeezed me tight and tucked my head under his chin. It was as warm as I remembered. Too soon he pulled back and smiled at me sadly.

"I wish we could take our time catching up, but we have more important things to talk about," Dillion told me.

"I have questions," I warned him, and he chuckled.

"When have you not? How about you ask a question, I answer it, and I'll tell you the important things?"

"Okay deal." I wrapped my arms around me and looked out the windows. It was then that I noticed that there wasn't anything around us. No trees, no barn, no grass, no sky, and no roads. We were in the truck that was floating in pure white space. "Where the hell are we?"

Dillion chuckled again and looked around us, at what I wasn't sure.

"We're in the In-between. It's a space in-between the spiritual and physical worlds. It's a bit on the nose, but it gets the point across. My turn. You know that I went to see Odette. The reason was that while I was stationed in Europe, I started to see things. People weren't people anymore. I started to do intense research that led me to her. I knew if I got caught leaving, I'd be imprisoned. So, I asked my CO for a leave of absence since he wasn't human. I was granted permission."

"Why did you see her though? You could have asked mom." Dillion shook his head before I had finished asking.

"I had no way of knowing that Mom knew about this. What if she thought I was mental and sent me away? I couldn't risk it. Odette was the know all see all; she was my only possibility."

"Do you know anything about where Sara and Sean disappeared to?" I asked. If anyone knew it would be someone who could see both worlds. But Dillion frowned at me as he thought.

"Surprisingly, I have no idea where they are… Which means someone is hiding them with magic. That could be either bad, or good… Odette would probably know."

I smiled slightly remembering what Odette had said about Dillion. He saw the smile and raised an eyebrow.

"Did you really try to swoon a three-hundred-year-old oracle?" I asked him, making him turn beet red.

"Listen here missy. I was a young man, and she was and still is, a very attractive woman. I gotta shoot my shot," he shrugged good naturally. I grinned and shook my head. He was the same as when he was alive. "She couldn't help me much. She told me who I was. What I was. She suggested that I go back to my life. That I should ignore anything and everything I saw and heard.

She warned me that I shouldn't come back into the world of the supernatural. 'Go back to being human' is what she said. I tried to. I really did. But when I got to the coast, there were creatures waiting for me."

Dillion trailed off and he got a haunted look as he recalled what had happened to him. I laid a hand on his knee, my thumb making comforting circles. He laid his hand on top of mine and squeezed it lightly.

"You don't have to talk about it," I offered, and he closed his eyes tightly for a few seconds before giving me a pained smile. It was then that I realized that his eyes weren't the deep brown I had known. They had changed to the golden yellow of a werewolf. They were an exact copy of Maxwell's. He sighed deeply before shaking his head.

"No, it's important. They weren't creatures exactly, but they weren't normal either. They looked a bit like the hell hounds Damon conjured up, but they had humanoid limbs. They killed me."

I flinched at the bluntness of how he said it. I guess he had four years to get used to the idea. But I had been under the impression that Dillion had been killed by stepping on an IED. That's what we were told by the Army.

"Why did they lie? You never made it back from your leave, so why did they tell us you died on duty?"

"My CO covered for my death. He forged the report and death certificate. I think it's because he let me leave in the first place."

I didn't know what to say to that. There were so many questions being answered, but new ones were popping up. Why had Dillion been killed in the first place? Was it a random attack or was it planned? With the evidence I had, my money was on a planned attack. More than likely by the same people who attacked me. The same people Samuel was involved with.

"Why couldn't we have been born to a mundane family? I know that I read a lot about fantasy, but I never wanted to be involved in it!" I sat back in the truck seat with a sigh.

Dillion smirked at me and crossed his arms over his chest, mimicking my posture from moments ago. Gone was the haunted look, replaced by laughing eyes and a curved smile. Dillion was aware of my reading obsession and knew what they were about. He knew what was in them.

"Perhaps you already met the man you read about in your books," he teased. I blushed furiously and looked away from him, making him laugh. "Hunter seems like a great man. For a minute there I thought you were going for Samuel."

My nose scrunched up in disgust. He was seven years younger than I was. I liked my men to be older than me. The brain wasn't fully developed until the age of twenty-five. Hunter was twenty-nine. It wasn't much of an age gap, but Hunter was more mature than the men I had been around in high school and college. Besides, Samuel turned out to be a bad guy.

"He wasn't my type," was all I said.

"Mmm good thing too considering he was insane. I mean, only crazy people shoot themselves."

"Wait. Pause. Samuel shot himself?" There was no way.

"Yeaaaaah. He orchestrated it all. There's a man here, in the In-between. Samuel used the man's dark magic to alter the weather. I can't tell you who the man was because he disguised himself. They were trying to jumpstart your powers. Obviously, it didn't work."

"I..." What the hell. What was it with people being obsessed with my powers? Now I was hoping I was a dud. It would get all these people off my back.

"From what I've learned, there's about a five percent chance you won't develop any powers," he frowned apologetically. "Sorry."

I was going to say something sarcastic, but the white light outside the truck flickered. Dillion looked around and swore to himself.

"Since you're in the In-between and in the physical world, if you make the conscious effort, you can manipulate what's happening. You can heal Hunter from here. Luke is healing you now, that's why the In-between is flickering. Luke won't have the energy to heal Hunter after he heals you. Damon doesn't have the healing capabilities to heal a plant let alone a fallen angel."

My mind went blank. I didn't know why I was surprised after everything that had happened. I had never asked Hunter what he was because it seemed rude. It hadn't mattered to me, I figured it would come up eventually. I just never imagined he was a fallen angel. Did that mean the flames on his sword were the flames of hell? Unbelievably, it made him more attractive. Oh gods, the book I was reading when we went to the village. It was about fallen angels and demons. I hoped Hunter hadn't realized.

"I don't even want to know what that facial expression is for. You need to concentrate on healing Hunter before Luke pulls you out of the In-between."

Now that Dillion mentioned it, I did feel a tug in my chest. It felt like a rope was tied around my torso, pulling me toward the physical world. An idea popped into my head.

"Could I bring you back?" I asked, my voice hopeful.

"You won't have enough strength to heal Hunter and bring me back. You would die if you tried, despite Luke healing you. But it's okay. I know you're in safe hands with those three. I can move on."

I imagined healing Hunter by picturing his neck wound stitching back together. The spilled blood was being replaced with new. His breath became stronger and easier. Dillion was right, I could feel myself getting tired already. But I could do this. Hunter and Luke would figure out a way to bring me back. Dillion had otherworldly information. Hell, so did Hunter, no pun intended. I visualized the rope Luke's healing had created and imagined wrapping it around Dillion. He would be so pissed if he figured out what I was doing. I felt the rope leave me and connect around Dillion and I smiled at him.

"Tell him I'm sorry and don't be mad," I told Dillion with a smile.

Dillion looked confused and then angry as the lights pulsed faster.

"Damnit Seine!"

Dillion faded to a transparent form just before he was ripped out of the truck by the rope. I sat back in the truck and pulled the stuffed elephant onto my lap. Smiling, I looked out the window. The flickering had stopped. If anything, they seemed to brighten now that I was by myself.

They'd like each other... Hopefully. I laughed quietly to myself. It was too late now.

THIRTY-ONE

Hunter bolted up as copious amounts of energy raced through his body. It felt as if his veins had been filled with ice. It was a vast difference from the usual fire that flowed in them. For a moment he had thought himself to be dead. Though as Hunter breathed in the cold night air, he knew it to be untrue.

He looked around the area for his companions- his friends. His Princess. His Kitten. He saw Damon conversing with Seine's friends- her would-be attackers. Hunter's chest burned as he caught sight of Samuel's crumpled form. He still held his blade, even if his body no longer breathed. Hunter had failed him. That was the only explanation as to why Samuel had tried to kill Seine. He was only eighteen; just a boy. Hunter had trained him since Samuel had first transitioned. That was six years ago. Perhaps someone had influenced Samuel before he was brought to the Academy. A small knot of unease developed in his gut. If someone had convinced Samuel to the wrong side, Samuel could have been a spy. He would have had insider knowledge of the Rudianda Kingdom. Which meant Seine had been in constant danger even when Hunter had thought her to be safe.

Where was she?

Hunter grabbed his fallen sword and spun on his knees looking for Seine. He saw Luke first. He was kneeling with his hands outstretched. His palms were glowing as they did when he was healing someone. Though his power flickered in and out as they diminished. The knot in Hunter's gut grew as he saw who Luke was trying so desperately to heal. Seine lay on the ground motionless. Despite the dress being a deep red, Hunter could see the blood that stained the fabric. Her eyes were closed and her chest was still

No. She could not be gone.

Hunter stumbled over to them both and fell to his knees, ignoring the pain in his chest. He picked up Seine's hand and held it gingerly between his own. It was cold to the touch and Hunter felt the tears roll down his face. I should have protected you better. I should never have left your side. Please forgive me.

Hunter thought of the little fur ball that awaited in his cat room. Hunter would have to care for little Hades. He would have to watch the kitten run to the door expecting to see Seine. He would have to see the disappointment Hades would have when he saw it was only Hunter. Hades would not understand that his momma was not coming back. Hades would be a constant reminder of Seine, but Hunter would have to deal with it. Hades was the only part of Seine Hunter would have now.

Hunter would never see Seine smile again. He would never roll his eyes at her really bad jokes. He would never see her blue eyes sparkle with joy when they were together. He would never see her face scrunched up in deep concentration. Hunter would never see her transition to her full powers. It was his own fault for leaving her alone after the Crowned Head reminded him of his lineage. That he would soil the bloodline. Hunter had not cared but knew he was making a scene so he left. Now Seine was gone.

"She sacrificed herself to bring us both back."

Hunter's shoulders tensed at the unfamiliar voice. He lifted his head to see a man approaching behind Luke. Hunter heard Seine's friends gasp behind him. The man was wearing the outfit of an American soldier. It was incredibly odd as they were over a thousand miles away from the States. The man was tall with dark brown hair cut into a short crop and his eyes were those of were-wolf lineage. He looked like a younger version of the Crowned Head. Tears were streaking down the man's face, it was the only reason Hunter did not attack.

"Who're you?" Luke asked in a raspy voice.

"Dillion, I'm- was- Seine's older brother," the man, Dillion responded.

"Weren't you supposed to be-"

"Dead? Yes. It seems that in the four years of my death, Seine still hasn't learned how to listen."

Hunter heard the fondness and tenderness with which Dillion spoke. He truly loved his sister as much as Hunter did. He looked back at the hand he was holding and watched as one of his tears marked the dirt on her skin. The polish on her nails had chipped during her fight. She had held her ground until the end. A proud feeling swelled in Hunter's chest.

"I know this is bad timing and all with the Princess dying, but should we be concerned about that?"

Hunter glanced at Damon and saw him pointing up toward the sky. Hunter looked at where he was pointing and his eyes widened in disbelief. The moon was shrouded by a darkness similar to what Damon's hell hounds were made of.

"Five lives lived and lost, ended before being awoken.

Ended unfairly, with sickness, by strife, in birth, by greed.

The sixth different from the last.

A sacrifice to be made when the earth bleeds red and the moon turns black.

Him or her."

Hunter repeated Odette's words from their meeting.

The others were silent as they absorbed the words. Seine's friends looked confused, Luke looked exhausted, Damon looked bored, and Dillion looked heartbroken. Hunter himself felt both concerned about the prophecy Odette predicted coming true and devastated about losing Seine. Minutes ticked by and Hunter was going to suggest making their way back to the manor. They had three bodies to carry back after all. Except something otherworldly happened.

Seine's body gasped for air as she pulled her hand from Hunter's. They went to her stomach, feeling for a wound. Her eyelids fluttered open just a crack. Hunter watched in shock as she looked around the trees, searching for something. Her eyes latched onto Hunter's and he felt the air leave his lungs.

She had transitioned. Gone were the blue eyes he had come to love. They had been replaced by glowing silver eyes with spinning orbs that matched the mark on her wrist. Whatever Seine had transitioned into, it certainly was not into a werewolf.

EPILOGUE

I didn't move as a hand was laid on my shoulder. Ever since I had transitioned, my senses had sharpened tenfold. It was too much sometimes and I would have to hide away. More often than not, when someone needed me I was sleeping in Naji's room. But I had to be here today. I had to make an appearance, it was only right.

I turned away from the cliff edge to face Dillion without saying anything. I had cried for days and was now tapped dry. Dillion on the other hand had tears to spare. He was crying for both of us. I had to remember it wasn't just me that lost Naji.

"It's time," Dillion told me and together we walked towards the others that had gathered.

Despite why we had gathered, a small smile graced my face before slipping. There was a rather large crowd that was there to see us sendoff Naji. I had even met Naji's parents earlier this week to prepare. When someone of dragon lineage died, they were cremated and their ashes were spread off the cliff. It was their way of allowing the dragon to soar the skies one last time.

Dillion and I walked over to the table that was draped with a black cloth. In the center of it was an emerald-green urn that sparkled in the sunlight. I picked it up and it was surprisingly cool. Soft music started playing as we made our way back to the cliff edge.

"The world will be emptier without your joyful spirit. I hope you'll be able to find many treasures where you are; I know you were mine." I removed the lid and approached the very edge of the cliff. My toes curled in the grass as I looked into the raging waters below. "Fly high in your travels and until we meet again."

I let the contents of the urn spill out and I let out a gasp of surprise. I had been expecting grayish ash to come out. Instead, there were purple iridescent flakes that drifted on the wind. My confusion must have shown on my face because Naji's mom approached me. She tucked a loose strand of hair behind my ear and smiled sadly.

"When a dragon is cremated their ashes represent their soul. My daughter was pure and light, so shall her ashes be."

I swallowed the hard lump in my throat and blinked away my tears. I nodded my thanks and we watched Naji's ashes disappear. Eventually, everyone left and I was alone staring into the waters. When the sun set I heard Hunter approach. Even with the grass cushioning his feet, his steps were easy to hear. It was no wonder I hadn't been able to sneak up on him before. I turned to face him without speaking. I tried not to react when Hunter flinched away from my eyes.

It had been Odette who had revealed what I had transitioned into. Odette had told me I was Crescent Born. That they were extremely rare, the last one being born over four centuries ago. Their powers- my powers- were undocumented and many people of the kingdom were scared of me. Hunter said he wasn't afraid of me. He said that seeing my eyes reminded him that I had died. And that he was ashamed of not being able to keep me safe. I had hoped he'd gotten used to it by now…

"We have to head back," he whispered as he wrapped his arms around me, resting his chin on my shoulder.

"I don't want to," I shivered in his warm embrace, I was always cold lately.

"You have to eventually," Hunter reminded me.

"I know," I sighed. Once I returned to the manor, I wouldn't be able to mourn any longer. I would have to hold a conference to discuss the future. We would have to train harder. I grabbed his hand as we made our way to our truck. I centered the small crystal ball with the bird knuckle on its chain. It was warm against the cold skin of my throat. "Let's go plan a war."

To be continued in...

LAST OF THE HELLFIRE

9 7 9 8 9 8 8 5 5 7 9 0 6